The Unwitting Journeys ∞∞∞ of the ∞∞∞ Witty Miss Livingstone

Book I: Journey Key

KENNEDY J. QUINN

FreeValley Publishing
North Bend, Washington
freevalleypublishing.com

ISBN: **1537732617**
ISBN-13: **978-1537732619**

DEDICATION

For the courageous and adventurous souls who reach out to see what's around the next corner, and who shape, not only their own lives, but create new communities and technologies that benefit us all.

With special appreciation of those that lived in and settled the Snoqualmie Valley in the foothills of the Cascade Mountains in Washington State. The native peoples, early settlers, and those who labored on the Milwaukee Road and other railways gave inspiration for this book, and their efforts and vision have left an amazing legacy in this beautiful place I call home.

And for my husband, whose steadfast love and ever-changing spark of life make my every day a fantastic journey.

CONTENTS

Gratitude   i

1   In Which Miss Livingstone Spies Hope of Relieving Literary Despair   1

2   In Which Miss Livingstone Loses Her Charm   8

3   In Which Miss Livingstone Garners Support for a Most Pressing Opportunity   15

4   In Which Miss Livingstone Makes an Enthralling Discovery   21

5   In Which Miss Livingstone and Janie Teeter through an Unwieldy Cover-up   27

6   In Which Miss Livingstone Employs her Inventive Nature   32

7   In Which Miss Livingstone Embarks on an Unwitting Journey   40

8   In Which Miss Livingstone Meets the Twisted Mr. Worthington   46

9   In Which Miss Livingstone is Not Quite Herself   52

10   In Which Miss Livingstone Uncovers Her Future Past   60

11   In Which Miss Livingstone Goes Home Again, Home Again   67

12   In Which Miss Livingstone Shares her Eccentricities - with Some Regret   73

13   In Which Good Logic Bows to the Dictates of Strong Intuition   80

14   In Which Even Sneaking Becomes Easier with Practice   87

15 In Which Miss Livingstone Stumbles upon the   93
    Supernatural

16 In Which Miss Livingstone Giggles Like a Schoolgirl   100

17 In Which Miss Livingstone Resolves to Jump in   107
    Heartily

18 In Which Miss Livingstone Flirts with Infinite   112
    Fantastical Possibilities

19 In Which Miss Livingstone Goes Flying   116

20 In Which Miss Livingstone Finds Avoiding Capture a   121
    Difficult Trick

21 In Which an Unforeseen Connection Casts Dark   128
    Foreshadows

22 In Which Miss Livingstone Thrills to Her Heroes'   135
    Heroics

23 In Which Miss Livingstone Tests Her Mettle   140

24 In Which Miss Livingstone Flees Forthwith   147

25 In Which Miss Livingstone Exposes Flim-flam Fare   153

26 In Which Things Become Rather Tangled   160

27 In Which Father Listens with Heart and Mind   166

28 In Which Janie is Cast for the Perfect Role   174

29 In Which Miss Livingstone Gains an Unexpected Audience   178

30 In Which Miss Livingstone Slips Away from Unwelcome Pursuit   183

31 In Which Miss Livingstone is Certain There is More to the Story   191

32 In Which Miss Livingstone Understands How to Move Forward - Or is that   198
    Backward?

33 In Which Miss Livingstone Receives an Exotic Gift   206

34 In Which Miss Livingstone Seeks the Fastest Escape   210

35 In Which Janie's Sweet Giggle Dispels the Horror   215

36 In Which Miss Livingstone and Mr. Scott Worthington Share a Magical   223
    Exchange

37 In Which Janie's Trust is Undeniable   230

38 In Which Miss Livingstone and Janie Nearly Bare All   236

39 In Which Some Things Never Change   243

GRATITUDE

Thanks go to my writing and reading friends in SnoValley Writes! and this year's NaNo to Publish group at North Bend Library. Special thanks to my critique partner, Sarah D. Burd and beta readers T.A. Henry, Victoria Bastedo, Rachel Barnard, and Casondra Brewster. I owe much to my ARC readers Jean Buckner and Sarah Salter. And I was surprised and deeply grateful for the abundant ARC feedback from my brother, and excellent line editor, Dave Walton, who observed, "reminding twerps they don't quite know EVERYTHING is what big brothers do best."

Special appreciation is given to Robert York who provided advice on the French dialogue and to Kathleen Gabriel who provided Robert York.

Thanks to Kay Rene at Snoqualmie Valley Historical Museum for a delightfully helpful chat and fun afternoon.

Extreme and humble thanks go to author, Jeffrey Cook, for making Miss Livingstone's (and this author's) dream come true by allowing her to board the *Dame Fortuna*. This generous lending of characters and scenarios from his brilliant novel *Dawn of Steam: First Light* to Miss Livingstone's story-world enabled the creation of a sweeter and more inspired adventure. And I'm pleased to have the honor of building on his well-crafted alternate history.

I would also like to extend sincere gratitude to the ever-patient and friendly wait staff and baristas at Snoqualmie Brewery and Taproom, Little Si Restaurant, and Pioneer Coffee NB, for providing countless hours of food, bevvies and atmosphere for my writing and editing inspiration and pleasure.

-Kennedy J. Quinn

CHAPTER ONE

∞∞∞∞

In Which Miss Livingstone Spies Hope of Relieving Literary Despair

The train whistle interrupted my tea. Where had the time gone? "Father!"

"You needn't bellow, Miss Caprice, I have Mr. Livingstone well in hand," Camille assured as she tried to clear my tea tray from the porch. I clung to it tenaciously until she let go. "Jaimeson is on his way to the automobile with your father's bags. He lit the pilot twenty minutes ago, so the Steamer's ready to roll. Quit worrying about your father and gather yourself so you don't make him miss the train."

"I..." didn't have a whit's chance against her demand. Camille was a wonderful housekeeper, but I wished she'd stop trying to be my mother. The way she and Father fussed you'd never guess I was twenty-three. She treated me like I was a dawdling toddler.

"Come dear," Father encouraged while carrying his work kit down the steps.

Jaimeson was at the auto as well, and I resigned to follow. What a shame to abandon my buttered scone for such a short trip. I savored one more bite.

The remaining morsel would be quite cold upon my return, even on this unexpectedly warm April day.

Snoqualmie seemed dismally small to me, though it didn't lack for trees and mountains. There was a lovely modern train depot, and hotel, and a decent general store. But the other structures in the few blocks of settlement were modest and the roads were muddy trails.

"I know it's only a few minutes, but we've had such little time together in your first couple months in town." Father took my hand and helped me up into his prized automobile.

"I don't know why we need to take the Steamer, Father. I worry people will find us pretentious." I grabbed my Garden Hat as Jaimeson set us in motion. I'd forgotten my veil to tie it down so had to hold tight to prevent losing the precious flowers from its top in the wind.

"You know I appreciate its mechanism not its status, dear. I realize it's the fastest auto available, but it was awarded to me by the Stanley twins for my advice on adding a compressor. There's no pretension in that."

"True, it's just the appearance."

He flashed me the look he gave my mother when she said such things. I used to do the same, but now that she's gone, I attempt to keep some sense of her propriety.

I was scolded back at Miss Preston's School for Girls for excessive imagination. It's a fault of mine without doubt. I was once set before the formidable Miss Preston herself and made to explain my thinking after my composition on topiaries took an unexpected turn into fantastical shapes. My mother blamed my father, but I credited him as the source of my sharp wit.

2

"How long will you be in Seattle, Father?"

"I shall be about a week – likely back on Friday – or sooner if I can manage it. Mr. Earling, the company's president is visiting. Among other things he'll hear of my Colossal Clock for the Oregon and Washington Station. It's to be ready for the opening in Seattle next year."

"How exciting! Is it progressing well?" I asked.

"Oh yes, yes, it's on schedule. And speaking of schedules, I've almost perfected my chronospacometer. I can measure the precise location in time and space, but the mechanism still sticks occasionally. Soon I can offer it to Earling to guarantee accurate tracking of train arrivals and departures throughout the Chicago, Milwaukee, St. Paul Railroad, as they require – with an extra dimension over the chronometers they have currently."

"You haven't even called me in on your puzzling or shown me your progress since I arrived." Unintentionally, I let him hear my regret.

"Yes, and I'm sorry for that, Caprice. And after I brought you all the way out here to the west." His silver-grey eyes misted slightly.

Woooot woooot. "All Aboard!" I heard the conductor's call as we arrived at the Snoqualmie depot.

"I promise to fill you in on everything when I return. Oh, but I must go."

"And not a moment too soon," I blurted. "I mean, I'm sorry to see you go, Father, but you must hurry and not miss your train," I clarified, with hopes not to upset him further.

With a hastily placed kiss on my forehead he and Jaimeson were off with his bags. I couldn't help but wish it was I who traveled. After the horrid train journey west... Horrid was perhaps a measure too strong. After all, I arrived just a day before the blizzard began. A mere five days later and I would've been stuck in the train for several days and then swept away in the Wellington avalanche. What a terrible thing that was!

Also I had the privilege to travel on the 20th Century Limited, so I took just under twenty-four hours to get from Boston to Chicago. We met with excellent company while staying at The Palmer House – a Mr. Chesterton of Chesterton Air. I had never thought to travel the skies, but his tales of airships had my mind flying across the tundra by dirigible. After that, riding the rails of the Milwaukee Road seemed a fantastic journey into the unknown – even if it was the long way 'round.

Woooot woooot. My heart leaped with excitement each time I heard a departing whistle. I longed to be whisked away to adventure.

"Farewell, Father!" I held my hat and waved my handkerchief until we were out of sight, as my mother used to do.

Homeward again – or what had become home. I was perfectly happy at Miss Preston's School for Girls. But Father missed me. Imagine letting a silly thing like affection get in the way of education!

Perhaps Father's workshop would provide some stimulus. He and I got on well in our ability to invent – mechanically and otherwise. Mother always said Father could talk himself out of any escapade and shine with intellectual prowess, whether it was scandalous or not – and likely it was.

"Oh!" A horrendous gust of wind dislodged my hat from my head. Miss Camille will scold for the state of my already unruly curls. And she'll have to pick the dark hairs off my light duster. Perhaps I should've chosen the darker coat she advised. But it's such a sunny day. At least with a quick grasp I didn't lose the hat completely.

Dear Mother, I have missed her so. She never would've let Father bring me to this far flung place. As a forward thinking woman, I couldn't wait to see what the future held. Now I'd stepped back into bustles!

I had avidly followed the news on the 1909 Model T New York to Seattle race and those daring enough to undertake it. So I expected more civilization when I arrived in mid-February. My new friend Mary Jane told me the Model T's saluted Snoqualmie as they passed last summer, and it was terribly exciting. But despite the new roads from the East, the West was still a wild place indeed.

The one glimmer of society I discovered here was Miss Mabel's book club – though I needed to introduce them to decent tea. Regrettably, I'd missed the Saturday meeting today to see Father off at the station. Quality young women, such as my friend Mary Jane Adams and I, usually discuss what literature we can find – which frankly isn't the best, but will have to do. And good or bad, we've read nearly the entire collection of books available to the group. If only Father had brought our full library west.

Although, just as I was teetering on the brink of literary despair, I saw a most promising development a week ago Wednesday. Down the street from the general store I noticed a sign in a vacant storefront window that read, 'Mr. Thomas Worthington's Most Excellent Bookshop.' It was hard to imagine a book shop of quality in these parts, but my hope exceeded my skepticism. I asked anyone and everyone I met if they knew when the shop would be open for trade. But no one seemed to know the mysterious Thomas Worthington, proprietor. So any date assigned for opening was purely speculation.

The fact no one knew him gave me higher hopes for the quality of the establishment. I deduced he was from outside of this town. And having enough books to sell implied an origin of well-developed commerce, namely a large city. Was it London? Or at the least New York City? My heart fluttered at the prospect of new literature. If one couldn't travel by dirigible, traveling vicariously through books was the next best thing.

I checked the storefront each day after my discovery, but they had soaped the windows so detection of detail was nearly impossible. I simply had to know what was coming, so I pieced together every clue. There was an area near the bottom edge of the window where the soap missed and left a small transparency. It was terribly awkward to peek through with dignity, but determination won the day. A splintery gash in the low window sill served to catch my handkerchief if I dropped it just so. I could then bend to retrieve it and gain a marvelous glimpse into the shop. Of course I didn't want to be seen leaning in an unladylike fashion for too long, so my vision was incomplete.

Dark wooden shelves with a polished gleam filled the shop with quality worthy of Boston. One could only imagine the cost to bring them here. And there were colorful volumes stacked everywhere. An enormous piece of carved furniture dominated the back left corner of the shop. I thought it was a desk? The visible drawers and cupboards were intricate with a lot of ornamentation – like a cuckoo clock – and I was consumed with curiosity of what they contained.

To the right, near the door there was a sectioned off area. The entrance was covered by a curtain of a bright yellow-green silk, the exotic type of color one might see in imports from the Far East. I wondered what was behind the billowing veil? It was an odd accoutrement for a man's shop. I thought he must be an eccentric fellow, or perhaps just well-traveled.

I hoped he'd offer stories to tell as well as those buried in the tomes he'd sell. It was thrilling! My imagination simply soared with possibilities.

CHAPTER TWO

∞∞∞∞

In Which Miss Livingstone Loses Her Charm

I missed being on Father's arm at church, especially since I couldn't duck out with him afterwards before Mrs. Allen caught my elbow and my ear. Though a dear woman, she does go on when planning our next box social. I'm all for raising funds to improve things, and the active Ladies Aid was why I chose to attend North Bend Baptist, but I had other things on my mind.

I wanted to check on the bookshop again to see if there was indication of the opening date. I had Jaimeson keep the Steamer at the ready so we could leave right after Camille finished serving us luncheon. Poor Jaimeson was likely tiring of taking me back and forth to town, but I wasn't sure I could endure much more talk of *The Virginian, A Horseman of the Plains* at the next meeting of Miss Mabel's Book Club. We needed literature.

I remembered to tie down my hat this time, and decided on the dark tan duster to protect my Sunday finery.

"I hope we'll escape the rain," I told Jaimeson as he helped me step up into the Steamer.

"Yes, let's away then, Miss," he replied. And he levered us into motion forthwith.

The Virginian had some merits, I suppose. The strength and tenacity of those who settled the west were undeniably admirable, but I wasn't sure why one would travel so far without a civilized destination? Although Mary Jane came through rather well despite coming from such stock. She had rough hands and was strong as a horse. But for these parts, she'd be a thoroughbred. Her long blond locks and lively blue eyes would gain more admiration than any debutante could if she was gussied up, and she wouldn't fall for anything foolish. With expressions like 'for these parts," I would soon be unfit to return to Boston. Perhaps it was a good thing I was becoming friends with dear Mary Jane. She preferred Janie for short. At school we might have called a girl Penn or Poole but never Bette for Beatrice or Kit for Katherine. It was all the rage to shorten names in the west. Perhaps it was a way to keep dirt from one's mouth.

"Jaimeson," I shouted through the breeze of speed. "Can you please let me off by the hotel?"

"Yes, Miss," he hollered agreeably. I'm sure it was no matter to him since he was going to pick up sewing from Camille's sister before coming back for me.

Hoping to restore my typically sunnier disposition, I'd decided to take a slightly longer stroll before reaching the interminably slow-to-open book shop. As I passed the general store, I happened by Abigale Reinig securing the door behind her. Her father owned the store, Reinig Bros. General Merchandise, and had been the mayor for five years. Abigale was six years my junior, but what she lacked in age she made up for in self-importance.

"Afternoon, Miss Abigale. We missed you in church this morning." I was admiring her plum skirts and crisp shirtwaist and wondered what she was getting from the general store. It was closed Sundays, of course, but since her young brother was in attendance, I surmised she was picking up something for him and not for her own fancy.

"Mother was ailing and Henry was restless, so we've come by the store to get her some Beecham's Pills."

"So glad we've avoided the rain; it looks as if it will hold off for a time. Best wishes for your mother's health."

"Thank you. Afternoon, Miss Caprice." Abigale nodded smartly when she passed.

I nodded politely in return, but it was grating to hear my given name. No one had ever heard of such a name for a woman. Sometimes my father's invention is a bit too clever. I much preferred, Miss Livingstone. And I wondered for a moment if they'd call me, Cappy? Until I came to my senses when I turned the corner. And something exciting caught my eye.

The door to the bookshop was just that much ajar. I was sure someone must be inside. I didn't want them to elude me, so hurried down the block. Pulling up my pace near the storefront, I moved the open door toward me with a nonchalant nudge of my foot into the gap.

One moment I leaned my head around through the widening doorway, and the next I looked up at a most mysterious character offering me his forearm on which to pull myself up from the boardwalk where he'd spilled me with an abrupt thump and furious jingling of bells from the wide-swung door. I was aghast, but took the offered aid. I failed to see through the gaping threshold to the hidden treasures beyond, so taken was I with the countenance of this man.

He had the fine kid gloves of a gentleman, and the grace to snug them securely before reaching out toward me lest I contact his hand. His attire was completely black, from head to toe. An immaculately tailored shirt and waistcoat with a dazzling large gold watch fob which featured a jewel of a quality I've never seen before. It was the deepest emerald tone and richly faceted. But his face... He seemed no gentleman at all, but rather a gathering of consternation and weather, so deeply furrowed was his brow and so gaunt his cheeks. Odd for a man who otherwise appeared quite young. And his eyes were as black as the cloth he wore, and as glittering as his gold and jewel. They looked through me, and I lost all thought and purpose.

Before I knew what had happened he had secured the door and there I was, flustered as a pea-brained fool, having missed my chance at ascertaining the opening date of the bookshop or details regarding its proprietor or even taking in a good eyeful of what lay beyond the window I'd been so persistently stalking. Of course, it was greatly his fault for not offering an introduction – or a proper apology. He knocked me bustle over teakettle for Pete's sake. And then I realized I'd lost the charm from my bracelet in my fall.

∞∞∞∞

"Whatever are you doing, Miss Livingstone?" Abigale's voice scolded, as she approached my rear. "I must say you're in an awkward position."

"Oh pardon me. I surely look a mess." I spun upright and straightened my hat which had slipped askew. "And you're correct I have no business leaning down so, but I lost my charm."

"Yes, I see." The girl gave me the most unsavory sneer.

I imagined her an overripe eggplant in her plum-colored attire.

"I'm referring to the gold charm that was attached to my wrist." I indicated the empty chain pointedly. "I took a fall and it must have come loose."

She looked at me as if my gears were loose.

I tried, "my father gave it to me before leaving Boston. It was my mother's. I'm terribly upset. And I was pushed..."

"Oh you poor dear! It's a good thing we decided to get more air before returning to Mother. Henry don't just dawdle by my arm, help Miss Livingstone find her cha – her keepsake."

"So kind of you to offer your brother to help. I think it may have been closer to that jamb. Perhaps under the edge of the door?"

Henry proved to be a thorough little fellow and soon located my heart, the golden one that is, as well as something quite unexpected. When I held out my gloved hand to receive it, he set the small charm at its center and then laid on top a sturdy pewter key. His blue eyes flashed at me from his slightly dirty freckled face, but he didn't say a word.

"Excellent work, my dear boy!" I praised him when I closed my grasp tightly around both treasures so as not to let them slip from my glove. His sister was too busy looking about for passersby to note what he had given me.

"Thank you for the rescue, Miss Reinig." I hoped she'd return to 'Miss Livingstone' permanently if I addressed her so. She apparently had little affection for me so needn't be familiar.

"Certainly. Our pleasure." Henry gave a small bow at his sister's words. "But you haven't explained why you were in need. You say you were pushed? Who on earth would push you and then leave you to falter?"

"Oh no, he – the gentleman – well, the man helped me upright before he left me. He wasn't aware – that is, I wasn't aware I had lost anything until he left." Then I felt completely lost, I didn't bother to add.

"But why would he push you to begin with? Did you quarrel? Was he trying to harm you? Miss Livingstone, really you..."

"Oh no, you misunderstand. It was all accidental." Or was it? "I was walking by the bookshop."

"We have no bookshop...Oh, so we do." Miss Abigale apparently saw what was before her for the first time.

"Yes, an exciting development."

"Being pushed?"

"Certainly not. The imminent opening of the bookshop." It was all I could do to leave off the name, *Silly*. "And technically he didn't push me, the door did. Though he was behind it."

"So he didn't mean to push you?"

"No. I'm sure he didn't. That is, he didn't seem to. I'm sure he was just –"

"Well surely he gave you an explanation. Who was he?"

"We've never met." I told her.

"Before, yes, but what is his name? Surely he introduced himself after knocking you over with the door."

"Well, not exactly, no. I –"

"What did he look like? Is he the proprietor, Thomas Worthington? Or one in his employ? My father says Mr. Worthington is a sturdy fellow but rather small in stature, and he has a remarkably red beard that's unfashionably long," she filled in, to my delight.

"Your father has seen him? But I thought you didn't know of the bookshop."

"I don't generally pay attention to Father's business. But I recognized his name on that sign inside the window. My father sees most everyone. Money talks, as they say."

She paused so long I encouraged her with, "yes?" But she didn't go on. "So he's bearded?" I tried.

"Oh yes, it made quite a conversation at supper last evening. Father thinks the man is rather eccentric. Is he the one that pushed you over and ran off without a proper word? If his oddities defy social civility, I shall suggest my father not do business with the man. Perhaps he's some kind of nut."

"I'm sure he's a worthy businessman." I wanted no threat to our bookshop!

"So it was he you met – or rather didn't exactly meet?"

"No, it was someone else." I was bursting with curiosity about Mr. Worthington until she reminded me of the eerie and magnetic stranger. "Perhaps it was an associate or hired man? He was tall, with the darkest eyes I've ever seen, a closely trimmed black moustache and –" My enthusiasm often ran my mouth faster than best, but I felt a keen caution in revealing how his countenance undid me. "A very fine suit. He was dressed as a gentleman, to be sure." But was he one? I wasn't so sure.

"Well that sounds promising. Perhaps it will be he that services patrons at the shop, and the uncouth Mr. Worthington will provide inventory. Though I'm concerned that this dark fellow didn't introduce himself. Did he speak to you at all?"

"No, not at all." Not with words by any account.

"How curious."

Yes, curious is indeed what it was. "It was nice seeing you Miss Reinig, Master Henry. I thank you kindly for assisting me so well in finding what I was looking for." Supremely well, since the unexpected key might give access to what I was really seeking.

"Yes, of course, Miss Livingstone. Come along, Henry."

The small boy looked back at me with a sidelong grin.

CHAPTER THREE

∞∞∞∞

In Which Miss Livingstone Garners Support for a
Most Pressing Opportunity

My fist released its tight grasp of opportunity, and I studied the promising key. It was all I could do not to rush over and try it at once. But even greater than this urge was my fear of losing the chance to explore by being discovered. Good sense dictated to come back when the street was less traveled. With regret I secured the key – and the charm – in my bag.

I puzzled how to delay riding back to our home when Jaimeson arrived shortly in the Steamer to collect me. I felt compelled to enter the shop later in the evening. Just to look around, of course. My dear Mary Jane came to mind straight away. Could I stop by her parents' home, just behind the general store, uninvited and unannounced? I had barely met them and had never been to their home. The emergency warranted such a breach of etiquette, I dared to think.

Walking along, I tried to look more nonchalant than I felt. Not that the townsfolk could guess my plan, but I was so intent, I believed they'd notice the scheming light in my eye. The cover of the tall evergreens, small maples and brushy rhododendrons on the edge of the Adams' property brought relief. The gurgling sound of the nearby slow-moving river was calming and seeped in to soothe me until the wide porch of the Adams' newly built home slipped into view. Anxiety resurfaced.

I climbed the steps and hesitated on the threshold. As much as frontier towns give the 'howdy,' my city sensibilities balked at knocking on a door, especially without escort. I had the absurd urge to pull out my calling card. But of course such niceties were inappropriate to the situation. I didn't want them to think me priggish. When the improper deed was done, my knuckles throbbed, and it seemed forever until I heard footsteps. I nearly turned and ran off the porch. How silly I would've looked dashing away down the stairs.

"Good afternoon, Miss. Is there something I can help you with?" The housekeeper eyed me dubiously – as though I was as loony as my current behavior. And her eyes scanned for my escort, as was no wonder. Oh dear.

"I... that is, I'm Miss Livingstone and I would appreciate an immediate, pardon me, an appointment with Miss Mary Jane as soon as it can be arranged," bumbled from my mortified lips. "I know it's Sunday and –"

"Certainly, I will see if she is available."

"Please hurry." My curiosity overwhelmed my civility. But the prospect of getting into that shop, especially after bumping into that intriguing man – I was near bursting, and thought I might if she was long in coming.

"My dear, Caprice, are you well?" Janie rushed onto the porch.

Near swooning with impatience was my only malady. "Mary...Janie, my dear friend. I'm so glad you agreed to take my call, and I'm terribly sorry to intrude without notice. I've had an

interesting afternoon, and I have a most pressing opportunity which requires support. If I may entreat you?"

"You know I'm yours any time you're in need." Her blue eyes were steady with the earnest pledge.

"It's not need exactly, but more of a... potential caper."

Her blue eyes clouded with concern when I mentioned how I'd fallen and went wide with wonder at my description of the strange gentleman. She pulled on her blonde tress, a habit of hers when intrigued, as I told her of the key. I saw the puzzle and temptation of the key consume her, and a bright gleam appeared in her gaze when I laid out my proposal for the evening. As I hoped, it was in the bag!

"However will we get away?" Her brow furrowed.

"I shall inform my driver, Jaimeson, that I'll be visiting with you until late."

"My friend, I will be pleased if you'd remain until the morning. It would be too much to travel after this venture," she extended along with a bright smile.

"You're so gracious. I certainly accept, and that secures my freedom for the undertaking. But we'll need a cover to escape the eye of your parents for a time, and after dark. Everything closes at sunset other than the pub, or I suppose I must call it a saloon. Oh my, not to worry, it's Sunday!"

Janie giggled, breaking the tension with her delightful ease. I tried to step back from the issue but quickly returned to scheming.

"What could we possibly offer as a ruse?" My mind was ticking furiously. "I've got it. Miss Abigale! We'll say we've been invited to her home to work on the upcoming Box Social. It's just on the other side of the store, so we'll express a wish to take the air on our way and demand to walk. Since there are two of us, they may let us go together without escort, yes?" It was brilliant.

"Well, Father usually won't let me walk after dark. I believe he fears a patron of the saloon or hotel who's overindulged might come by and harass me. And it looks like rain." Janie dashed my hopes.

Perhaps she saw my face fall, because she instantly worked to repair them. "But I could go if we're escorted." She tugged at her hair furiously. "Our driver, Solomon, is usually up for intrigue. He's aided me in sneaking out on other occasions."

"Janie!" She smiled at my renewed enthusiasm. "I didn't know you did such a thing as *sneak!*" I let her look sheepish for the smallest flash of time. "But I certainly hoped so!" Our laughter mixed merrily. "You always have the most Puckish ideas when commenting during the book club discussions. I could see that spark of enterprise waiting for some kindling. And I do believe the rain won't fall hard until late in the night."

It's a miracle our laughter didn't bring the whole household running. But her countenance clouded again.

"You don't suppose we'll be in danger?" She was to the point, to be sure.

"I can't imagine the man I bumped into or Mr. Worthington would return tonight. That's why I've pushed with such urgency. But now I must meet Jaimeson by the train depot."

"I'll get Solomon to take you to your car, and I'll fill him in on the plan for later. What is the plan exactly?"

"Just tell him we'll need his assistance to get out of the house this evening, and I'll contemplate details as we stroll to meet Jaimeson and return."

She led me through the hall to be seated in their pleasantly appointed peach-toned parlor, and a shiver of humiliation rushed over me with the realization we'd been conversing at the door jamb. It was utterly batty! Before I knew it Solomon's bow broke into my preoccupation, and I jumped. I hoped he wouldn't think my upset due to his dark complexion for I had no concern of such. His height and girth could also have been daunting, but his rich brown eyes spoke of intelligence and integrity.

"So sorry to startle you dear," Janie set her hand on my tensed shoulder. "Solomon is ready to escort you now."

As we passed through town again, I had Solomon lead me by the bookshop. A gaslight glowed in the misty rain and shone into the nearby window. I noted that with the soap to disperse the light, we'd be able to see throughout the store without calling attention with a lantern or candle inside.

I was almost in to see what I had wondered about for over a week. Janie and I would return tonight. I trembled with anticipation.

∞∞∞

After I waved Jaimeson off at the depot, Solomon led me back across the street and along the block. My thoughts returned to the mysterious man and the jewel on his watch. Why would he carry such a rare item? Especially in this town where, though it was civilized, there were many rough characters. Lumbermen came down from the camps and the railroad men were not all savory. Even the mill workers were hit and miss for civility.

"Easy miss," Solomon's deep voice rescued me along with his elbow.

I wasn't watching where I was walking and had nearly tripped on a crack in the boardwalk. It was remarkable how the strange gentleman's eyes haunted my thoughts so deeply – like he saw something beneath my exterior that I hadn't fathomed yet. A future or past or...

Solomon and I were close to the Adams' house now, and I picked my way through the trees in the rough mud of their drive. It was uncanny how that mesmerizing dark man had knocked me down, I'd been given the key, and next thing I knew I had knocked on the door of a new friend – an imposition of catastrophic measure had she been less gracious.

But my dear, Janie – for I resolved to remember her name as such – had risen to the demand of my infamous fancy. What fun we would have had at Miss Preston's School for Girls.

CHAPTER FOUR

∞∞∞∞

In Which Miss Livingstone Makes an Enthralling Discovery

After a delightful tea complete with aromatic rolls of cinnamon, Janie and I left the house under Solomon's wink-and-a-nod care. The heavy rain had indeed held off though the air was damp with gathering clouds. We'd convinced her father and mother of the urgency of a work bee with Miss Abigale Reinig for the upcoming Box Social. I realized anything more prestigious would stretch the bounds of believability due to my afternoon attire. Also, Janie's parents were always supportive of anything to strengthen the community. I've learned when inventing explanations to consider the sensibilities of those who are listening.

As we approached the front of the bookshop, the gas lamp's light seemed to reveal too much. I knew Janie also feared discovery when she grasped my elbow and pulled in close. The energy of the conspiracy filled me, and my fear was lost in the thrill of pushing the promising key into the keyhole – a port of welcome possibilities.

For a moment I thought it was all for naught as the key stood firm against my desperate attempts to turn it. The satisfying *click* of the sticky lock's release produced a shot of adrenaline, and Janie heartily patted my back as the door squeaked open on its hinges with a soft tittering of the little brass bells attached within. We jumped inside and waved Solomon off to wait for us as he wished. He declined to come inside as his penalty would've been more severe than ours if caught.

Securing the door quickly, I observed the shop was lit as I expected. It was like moonlight at the full – perfect illumination for intrigue. The stacks of tomes went from near the doorway to the very back, and Janie fell to examining the ones in the middle. But I was drawn to my left and moved without conscious thought past the sales counter toward the back corner. There was nothing worthy of my attention but the fantastically enthralling desk. There were indeed drawers and cabinets built into its tall and exceptionally deep back, and their number and variety of size was beyond any I had ever seen. Remarkable does not begin to describe its allure. And though I knew it wrong to snoop so deeply, its full form before me birthed vivid imaginings of what lay inside. There would certainly be hidden compartments, especially given how far the cabinet protruded from the wall. I was driven beyond reason to begin the search.

I pushed on a carved fluer-de-lis and tried to lift the bars above the doors. I touched, bumped and prodded other decorative items on the desk's face. There were many slots and crevices that seemed like they should give, but they wouldn't budge, even when I tried prying with the key.

Next I tried the drawers. Pen nibs and blotting paper, parchment and bookmarks, all of the things one might expect were present. As if drawn by fate, my gaze fastened on a strange symbol at the crown of the ornate carvings. It looked ancient and I felt sure it meant something. It was far above my reach, especially when leaning across the desktop. A small table and a few stacked books would propel me to the desk's pinnacle. Janie glanced as I built my platform but pursued her own curiosity. She stroked the ends of her blonde hair while on her way to the other end of the shop, where the small room was partitioned off. She disappeared to her left into the room behind the silk curtain near the shop's door.

With a mighty effort I climbed and stretched to my full reach. My fingers investigated every facet of the rich carvings and were rewarded with detecting an obscured crack. The unusual ancient-type symbol nearly covered the gap. I'd never seen the pattern before. It resembled a striped parasol joined to a fence. I pushed it to the right, but nothing happened. So I pushed to the left.

With a mighty whirring, gears hidden to my eye raced into action. I jumped from my perch in surprise as the various carvings and whole sections of the desk's front traveled across the surface of the wood in the grooves and notches I first observed. They ultimately came into alignment. A startling *click* sounded and the portion of the desk above its writing surface swung open before me. Had I not left the platform, I would've been knocked silly. Two thick wooden doors hung wide with tantalizing invitation to see what was inside.

The hidden compartment was lit with a soft glow. I couldn't see a source, but that puzzle was lost in awe. My breath caught as I beheld a collection of large gemstones shimmering in the golden light. "Mary Jane!"

Janie didn't answer, but I climbed back upon the perch to see more closely. Terror of being caught looking inside gripped me, but they were irresistible. Beautiful! An opaque rust-toned oval stone sparkled as if filled with a thousand stars. My hand reached toward it of its own accord. Silly me, I almost contacted it, but gathered my wits and at last remembered some caution. If I was caught holding a gem, all of my ingenuity wouldn't convince anyone my intent was not thievery. And I needed to find Janie. Why had she not answered?

I stepped down behind the platform I'd built. The urge to touch the stones was impossible to endure without some prohibitive space between myself and them. I could hardly tear my eyes away.

"Janie!" I propelled myself further from the enticing glow and appealing gems and closer to the small room and the curtain. It's vivid yellow-green transformed to a ghostly grey veil in the filtered lamplight's radiance. A chill shook me and I was deeply reluctant to move it aside. "Janie, dear?" My voice dropped to a whisper. Again there was no answer.

The twilight sheen of filtered lamplight pushed in on me feeling suddenly dark. The stacks of books loomed, ominous in their haphazard placement and their weighty forms. My hand quaked as the sumptuous texture of the silken fabric met my hesitant touch. I was loath to leave the light of the stones behind me.

"Whatever are you waiting for, my dear Caprice?"

Janie's crisp shout nearly threw me upon my backside with my heart swallowed to my toes, so much was it lodged in my throat by her sudden exclamation.

"Aren't you curious what's here behind the..." her question trailed off when her head popped into the main shop, and she regarded me with the veil draped around her shoulder. The warm glow of a candle radiantly highlighted her figure. "Are you well?" Her eyes wandered the dim room along the front portion of the shop.

The desk was at an angle hidden from her, and I confess I wished to push her away. A strange possessiveness enveloped me, and I determined to hide what I had discovered – at least until I learned more.

Janie's demeanor, so bold the moment before, retreated into the dusk. "What's the matter?" She whispered, close to my face.

"Nothing's amiss," my voice burst out much too loudly.

The shout sent Janie teetering backward like a shot. Unlike I had, she was unable to arrest her shock from the surprise. Her heel caught and she knocked over a stack of books, spilling them in a wide swath as she sprawled on her back on top of them. "Oh..." came from her like the *oof* of a fireplace bellows.

"Oh my! Janie, my apologies, I –" It was my turn to *oof* as I took her proffered hand and hauled her upright, backing out partway through the curtain.

"How ever will we pick up all of these books?" Janie lamented.

It was rather a dilemma. Our clothing didn't facilitate bending readily. My finger went to my lip and my head cocked to the side – my customary pose when contemplating a solution. With this peculiar tilt of my head the enticing incandescence emanating from the desk's cabinet caught my eye as I took another two steps back. It was so...

"...and, are you well?" Janie's words broke into my apparent trance. I wondered how much I missed. The curtain had fallen between us, and I snatched it open again.

"Yes, yes of course," I tried, though I was sure my fluttering heart thwarted my appearance of control.

"Well?"

"Yes. I said yes." She looked confused. I surmised she meant the other type of well. "Well what?"

Janie's clear blue eyes clouded with consternation. I was always ready with the next idea – a review of our author's latest contrivance, suggestion for a pastime. In the weeks we'd known each other, she'd become accustomed to my sharp wit. I was at a loss. And apparently so was she.

"I... I'm afraid I missed that last part. Well, actually I got the very last part, which I've answered. I've never been better. But you were saying?"

"I asked if you had something to show me first or if you'd like to see what I discovered behind the curtain? It's really quite fascinating. I..."

Just that quick my attention was drawn to imagining the stones and away from her words again, but I snapped to. "Yes, of course. Please, my dear. Let's see your discovery forthwith."

CHAPTER FIVE

∞∞∞

In Which Miss Livingstone and Janie Teeter through an Unwieldy Cover-up

Janie presented her literary feast with a flourish. I laughed with joy as I uncovered the complete works of Jane Austen and gasped in delight at the many rare and delicious treats I'd only heard mention of in the posh literary circles of Boston. This was an excellent bookshop indeed! And the brand new books, crisp in their unblemished cloth and leather bindings – I hadn't seen such a thing since my arrival. My imagination launched away to lands and concepts yet to be encountered. New literature! But even with such ambrosial offerings my mind was drawn back to the stones. I couldn't shake the compulsion to hide the gems.

Janie tackled the task of re-stacking the monolith of books she disturbed with her fall. I came to her aid but was merely lingering until she became intent. She focused lest she lose balance in her wide skirts, and with guilt seated in my stomach, I eased back through the jumble and slipped outside of the curtain. Alighting upon my makeshift platform, I tried my hand at closing the doors. A simple nudge on the rich wood, set the doors swinging deliberately inward, with a whirring sound. A counterweighted mechanism apparently brought them to original position with slow precision. Marvelous to imagine and too complex to visualize. Perhaps Father could create such a thing.

Janie continued with her task, oblivious to the desk. "Oh!" I hoped my outburst wouldn't bring her running. My own displaced table and books required replacement. I hurried to disassemble my platform lest it give me away.

I completed the cover-up just before she emerged. Both of us were rather winded, with all the stooping in our unwieldy garments. It was a wonder how women would ever progress here in the West weighed down by all this fabric. A noble mission for me to propel them forward to the new lighter styles embraced back East.

"Did you remember the candle, dear?"

"But of course," she confirmed – ever faithful.

As we stepped from the bookshop with a jingle and a click, large raindrops began to fall. I wriggled the key securing the stubborn lock and dropped the precious molded metal in my bag. My body shook as though I'd burst apart at the seams.

"Oh my!"

"Sorry, dear!" Janie apologized after rankling my nerves further by – of all things – whistling briskly between two fingers, at which signal Solomon returned to escort us home.

∞∞∞∞

My longing for a short slap of brandy had grown as large as the surrounding cedars by the time we reached the Adams' home. We certainly needed something to warm our bones from the chill rain. Though we managed to gain the porch before it poured in earnest. Mary Jane requested tea, and I wished it would be Mariage Frères, my father's most lovely discovery in Paris. But Twining's was not a disappointment. I wasn't foolhardy enough to hope against reason. At least it was British. Some things like lesser teas, and perhaps ladies whistling, were just part of the territory here. But mediocre tea or the finest of fine, nothing calmed my mind. Even the brandy may not have done the trick.

Within the hour, Janie was resting with the daintiest of snores while I lay awake listening to the rain pound on the roof. And I was thrashing about mercilessly the whole night despite the excellent accommodations Janie's family provided for me – and so graciously on a moment's notice.

∞∞∞

I was spellbound by thoughts and visions of the stones from the moment I saw them. My unnatural preoccupation blurred breakfast, though it was lavish and lovely with thick cut bacon, and biscuits that were uncannily both flaky and hearty. The rain had cleared into a light fog, but I hardly noticed. When my car arrived, I fell off the step when bidding adieu to the Adams. My absentmindedness may have been maiming had not Jaimeson dutifully caught me. The depth of my obsession was queer and somewhat frightening.

Regrettably, I left an awkward impression on my new friend's kind family. But they seemed truly cordial when my trance was shaken off long enough to give them a genuine wave as we pulled away. The formal ways of Boston could be bettered if affection was allowed more expression and there was adequate freedom for a woman's curiosity to be pursued. A little less scrutiny and a little more passion, perhaps? It warranted reevaluation of my measure. But that would have to wait. I strategized how to get back into the shop and look more closely at those glowing gems.

Thankfully when we arrived back at our manor along the far reaches of Snoqualmie I had hopes of sitting undisturbed. Father was still away meeting with Milwaukee Road's president in Seattle for a few days, and Camille and Jaimeson were used to my moods. For all of my whimsy, my routines were quite readable. Sitting solitary on the porch indicated my considering something without wishing to be bothered with anything else. Shamefully, I'd snapped at Camille last

29

week for intrusion. Her plump cheeks flushed with anger at my scolding. It was not the best way, and I later gave my apology, but at least it instilled deference to my required contemplation.

My return to the bookshop was simple in mechanics but difficult in principle. I keenly desired the freedom of a gentleman to come and go as I pleased without escort or permission. Instead I had to be wily and perhaps even deceitful – or inventive, I'd rather say.

I'd noticed the currier's son, Master Seth smiled sweetly on me ever since I helped to repair his favorite harness. He seemed to admire my independence in grooming my own mount from time to time, as well. Perhaps he could be persuaded to help without giving me away. I determined to sneak off as soon as we arrived home to arrange for him to meet me with a horse later in the evening.

∞∞∞∞

Master Seth agreed to respond to my signal of lighting the lantern outside the barn sometime after dark. He'd saddle up my mount while making the final check to secure the livestock for the night. Then he'd come to the light to help me into the saddle and on my way.

I settled into my place of contemplation on the cane-bottom chair on the porch, and accepted Camille's offering of fine tea. She delivered the libations in respectful silence.

The beginnings of a plan took shape, but there was one point I couldn't decide upon. The secret strained me near to breaking, and it would be such fun to have a companion to share further adventure, but each time I thought of bringing Janie into my game, I shied away from it.

The possessiveness overwhelmed me when I thought of the contents of the cabinet. It wasn't my nature to horde knowledge, but I couldn't overcome this compulsion. And to compound my hesitation, the haunting visage of the dark man hung over me like a sultry mist. It oppressed me with a mystery both captivating and daunting. And I was convinced he owned the magnificent desk and its mystifying contents. Fear for my friend's well-being gnawed at me. It was risky if she accompanied me, especially given the...*inventive* nature of the quest I'd planned with hopes to learn more.

But it was only logical to leave a trail for someone to follow when I entered the shop – to provide potential rescue. Janie was my chosen confidante. The puzzle was how to get her the information too late to come along, but in time to save me if the caper went awry.

"I've got it!" Timber was terrified by my eruption, poor cat. His over-sized grey-striped form flew right out of his nap and over the side of the porch into the rhododendron shrubbery. I really needed to learn to contain myself. If capable of startling that imposingly calm character, I could bring someone to their death with a sudden heart fibrillation.

My *Eureka!* entailed using the book club to transfer information to Janie with just the right delay. We shared the books – I was about to pass our current tome – and Janie was next on the list to receive it. Jaimeson could deliver it to her shortly after I went out to achieve my scheme. And I could tuck a note just far enough into the next chapter so she'd discover it right when I might need support. Janie's voracious reading assured she wouldn't delay in reading the next segment of *The Virginian* as soon as she received it. The plan was infallible.

I was set to affect the first part of the caper. But wondered if it should wait until after tea? My impatience to begin was nearly unbearable, but nightfall wouldn't come any quicker on an empty stomach. And if successful, my ruse would certainly lose any chance I had for ingesting Cook's delectable cucumber sandwiches and iced biscuits. Any adventure would benefit from a fully satisfied appetite.

CHAPTER SIX

∞∞∞∞

In Which Miss Livingstone Employs her Inventive Nature

"Arghh...Ohhh," I groaned and cast myself upon Father's Chesterfield in the parlor. After my fifth attempt, the wail still wasn't loud enough to gain Camille's or Jaimeson's attention. If I'd caterwauled any louder, Cook would've run in from the kitchen, and rather than putting me to bed they'd have insisted upon taking me to hospital.

"Mmmm...Ohhh." I heard footsteps padding down the hall toward the parlor at last and grew still where I reclined.

I couldn't wait in the darkness of my closed-eye state much longer. Even with rising impatience, an enormous yawn escaped me evidencing distinct danger of falling asleep. The recent excitement stretched my physicality, no matter how lively my mind. A quick spy from one slit-open lid showed Camille approaching at last. What took her so long? Suppose I'd really been ill? "Urghh." This was thrown in for good measure. Just in case she hadn't heard the other groaning and had come by incidentally.

"Miss Caprice! Whatever is the matter?"

My eyes opened to Camille's brow-furrowed concern planted rather uncomfortably close to my face, and at the same time a startling *phlumff* that shook the Chesterfield and rattled the china on the side tables. The woman threw her sheets to the wind to come to my aid – so to speak. Our once crisply folded linens would go back to the ironing board. I was riddled with guilt. But the eerie illumination and fabulous gems in the bookshop floated before my mind's eye. It was only laundry, after all.

"Ohhh, I've the most terrible headache. I'm sure I can't endure company. Can you please help me to my room?"

Camille hoisted me off the furniture.

"Urghh." That was for emphasis.

"You poor dear," she soothed me. "I hope you're not taking ill, and with your father away and all."

"Rest and quiet. Just rest and quiet." I didn't want her to procure a doctor.

Camille eased me through the hallway to the stairs with uncharacteristic gentleness. I was apparently quite convincing. She followed me up the steps and I took note of squeaking boards to avoid later. The concerned housekeeper helped me strip down to petticoats. Further bed dress was thwarted by moaning and beseeching her to let me rest. "Ohhh." Partial dress was crucial for ease of my upcoming exit.

"Can I get you anything else, Miss Caprice, dear?"

"Please...quiet...no more noise," I raised my hand slightly and let it fall weakly to the coverlet.

"Yes, Miss. I'll see that you're not disturbed," she whispered as, finally, she left the room. I followed her progress down the wooden steps by the pattern of three squeaks. The final sounding with a loud whine on the bottom step.

∞∞∞∞

I was still as long as possible, in the attempt to be quiet. The comfort of repose tempted me to slip from consciousness, but I fought off slumber. It was worth the risk of a lit candle in the dusk dimmed room to rouse my senses. The shadows loomed large and threatening, but I worked my way back into my clothing. It was impossible to properly place everything on my own, and I needed to ride, so I wore my tea dress to skip some of the more confining elements of my usual garments. But I didn't leave my gloves or hat. The preparation was for fight or flight. The suspense of what I might find alone in the dark grew heavy on my mind.

In proper attire for adventure – my light cloak adequate for riding – I peeked from my door and set my ear to its edge. I heard nothing at first. Then I heard soft footfalls padding toward...but then, there was nothing. Why would someone tiptoe and then wait in the hall at the top of the stairs? Why would someone else be sneaking through the house at all, for that matter?

I pulled the door to and listened against it. I heard nothing but my beating heart. As the thumping slowed, the air circled in my ear like the sound of the ocean deep within a shell. Venturing to crack the door again, I dared a narrow peek down the hall. A little wider, and I confirmed the way was clear. "Oh!" I nearly squealed when something nudged my leg firmly. I'd failed to look down when I scanned the hall. Timber, the big grey lurker, infiltrated my space with his soft paws and lay upon my shoes. He stopped me at the threshold.

I shut the door and shooed the cat with a soft kick to his ample middle, and then returned to my bed. Perching on its edge, I struggled to regain my nerve. Timber had quite undone me. He returned and curled around my toes, still unwilling to let me move freely. His purr was soothing, and I laid back taking deep breaths to ease my anxiety.

Timber jumped up beside me, and I let my mind wander and rested into the rhythm of the feline's comfort at my side.

I was brought to my senses by Timber's warm furry body moving away. I had fallen into a doze! My adventure with Janie must've worn me out more than I realized. The room was nearly dark, and the candle guttering its last. Timber was a shadow at the door waiting to leave. I shook the sleep from my addled brain and rekindled a candle to carry. At least there was no time lost in dressing. With a gathering of my skirts and my courage, I joined the cat at the door again.

Under the full cover of night my caper was more likely to succeed. My impatience may have ruined it for me earlier. "Good kitty." When I scratched around his ears he gave me the most knowing look. "Yes, you were quite right to delay me, though it's not polite to gloat." He sauntered off as soon as I cracked the door. The cat could provide distraction to hide my unavoidable trip through the house before escape, I hoped.

Ding dong dong ding, gong... gong... Perfect, I hurried to hide the sounds of my steps in the grandfather clock's chime.

My creep down the steps went smoothly, and I skipped the last with a hop to avoid the loudest squeak. But just then the last of the ten gongs chimed. I inhaled deeply and tiptoed through the kitchen without an exhale. And out the back door into the night!

Launching from the bottom step across the yard, I'd never felt such freedom. But I confess, there was some self-doubt – very rare for me, to be sure. The constraints of womanhood often buoyed my confidence with resolve to overcome. Set free upon the world, I felt suddenly small. And it was cold! If my mission was less compelling I might have turned back. But as if mesmerized, I simply had to see those stones.

The stars stretched out in the open sky above the evergreens as I sheltered the candle flame on a lonely walk to the barn. The wind was low in the chilly night, and though it flickered, the flame arrived with me to spark the lantern's signal. It seemed a shivering solitary eternity before Seth arrived.

"Evening, Miss Livingstone," he dropped his grey eyes shyly. "I thought you was never gonna make it out here. But I've stood at the ready."

"You're a steadfast gentleman, Master Seth." I answered to the mass of his wavy blond hair. Faced with his gentleness my pluck returned.

He busied himself with the task of untangling the tack, perhaps to hide his awkward admiration. I didn't press him further with conversation.

"Here she is Miss. I know Summer's Girl's your favored mount."

"Yes, she's perfect."

"Be sure to secure her to the hitch, Miss. She's as gentle as a lamb when you're riding, but she gets restive when she's made to wait. If you hitch her where there are other horses, she'll behave better," he advised while helping me into the saddle. A smile lit his features with just the amount of admiration I could see but not enough to acknowledge. "Are you sure you'll be alright, Miss, your skirts are kinda' light for..." he blushed.

"You have my gratitude, Master Seth. I'm fine and will certainly take your instructions under advisement." I gave him a smile with just the amount of personal attention that he could see but not enough to follow up on.

"Now you're sure you don't need an escort, Miss Livingstone? I'd be mighty pleased to come along and make sure of your way. I can stand aside while you accomplish your task, whatever that may be."

"No, you've done enough, truly."

"Alrighty then, Miss, just remember I'll be waiting for your signal when you return. Bring her to the stable and then toss a stone by my window."

The term *stone* startled me for a moment, but of course he hadn't meant one of *those* stones. "Certainly, my thanks."

"Just mind you don't hit the glass." His eyes sparked with his tease.

My laugh rewarded his easy charm. "I'll be certain to let you know with careful precision when I return." I gave him a genuinely appreciative nod.

I rode into the night feeling free and a bit exposed. I'd always dreamed of doing this, but didn't imagine it so dark or so quiet. The glow of moonlight was a small comfort. My heartbeat filled my ears and warmed me with anticipation. The frogs' chorus rose as the trees gathered in a dark mass near the winding river on one side of my path. It would be frightening to disappear into their depths, where even the moonlight didn't reach. But Summer's Girl had my faith she'd carry me safe and sure.

I focused on arranging my plan. I preferred to stop by the Lucile Hotel, but decided Summer's Girl needed to be hitched near the saloon even if I could be accosted by passing patrons. As a bonus, it would remove any suspicion raised by a horse alone by the bookshop at night. If I could hitch her and disappear, anyone in the saloon could assume the horse belonged to another.

∞∞∞∞

Summer's Girl was securely hitched next to a roan at the saloon. I assured her I'd be back soon and shook my way down the block to the bookshop – whether shivering more from cold or fear I couldn't ascertain.

The dark pressed in on me with more gravity than when Janie accompanied me, though the same gas lamp glowed faithfully, shining on my gateway. It gave the soaped windows a ghostly presence. There was nothing for it but to shimmy the key into the keyhole. But my quaking hand labored the task, exposing my invading figure on the threshold for way too long. When the stubborn lock finally gave, I disappeared from the street with a ringing of bells and a snap of the latch.

I'd been holding my breath! The must of old books and delicious smell of new ones wafted in as I pulled a long draught of air through my nose to compensate. Slight dizziness for lack of air shifted rather than left me. I was flushed with heat – the cold of night left behind. It was the enticing lure of the jewels. Being so close to them stirred a magnetically deep desire. Even at my most curious, I'd never encountered such a force. It drove me toward the cabinet.

I slid the table and hopped upon my makeshift platform like a springtime rabbit. I couldn't wait another moment. Without adding the layer of books it was hard to reach the correct spot at the cabinet's top. I strained with all my might to set off the ingenious mechanism within. The whirring put my heart in my mouth. I stumbled down again to await alignment and the accompanying *click* of opening. The anticipation was nearly unbearable, being so close to what I'd longed for since the prior night. Had it truly been only one day I suffered in waiting?

The doors stood open before me, and I must confess I was unable to move or speak for some time. Now that it came to it, I hesitated to touch the stones. The glow of light from the cabinet was as irresistible as the aroma of those lovely buns with cinnamon we had at Mary Jane's. But the level of intoxication I felt raised my caution.

"Oh my, why didn't I notice that before?" I spoke aloud. The design on the sash across the inside of the cabinet was formed from intricately embellished letters. I'd never seen such script. Exquisitely rendered but camouflaged by its own detail. Close inspection would've failed to decipher the letters, but my strange trance-like mood made them vivid like a prophetic dream:

If you are inclined to roam, always take a steam train home.

How strange. And yet, I understood – as if the words were meant for me.

CHAPTER SEVEN

∞∞∞

In Which Miss Livingstone Embarks on an Unwitting Journey

I resolved to force my fate and move ahead with eyes wide open. I stepped onto the platform to choose a stone for inspection.

When they were at my fingertips I had an intense desire to grab them all and run. But then there'd be no escaping the label of thief if I were caught. I fought the irrational urge.

Besides, something important had escaped my keen eye on first discovery. There were two spaces without stones. I would most certainly need them all before any high risk was worthwhile, I thought. Though again, the rationale for this escaped me. The indentations waiting for stones were not uniform, but had complex shapes – perfectly suited to their potential occupants.

I was puzzled, but it was the rust stone with the sparkling stars that again drew me in. I attempted to pick it up. "Oh!" As it slipped through my gloved fingers and settled back into its place on the small block, I saw a flash of light from beneath it. It was most unsettling, the feeling that light brought me. I determined to leave that one in its place and try another.

I was overwhelmed with hesitation – it bordered on trepidation. Besides the odd sensation I felt from the light, a stab of fear had gone through me. I'd imagined the stone might fall to the floor as it slipped. Although the oils of my fingers might smudge the stones, removal of my gloves was required to examine the gems properly. How convenient I wore my tea dress instead of corset and bustle. I tucked the gloves in the pouch-like pocket in front. But what a frightful excuse for a lady I was if the proprietor caught me bare handed with nothing under my frock and a pair of gloves at my bosom. I loosened the collar fastener and drew my cloak in a double layer across my chest protectively.

Enough stalling, I chose the faceted piece of emerald – attracted by the depth of its fresh green. It looked rich with promise and brought me comfort somehow.

As I reached out for a second time, my exposed skin descending toward the emerald, my mind ran off again wondering if that strange dark man owned them all. And when I lifted the gem, I turned my head toward the door, filled with chilling worry he might be there. But not only was he not there, neither was the door...nor the shop...nor anything I expected at all. When I turned my head back toward the cabinet, I reacted in an instant, throwing myself to the side on hands and knees to avoid – an automobile? It was certainly no carriage!

The horrified gasps and coos of relief from those on the boulevard buffeted my ears as I flew through the air and landed in a heap. But did I also hear my name? The question puzzled...

"Miss Livingstone... Miss Livingstone, are you well, lass?"

Yes, I heard a rich and reedy voice with a distinct Scottish accent asking after me from somewhere at my back. Thank heavens I managed to keep a grip on the emerald. A sharp pain stabbed from my knee as I labored to prop up on my hip and gain my composure. My skirts were in a tangle around my legs. It was a strain to see where

I was. The low sun shined in my eyes, and I wasn't able to ascertain who owned the unfamiliar voice that clearly knew my name. As I gathered my wits a ring of concerned strangers came into focus around me. They were oddly dressed. I tore my gaze from a woman's sheer stockinged legs. She was practically bare!

When I looked about...

"Miss Livingstone," came to my ears more loudly.

I still didn't see who was calling from behind me. But I knew exactly where I was. I recognized buildings I had left behind and the edge of the Boston Public Garden. It was my dear Newbury Street. My home, Newbury Manor was across the way – although changed somewhat. And there were so many automobiles. Their design was strange to me. Not a horse to be seen. The smell of steam and noise of engines – it was overwhelming. And the ladies, they had such different garments – too short, austere, drab, with no draping or embellishments. Like the world had turned to a sepia toned photograph, but with lips painted the most garish red! And their hats...

"Oh...Oh dear!" I straightened my oversized hat with my free hand. I was certainly glad I didn't leave the house without one. But my exposed hands and arms, lack of proper undergarments and – "Oh!" – the bundle of gloves protruding at my bosom! I was all aflutter. I tried to smooth this and hide that and...

"Miss Livingstone?" The accented voice was calming, and my wild attempts at decorum were tamed.

I found his face at last in front of me – blocking the sun – along with an insistently extended hand. I obeyed and took it.

"Whoa!" I was swooped gently but firmly from my awkward place on the walkway to my rather wobbly feet. I was terribly and thrillingly conscious of his hand in mine. But, "Oh!" He released my hand and caught me around the waist. My propriety wished to pull away, but the curl of his arm and grip on my side were the only things keeping me from going down again. I hung at a precarious angle at the mercy of my captor – or was he my savior?

I let go of the quandary and caught hold of my senses – and promptly attended to my balance. My upright form dispersed the crowd. I was suddenly keenly aware of the emerald in my hand and tightened my grip.

"I'm sorry, I didn't know precisely when you'd be here, lass. If I could've pinpointed the moment, I'd have grabbed you rather than let you dive. Although I'm not sure the twist would've been safe, it seems worth it to have saved you the nasty scar on your knee and the pain you'll have for the next days." This gibberish came from the older man who finally released me. His garb was equally strange as the others' on the boulevard, and his fiery red hair laced with grey was accompanied by a remarkably long thick beard.

"Mr. Worthington?" Though my mind was addled, my quick wit followed the clues brilliantly.

"Taing dhan Aig! you recognize me. Yes, lass. I... but wait, you told me this was the first time you met me. How...?"

"If it's the first time I'm meeting you, how could I have told you so?" I was beginning to feel very dizzy so took a wider look around and a deep breath, avoiding the spot of sun. "The trees! They're huge!" That was the difference by my Newbury house...

"Here lass, take m' elbow. I'm sure you won't appreciate me holding your hand." He gave me an overly familiar grin, like this was an understanding between us. My protest was stopped by, "We need to get you off the street and tell you how it is. I'd carry you if you'd allow it, but you'll have to endure the pain of a few blocks walk. I'll support and lead you along."

"Elbow or hand, I'll not allow you to lead me anywhere. We haven't even had a proper introduction. And..." my eyes swung wildly around the foreign street that should have been the one I remembered. Except I was supposed to be in Snoqualmie. "Where am I?"

"That's what I'm trying to tell you, lass. And the question is actually, 'When?'" He smirked and his amber eyes twinkled merrily through a quirky squint.

For fear of swooning, I was forced to hold his elbow to steady myself. And, next I knew, he broke into a jaunty stride which I trotted alongside. My left knee was stabbing with pain beneath my skirts. I couldn't carry on for long.

"I'll get you your proper introduction at MacGinty's, lass. It's not far now, but you ought not tell Angus about your – em, journey. I'll just tell him you're a traditional lady and won't have a drink with me unless he makes us better acquainted."

His pace, the pain and my racing thoughts left me too breathless to reply. But he stopped at last before a green-painted door. A string of brass bells hanging on the inside jingled loudly upon our entrance, bringing a bulky but jovial-looking dark-haired man out behind a well-stocked bar. I lost focus again and only vaguely heard Mr. Worthington ask about introductions. He gave explanations I didn't follow. Suddenly through the fog I understood the bartender had addressed me.

"I beg your pardon? I'm afraid I didn't hear what you said, sir. Can I trouble you to repeat it?"

"Oh, she's very good." He nodded and smiled widely at Mr. Worthington. "I was asking if I might have your full name and the honor of introducing you to my esteemed friend here, Miss?"

The men exchanged an amused glance – at my expense!

"I believe, Miss Livingstone, will be adequate." I mustered the best look of dignity I could feign.

"Very well." He gave me a slight bow and raised one hand indicating the man that pulled me from the boulevard walkway. "Miss

Livingstone, may I present Mr. Thomas Worthington, bookshop proprietor, and man of many talents and travels."

Eying the two men dubiously, I shifted my weight briefly onto my sore knee but returned to leaning on my fatigued right leg. Silence seemed the best response.

"And Mr. Worthington, may I present the beautiful Miss Livingstone, who doubtless has many talents of her own." His brows were frozen in their arched position as he continued to extend his hand toward me, waiting for my validation of his words. Mr. Worthington stood firm with the most twinkling eyes I'd ever seen. Most amused, apparently.

The *humph* I planned to huff at the man's insolence stuck in my throat as my mind flew away on the supreme compliment of an introduction as beautiful. Though prized for my wit, I was never praised for my beauty. A downside of being sequestered at Miss Preston's School for girls, perhaps. When I quelled my pleasure, the moment for a *humph* or any other appropriate expression of disgust had long passed. "I... em..."

"My pleasure, Miss, to be sure," interrupted my squirm.

I opened my mouth with new intent to scold, but the sincerity in Mr. Worthington's eyes arrested my ire. If he was making fun, why did his gaze offer respect? My mouth formed a firm line, and I dropped my eyes as well as a small, somewhat painful, curtsy.

Mr. Worthington's warm smile acknowledged my concession.

Angus set a bottle on the bar and chuckled deeply as he filled a glass with scotch. "And for the esteemed, Miss Livingstone?" he asked.

"Brandy, if you please," I boldly declared. If this day – wasn't it just night? – was going to take such sudden turns, a small slap would do me good.

CHAPTER EIGHT

∞∞∞

In Which Miss Livingstone Meets the Twisted Mr. Worthington

"So alright then, to *when* have I gone, sir?" Thomas' insistence and my own eyes finally convinced me to suppose I traveled in time. The apparent fact of night turned to day and the changes on Newbury Street were indisputable. And though I found it uncanny, logic dictates the theory that best describes observable facts is the most likely truth. Grown trees, unknown fashion, and overwhelming advancements in technology evidenced the future. Either that, or I was having the most fantastical dream. Since my dream would be a smashing adventure with the assumption I'd traveled to 1941, as Thomas claimed, there was no reason to reject that supposition. However, denying I was in the future and insisting it was a dream would bring grave danger of classification as a lunatic. The result of that designation would be unpleasant indeed. So I sided with logic and the scenario I fancied – with prudence of continued observation, of course.

With more difficulty he convinced me to call him Thomas. Though once I began, it suited me well to do so. Much more efficient. He said it was the fashion among friends and anything more would seem out of place to those around us. We had apparently known one another for many years. My intuition felt familiarity, but my mind rebelled. This couldn't be so. I hadn't yet met the man...Well, other than Angus' recent introduction. And who was Angus, after all? It'd been a long day – night – day.

"You have remarkable intellect and spunk, Li... Caprice."

I jumped in my seat. A sharp pain stabbed through my knee. Hearing him call me that would take serious adjustment. I didn't like it at all. I shivered.

"But if you had a shop in Snoqualmie, em, Thomas, why would you be in Boston?"

"I left some grief behind, and hoped to reunite with and encourage an old friend." His smile crinkled into well-worn lines of care. "Here lass, put my waistcoat around you, you're shiverin' like a newborn pup."

He wrapped my shoulders with his generous coat and I suddenly missed... "My cloak!" I scrambled wildly throwing my hands and arms over my terribly exposed body.

"I'm afraid it was lost in the fray. My apologies, though I'm sure the gutter left it hardly worth rescue."

"But what am I doing here? I..." I was at a loss for words, that's what I was. Miss Livingstone, with no words!

"I know it's a lot to take in, lass." Thomas set his hand on mine, and mine pulled away by reflex. I wished I allowed the comfort. He looked at me with caring not unlike my father portrayed when I was afraid or displeased. A tear fought for its life at the corner of my eye, but I didn't give it form.

"I'd like to fully embrace this, it's just so difficult." I kept my voice steady.

"Well, I know you'll listen to nothing but logic, so think it through. I know your name, even the part you didn't share in your introduction, and I knew where you'd appear sometime today. This implies I've met you in the past."

"Yes, it's a reasonable theory." A deep breath sniffed back my final threat of tears. "Or you could've read about me in the newspapers." I managed a feeble laugh. Thomas mirrored my humor but without his sparkle.

"Since we both lived in Snoqualmie in 1910, it's likely our past meeting was there, yes?"

"I suppose. I heard about you from Miss Abigale yesterday...or whatever day that would be now...and it's likely I'll meet you in 1910 Snoqualmie once the book shop has opened. It's a small town...But do you know how I got here?" My cheeks flushed with the guilt of breaking into his shop – and even into his cabinet. Was he aware?

"If you can believe you'll meet me there, can you also believe that we'll become friends?"

"That one is easier to entertain than the others."

Some light returned to his eyes.

"During our friendship you shared many things, including the tale of meeting me briefly in Boston in 1941. You'll find it amusing that when you told me that as a man of twenty-eight years, I was just as hard to convince as you've been. But you showed me a piece of evidence that was hard to refute. A souvenir of sorts. Something that couldn't have come from 1912, which was the year you showed it to me."

"So you know my future. My future between 1910 and now – 1941 that is? Oh my, these questions are swirled in problems with time references, are they not? Currently, for me, that would be less than a day's worth of story. But if what you are telling me is true, it has been thirty-one years of history for you. And the grey in your beard – which was missing from Abigale's description of you – evidences that's so. How old are you? If I may be so bold?" My curiosity wound up grandly once I accepted the premise, and my addled brain wouldn't calculate the figures.

His eyes crinkled in that quirky way, and they smiled with twinkling golden light.

"Do you laugh at me, sir? If we are friends, don't make light of my questions. I ask with sincerity. It's just there's so much I don't know..."

"...and long to understand. Yes, I know, I know, lass."

His broad smile goaded me with frustration. "I fail to see the humor —"

"It's just you always say that, and it's been so long since I've heard you hot on the heels of quenching your curiosity. It's good to see you again, my dear, Lizzie...Oh —" He drew his hand to his beard and pulled it with a stroke.

The motion soothed me. "Lizzie? That was my grandmother's name. And my middle."

"Given you by your mother...I was trying not to give things away. I barely managed to call you by your first name a few moments ago. I guess there's no harm in telling. You asked me to call you Lizzie shortly after we met. Seems once we were beyond, Miss Livingstone, Caprice was not to your liking on a regular basis."

I dropped into silence. It was like he knew my thoughts of the last few days. But of course, he likely knew my thoughts of the next few weeks.

"So when I told you I traveled here, did I tell you how long I was gone? If your story is true, I must have returned within the year." I could feel my brow knot but couldn't seem to shake the weight of my growing understanding.

"I don't think I should give you too many details. But I first met you the day my bookshop opened in Snoqualmie. I'll never forget it.

You were with Miss Mary Jane Adams and wore a striking dark green tailor made suit. You had, of course, already met me here in passing on your travels, though I hadn't met you. I was anchored to the slow passage of days. I have long awaited this one."

I had no words.

He continued, "although things may be different now than they were the first time around. I created a twist by meeting you on the boulevard today. According to what you told me in the past, today is the day before I met you in Boston that time. I wanted a chance to truly talk with you – for you to get to know me – instead of just our brief encounter, and I hoped... You told me that twists can be risky, but... I guess I've caught some of your impatience. I didn't want to wait for fate to bring us together, in its own way. I wanted things to be different."

I swallowed hard, remembering my decision to force fate just before I touched the stone. The stone that was still in my hand. It had grown warm, and I wished to lay it down. But I wasn't certain I should reveal it.

"Did I tell you how I came here?" I searched his amber eyes.

He almost spoke, but hesitated. His eyes shifted.

"No," he admitted.

There must have been a reason. I allowed the stone to feel overly warm in my palm, and waited to understand more. Telling him could've inadvertently destroyed my chances of returning home. There were so many unknowns on this outlandish journey. My whole life may have been whisked away as quickly as I was whisked from the shop to Newbury Street. I would look for an opportunity to secretly try going home by wishing for Snoqualmie with stone in hand, but checking my option of returning by train, like the strange carved message suggested, was prudent as well.

My mind sharpened, at last. "Is there still a steam train in Boston?" I vaguely recalled the city smelled of a steam locomotive earlier as we walked. Though there were so many steam autos, it was hard to be sure.

"Well of course, why wouldn't there be? Things have progressed not regressed. There's a station just down from my bookshop."

"You mean you have a shop here as well... in Boston?"

"I left Snoqualmie, not my mind. Of course I brought my books."

We shared a look of delight, and he broke into a rich laugh.

"It's well-known for its extensive collection, especially of historical books and early editions. We can use that as explanation for your strange dress and manner while you're here. I can say you are advertising the period texts. Come to think of it, you told me you were on the way to the train..."

He trailed off too late. I deduced I'd found his shop on my way home, and I met him there when I was here last. Or at least that time. Who's to say I didn't go back and forth between these places and eras all the time?

"Strange dress and manner!" I protested, but the complaint was half-hearted. My mind was somewhere else.

CHAPTER NINE

∞∞∞∞

In Which Miss Livingstone is Not Quite Herself

The brandy mixed with the expansion of possibilities set my mind awhirl. Although I'd seen my home nearby on Newbury Street, it was likely no longer my home. My father kept Newbury Manor when he moved to Snoqualmie in 1908, for sentimentality over the loss of my mother. It's the home they'd moved to together not long after I was born in London. We had a willing staff who was left behind for its care, but that would be thirty-three years ago.

Father would be a terribly old man in this year! Was our Boston home sold off as part of his...his estate, at his passing? Unimaginable that this world would not contain his dear soul. But surely he would've passed the property to me.

"Thomas, do you know...Is the property on Newbury Street where my family was once settled...mine?"

He was slow to answer, and I realized he had been lost in thought, just as I had been.

"I'm not sure where you stayed, or will stay, when you come here. But you told me it was nearby on Newbury."

"And when I met you here before, what time of day was it, did I tell you?"

"Yes, I've imagined the scene you described many times – with the morning light on your curls. Oh pardon, Miss Lizzie. I can see by your wide eyes that is far overstepping our current familiarity. It's just difficult when I've known you for so long."

I let it pass, though such familiarity made me wonder how close we'd been. "Are there any more passenger trains leaving this evening?"

"I don't believe so. There will only be arrivals by this time of day."

"I hate to trouble you, but could I be allowed a place to freshen up? Now that I've regained my wits, I'd like to check my dignity."

Thomas' laugh was filled with fondness and he waved me to a small door. I could try to travel home in privacy there.

"Don't worry, I'll be back soon," I assured.

I heard uproarious laughter in the mixed tones of Angus and Thomas fade as I closed the door.

"Oh dear!" I hadn't thought through the absurdity of my assurance. I merely wanted him not to be concerned if I disappeared, as I likely could.

The water closet was befitting a man's bar and had little light and stuffy air. My dignity certainly needed checking. The young woman in the mirror was disheveled and had the most ridiculous dark curls flying off in every direction. I looked in her eyes and then squeezed them shut with an equally hard squeeze of the emerald stone in my hand. I wished for Snoqualmie. But when I opened my eyes again, all I saw was the same dark and dreary water closet. I would have to try the train in the morning.

As I left the privy I announced, "so I need a place to stay tonight and – "I held up my hand to halt his interruption which undoubtedly contained an inappropriate offer of lodgings at his home. "I need to find a proper place."

He gave in immediately, which assured me I'd kept my propriety in our past, since he expected nothing less. Seems I'd managed to do mother's memory proud.

"I'd like to pay a visit to Newbury Manor to discover who currently holds its charge. It's my hope to stay there for the night. But who shall I say I am? I would be, oh dear, old, if I was myself. No offense intended for your regular aging, Thomas. It's just a wee bit shocking to gain thirty-one years in a day."

"No offense taken. It's wonderful to see your youthful beauty again. How strange it must be for you to see me so old. Or I guess it's different for you since you've met me this way first. I hadn't thought of that."

"Yes, yes, we could go over these oddities all evening, but I need to go to Newbury Manor at once. Do you suppose they'd believe I was my own daughter? But they might know I don't have one…or perhaps I do? Oh my!"

Thomas put his hand on mine again. The secret jewel was embedded in the knot of our union. I allowed his touch to remain. Tears sprung to my eyes, and I needed his kind strength.

"Did I marry?" I asked him softly, and was surprised to see water spring to his eye. Was it in response to the tear in mine?

"Your daughter's name is Elizabeth."

I was stunned. "So perhaps Lizzie for Grandmother and Bessie for Mother," I surmised. "Does she go by Lizzie as I will do? …I'll go to Newbury Manor and present myself as Elizabeth but will ask them to call me Lizzie. I'll have to risk the chance she's known to them and I shall be found out."

He waited patiently through my rambling and then assured me, "I'll have a cabby at the ready to whisk us away to my shop if things go wrong." He called loudly without looking away, "Angus, can you call a cab?"

Thomas' eyes shone with feeling. Surely he knew who would be my husband. But I wasn't ready to digest more just yet.

"Let's go now," I pronounced. "It's important to arrive well before darkness falls."

"Agreed." He stood and approached the bar. "Angus, mate?"

I heard Thomas call his friend, but was focused on how my hand grew cold when his left mine.

Finally, I could find a place other than my palm for the stone – a unique and fearsome treasure. The emerald's power brought me to this place, certainly. I should have put it away while in the water closet, but a secure place was required, and I was reluctant to let it go. My tea dress had only one pocket, and it wasn't covered or closed. But it was very deep – a pouch really – at the waist. With trepidation I released the gem into its depths.

"Our taxi will be here presently. We can wait outside if you'd like, Lizzie," Thomas' voice reached out to me.

I stood as if entranced – bereft without the stone in my hand. Or perhaps it was more than that. The simple and curious girl I was when I awoke that morning was lost in the wide journey of time. But I had traveled through time! The thought ignited my flame. I pushed my arms with vigor into Thomas' coat. Curiosity and longing for adventure spurred me onward.

∞∞∞∞

The taxi ride was enchanting. The vehicle was a marvel of invention beyond even my wildest fancies. There were materials I didn't recognize, and although the locomotion was still achieved with steam and gears, the efficiency was a humdinger. The conveyou, as Thomas called it, was quiet and near odorless on the interior. I would have liked to ride across the world examining its workings, but we were to Newbury Manor in no time.

Thomas opened my door, extending his hand to help me from the cab into the fading light of evening.

"Here's your coat, sir." I swung it from my shoulders, confident to try my hand at being a modern woman. "Thank you kindly for the loan."

He donned it, looking rather dashing I noted.

I walked a couple steps and looked back longingly at the conveyou, until I turned to see what awaited us – the fine steps of Newbury Manor.

"I'm so pleased to see how well kept the property is. The warm brownstone columns and brick steps are clean and inviting." I was moved by the noble structure, so extravagant compared to the wooden buildings of my new home in the West. Whoever was in charge obviously loved the place as I did. It was just as I remembered. The only difference was the high red doors were darkened by long shadows, cast by the eerily mature trees that seemed to have grown up in a few months from my perspective. It gave me pause.

"Come," Thomas softly urged.

He gave his elbow to escort me forward, but when we stood on the porch, another significant change set me back. The heavy brass door knocker with father's initials had been removed. Fear sunk its black teeth into my heart. The mark of Father had gone from this place. In addition to my dread, I didn't know how to knock loudly enough without it.

"Push the button to the right of the door." Thomas' gentle instruction from behind my shoulder made me jump like an arrow from a taut string. His advice produced the loveliest tune played through the door on what sounded like a tiny steam-pipe organ.

"A doorbell," he supplied.

"Certainly a far cry above a bell," my wonder was renewed, and my stress subsided.

The crimson door swung wide. "May I help you? Oh my...Miss Elizabeth! Why didn't you tell us you were arriving from Scotland? I would've prepared, I would've – Oh...My Dear!" The unfamiliar woman threw her arms around me and squeezed like I was her own lost child. I heard Thomas' soft chuckle from behind.

Unsure what to do, I returned her embrace, taking the part of Miss Elizabeth. "So good to see you...dear...but please, I go by Lizzie now."

"You've taken the nickname of your mother? How...Oh..." Tears sparked in the woman's expressive brown eyes. "It's so good to see you dear, and I'm forgetting myself. Please do come in. And your gentleman friend here is?"

"This is Mr. Thomas Worthington, a friend of...my mother's. I met him in connection with his bookshop, and I stopped there on my way from the train. As I had no escort in the approaching night he insisted on calling a cab and delivering me safely home." My quick wit had indeed returned.

"A pleasure, Mr. Worthington."

An uncomfortable pause settled, in which I knew I should present her to him, but I didn't know her name. She noticed my discomfort. I hoped she'd supply her own good reason for its cause.

"I'm Mrs. Phoebe Carrington, housekeeper and onetime nursemaid to this precious young woman," She graciously filled the gap. "I was heartbroken when she...but here she stands again before me." Her tears escaped down full cheeks, dimpled with her joy.

"Yes, it's good to see her, and it's my pleasure to make your acquaintance, Mrs. Carrington." His brow was up and his eyes wild with light. Perhaps he'd heard stories of this woman from me?

"I'll take my leave now that L... Miss Livingstone is home," Thomas excused.

"Miss Livingstone? But her last name is..."

"Oh please, pardon me," Thomas jumped in with abrupt intensity, "it's just she reminds me so much of her mother when she was young. Ladies, I'll leave you to your reunion." He all but ran from the porch.

"Oh, of course." Mrs. Carrington was convinced by his quick save.

I could see why I liked the fellow.

"But don't you need to have the cabby bring in her luggage?" the caretaker called after him. "She doesn't even have a coat."

"Oh, I... em...I had my luggage sent on," I improvised. "You see, I'll be leaving on the train tomorrow." I missed my cloak desperately. Thomas' departure left me feeling bare.

"Tomorrow! But whatever for? Oh sorry, dear, of course you must proceed as you need. May I ask what's so pressing?" She rolled her eyes toward a stray lock of dark hair and wiped it back away from her forehead.

"Em...I'm in Mr. Worthington's employ as a finder and book buyer. There are more journeys planned. I'll bring the tomes I find on my travels to his most excellent bookshop for sale whenever possible. It's a famous collection, you know." I had a vision of my soiled cloak in the gutter where I'd fallen. How odd.

"Oh, you're so like your mother. I should have guessed by your out of fashion gown. She spent her whole life disappearing here or there on her infamous adventures. I just knew her bedtime tales would set a seed of wildness in you. But it can't be helped..."

The woman babbled on as she tried again to paste back her wayward black wisp of hair.

I turned to see Thomas standing by the cab open-mouthed in astonishment. Perhaps he got more than expected while waiting to bid us good evening.

"I'll stop in again at the shop on my way to the train tomorrow, Mr. Worthington. My sincere thanks for the gracious and unexpected escort home."

"Oh, one last thing." He approached, pulling a small stack of papers from his pocket. "Be certain to give my card to the cabby for ease in return to the shop."

Thomas' face crinkled into that merry shine again as he pressed several cards into my palm. It was apparent he desired me to visit more than once. "Oh!" And there was money to pay...

"Oh wait, Mr. Worthington!" I called, but stopped short as my injured knee protested my lurch toward chasing him down.

He turned after his retreat and waved off into the conveyou with what could only be described as a mischievous grin.

CHAPTER TEN

∞∞∞∞

In Which Miss Livingstone Uncovers Her Future Past

I stumbled over the threshold throwing Mrs. Carrington into a ridiculous deal of fuss over my stiffening knee. She refused to return to her dinner until I was properly nursed. I suffered a nasty gash very near the knee cap, but it was much improved after her kind attendance.

After a late dinner filled with squirming and quick thinking explanations, Mrs. Carrington's immediate prying for news was diverted without further faux paus. Her husband and son joined us at the table but didn't speak at all. She gave them no opportunity. I tried to quell my curiosity and avoid prying on my own part, but without trying I learned that Elizabeth was born in Scotland, and at some point I brought her to Boston for Mrs. Carrington to raise. Elizabeth was upset by this and, as soon as she was of age, left for Scotland to find her family and, in the caretaker's words, track her mother down. The woman criticized me for a good deal of time and bemoaned her time away from Elizabeth. It does seem a strange decision since I apparently came all the way from Snoqualmie to Boston first. Why would I come back home to the east just to leave again? And why Scotland? The only connection I could imagine was Mr.

Worthington's Scottish background, but he implied I was without him, and Mrs. Carrington clearly didn't recognize him at the door. She would've known him if he was my husband. My husband! What strange directions these riddles took. But I accepted temporarily that there were many things I didn't yet understand. To think before this journey I thought myself well educated. Piffle!

Mrs. Carrington revered her role as caretaker and was given charge by, apparently, myself. So somewhere in the world, my older self still existed? Or actually, she didn't say that. She said she continued to receive the payments I arranged. That wouldn't preclude my death. I couldn't very well ask her such a question as it defied verity for a daughter not to hear of her own mother's passing, especially if we were in Scotland together – which seemed likely. I couldn't find out more since the family didn't communicate with Mrs. Carrington, as she lamented ceaselessly.

I wondered if Thomas knew whether or not I was still living and my older self's whereabouts. Perhaps another thing he'd be reluctant to divulge to me.

My chief mission had been to convince Mrs. Carrington to extend me lodging for the night, but I could see the difficulty would be in getting her to let me go with minimal drama. I reminded her repeatedly that my bags had gone on before me. But rather than causing logical acceptance of my departure in the morning, it caused an enormous outpouring of sentiment profusely punctuated with 'poor dears.' It also resulted in a lavish store of comforts pressed upon me. My room was stocked with everything I could desire.

I must admit a show of sentiment on my part when I climbed upon the high carved bedstead. What a pleasure to lay back in the gloriously familiar room that was my own many years, or a few short months, before. I was moved by the obvious care with which all was preserved. It was good to be home.

I had taken the stone from my dress so as not to lose it, and I held it on my palm and regarded the common-looking faceted emerald. Squeezing it, I once again tried to travel to Father's home in Snoqualmie. After no result, I tried the bookstore there. It was no use. I would have to wait to try the morning train. I set the stone on the nightstand and wished it was as simple to set aside my worries regarding Summer's Girl and Master Seth. Nevertheless I would do my best to sleep like one did in one's favorite place after a long and eventful day. And afterward, to listen much and say little at breakfast.

∞∞∞∞

It wasn't hard to avoid difficult explanations while we devoured poached eggs and sweet biscuits. And I was delighted by a perfectly hot cup of Mariage Frères breakfast tea. It was part of the prescribed budget to serve nothing but that brand in the household – which convinced me more than anything else it was I who gave the woman her charge.

Mrs. Carrington was completely focused on her distress at losing me again. She tried every angle to learn when I'd return, until I assured her it would be soon. Thomas implied I came here more than once, and although I didn't know when, it was better to leave this door open. Besides, the woman would hear no other answer.

After breakfast, Mrs. Carrington insisted on redressing my wound. Bless her fussing soul.

So, once again I limped off to adventure. When I told Mrs. Carrington I would take a cab to the station she immediately telephoned for one. I did my best to hide my astonishment when she picked up what was obviously a transmitter and receiver in one handle from a small squared off base that was freely sitting on a table. This, more than anything so far, evidenced the future era. Additionally, she offered her son to escort me, but was not ruffled at all when I insisted on going alone. Apparently women in this era achieved much of the independence I craved. Next they'd have the right to vote! I determined to move forward upon my return to

62

Snoqualmie and never wear a bustle or corset again. The sooner we changed the better, and the precedent had been set on the east coast, though I was oddly slow to pick up on it. It seemed improper until now when I keenly felt its utility. Although I was rather chilly on the clear morning without the extra fabric, with only the emerald's burning presence in my bodice to keep my mind off the cold.

My tangent brought me shivering to the doorstep of Thomas Worthington's Rare and Collectible Books. It's not a wonder I entered it on my first journey without his intervention. Curiosity about the possible connection to the unopened shop I had snuck into back in Snoqualmie would have captivated me. In addition, it was a fabulous bookshop – a place irresistible to me under any circumstances.

The elegantly painted flip-sign on the door invited, *Please Come In.* And a lovely steam-powered doorbell was tripped as I stepped inside.

Thomas' glowing smile greeted me, but he was quiet while the minute steam organ played its tune. I could see the fascinating mechanism creating the notes, and expressed, "what a lovely song." It truly was.

"It's called, *My Melancholy Baby.* It will be a favorite in 1912." His face clouded, and I noted his attention drifting away somewhere.

"So music hasn't changed much then?" I had quite forgotten my chill.

"Oh, on the contrary, it's changed remarkably. I'm sure you'll encounter it. I'll let you discover it on your own. But I have a tendency to cling to the past, like an old fool." His eyes were downcast.

"You're not a fool," I tried to comfort him. "I'm sure that's the secret to your immaculate book collection."

His glow returned, "That and your good eye. Many of these are your finds, you know. Past and present."

I shivered again in reply.

"You're cold, and well you must be with no coat. Please, I insist you wear this. And don't mind about its return." He pulled a rather short and scratchy beige wool jacket from a shelf nearby. "It was my brother's. I have no need for it now."

He set it around my shoulders with a reverence I failed to grasp. I was immediately warm through.

"What is this pin at the pocket?" I asked about the strange colored bar.

"It marks his service...In the war."

"The war...?"

"Yes, no matter. We're at war again as a matter of fact, but not here in America, you know. Please don't mind –"

"Oh my! *History of Women's Suffrage, Volume 6*," I shouted as I fingered the book. I was fully distracted and lost his thread. "Have we succeeded?"

"Yes, you have the vote, and other rights of employment and equality ...1920, I don't think it will harm you to know. I recall how passionate you were when speaking of attending the Women's Suffrage Parade in New York." He smiled indulgently.

"In 1905. You remember...Amazing. But, back up a moment. That's why you had that surprised look on your face last night when I invented the story – I'm in your employ already, am I not? I hit on the truth...or at least what later becomes the truth. Do you suppose I got the idea in the spur of the moment when cornered by Mrs. Carrington the first time?"

"I wouldn't put it past you, Lizzie. I thought it was my idea, but you're such a wily lass you may have just let me think so."

"Thomas! I may be witty, but I strive to be truthful. Yet, I must confess, if things were working out well, I may not have corrected your supposition that you offered me a job. But, well, are you?"

"Certainly, I wouldn't have it any other way! Books are the beginning and the glue of our friendship – one of the high points of my life – I would repeat it all again in a moment."

I gave him an unabashed grin of excitement. I'd never had a job, and this one sounded downright thrilling! He returned it with a look of careful reserve. He was holding back something big.

In turning from his discomfort, a large piece of furniture caught my eye in the back corner of the shop. It was none other than the remarkable writing desk through which I'd traveled to this place.

"Ah, that behemoth of a desk," Thomas remarked, "I would never have kept it if it weren't for you and... a possible entanglement. It does add a certain flavor and authenticity to the shop. A great collectible it is, no doubt, but I've never understood why it needs so much bulk. It cost a fortune to transport it here from the West. But you asked me to keep it, and when my partner disappeared, I was never certain if he might come to claim it from me. It was a family heirloom of his, you see. And he was not the type of fellow –"

"Your partner!" Oh my, I did that over-exuberant thing again, cutting him right off with an unladylike shout.

Thomas' eyes were merry.

"Yes, my partner." His look became serious. "Do you know of him?"

"I believe I've bumped into him in town – at home. Is he a dark fellow?"

"Yes, that describes him in a nutshell."

"You say he disappeared?"

"It's remained a mystery where he went or on what business. He left right after... Do you know his fate? Or no, I guess you couldn't yet." Thomas scrutinized me with a hawk-eyed look I hadn't seen from him before. It was my first hint he could be a shrewd man if required.

"No, of course not, we haven't even been introduced." We both fell silent, and I wondered – as Thomas likely did – if I would know eventually.

CHAPTER ELEVEN

∞∞∞∞

In Which Miss Livingstone Goes Home Again, Home Again

"I'm afraid I need to proceed to the train station. As exciting as this excursion has been, I'm anxious to go." I'd forgotten for some time to consider those at home. Their worry would be excruciating.

"Will you tell me your destination, Lizzie?" His face once again revealed well-traced lines of concern.

"I cannot, I'm sorry, Thomas. I wish I could." I didn't know myself for certain. "You've been more than kind."

"So your secretiveness, at least, has not changed with my meeting you sooner. Perhaps the twist will change nothing at all."

"I can't see why you'd want to change a thing. Your shop is marvelous. I can't wait to help in supplying books to you."

"Yes, it will be a dear journey, once again. No matter how it ends." The warm light from his eyes penetrated my heart. It was quite disarming, and I pulled my gaze away to once more fall upon the desk.

"Oh!" I cried out again, but I couldn't help myself.

"What is it dear?"

"The trim on the desk. There – along its side? Do you see it?" The letters I deciphered in that moment had become almost imperceptible in the intricate design again.

"It's an intriguing design, but I'm not sure what you're asking me to notice." He cocked his brow in confusion.

"Oh, never you mind, I just imagined...It was nothing."

He stared at the desk again and then shrugged. "Please allow me to escort you to the station. Shall I carry you?" he teased.

"You'll do nothing of the sort! My knee is much improved." My indignant toss of the chin didn't quite hide my giggling grin.

"Perhaps a tow upon my elbow then?" His eyes twinkled golden under his raised brow.

"Certainly, Thomas. I'd like that, indeed."

He and I stepped out of the shop together as he flipped the painted sign to, *Please Return Another Time*. He turned the key to lock the shop, which for all-the-world looked like the one deep within my dress pocket alongside the stone. As we strolled at a gentle pace, he chatted about books and the shops along the boulevard and other pleasant things, but my mind could only ponder one thing:

If you travel where you've been, you'll wish you had it to do over again.

Once again I felt sure. The message on the cabinet was for me. I didn't understand this message or how to put it to the test. But in a short time, I would check how the first message from the desk applied and board the steam train hoping to go home.

I chose the next train leaving the station. My anxiety was at a pinnacle. All I could think of was rescuing my dear Summer's Girl. It was no matter for what destination the train was bound. I was counting on a power I didn't understand. There was nothing within my prior logic that could explain my displacement from standing on that platform of books to standing on the platform of South Station here in a different time. But my paradigm stretched to include the heretofore impossible. I believed I would just as inexplicably return to Snoqualmie as long as I followed the instructions revealed to me by the desk.

Thomas, the dear man, bought my ticket – I would need to carry a bit of money with me if I was to declare independence. He offered to linger until my departure, but I requested he get back to his patrons. It would be a shame for him to miss a sale on my account. He gave in to practicality but his farewell nod was rather wistful.

I was looking forward to meeting Thomas back at home. I'd become fascinated with the weaving story of my life after this remarkable glimpse of my own future. Although just as I was intrigued with what Thomas could tell and not tell, I was further enticed by the mystery message which implied I could change it.

My knee complained as I boarded the train to Chicago and stared down the porter's snub at my lack of bags. My thoughts kept returning to Thomas' sad eyes when he spoke of his past and my future. He claimed to be happy and want to repeat it, but there was something that hurt him. If it was on my account, I was determined to do what I could to bring about his full happiness. His esteem, and dare I say affection, for me was obvious, and I already felt indebted to him for his kindness.

I found my seat and must confess pride in being there on my own. Several amused glances at my antiquated attire – a true oddity with the addition of the strange jacket – sought to discomfit me, but I felt progressive in my status as a woman without escort on a journey. Even in this era, most women were with their husbands, or at least had a female companion at their side. There was one other who stood upon the platform and boarded alone, though she was older than I, judging by appearance. Of course, that was dependent on whether my age was judged by birth date or number of days I had thus far lived. How odd to consider.

I was looking for what I would call – for lack of a better term – magic around every turn. I would define it eventually. For now, aboard the train, I expected to be whisked home any time. When I settled in, the terrible realization struck that I could literally have to return by train – all the way to the West. It was a good thing I accepted the additional monies Thomas pressed upon me. My acceptance leaned on my expectation to return the excess value to him immediately upon my return to Snoqualmie. As soon as I made his acquaintance, of course. Or rather let him make my acquaintance since...oh dear, this got quite silly, didn't it? If I had to spend it, I could have him take it out of my wages. Which we didn't even discuss. I wasn't doing well with my first employment. I didn't even negotiate wage. Of course, he wasn't doing well as employer not to confirm the contract. Perhaps it was akin to a gentleman's agreement between friends.

With that agreeable thought – he and I as respectable colleagues – I dozed off, apparently for some time, and had the strangest dreams. Though hardly any stranger than what occurred in that last twenty-four hours. I hoped they hadn't missed me at home! I could be so self-focused when there was mystery to be solved. There was nothing for it but to get home as quickly as possible. If only I could've sped the process.

All in a flash, the answer came. I pulled the emerald from my bag as I whispered. "Home again, home again, clickety-clack."

Pshshshsh, the familiar sound of steam's release brought me back to my full senses in the stopped train. People around me were rising to disembark at the station. They were dressed in the lovely colors and inconveniently ornate dresses and assertive tailor made suits of my own time. I saw the station marker out the sun-filled window. 'Snoqualmie,' it stated clearly and dearly. I almost squealed in my excitement, but for once I held my dignity.

I cradled the emerald in my bare hand, and as I stepped toward the platform, I suddenly found myself on my platform table within the bookshop, still lit with the dispersed lantern light from the gas lamp outside. How odd to change from day to night in an instant.

I set the jewel in its place with reverence, and fought one more wave of temptation to take the group of stones. Suddenly I felt hurried to leave before being discovered. Stepping down gingerly to protect my knee, I touched the door of the cabinet-desk. As hoped, it whirred and snapped closed on the end of my journeys. Or at least on the first one. If what Thomas and Mrs. Carrington said about me was true, there would be many.

While moving the table back into place, I didn't once think I'd been dreaming or suffering delusion. Many would doubt my experience was real, but if there was one thing I trusted, it was my wit. And I didn't doubt what I saw with my own eyes. "'That which is sensible has simply been explained already,' Father always said, 'and that which is outlandish will be sensibly explained tomorrow.'" For me, tomorrow had come.

Oh, my goodness, it was indeed coming quickly. There was some passage of time in Snoqualmie. I left the house during the chime of ten of the clock and arrived at the bookshop about fifteen after the hour, but the bookshop clock was clearly displaying thirty minutes until midnight. I hoped no one had risen to peek in and see if I was distressed in my sleep.

I hurried out onto the boardwalk to the jingle of the bells and found the key, still safe within my bodice. The stiff-turning lock was becoming routine to me now, and its *click* left me feeling secure momentarily, with my trespass behind me.

Brrr, a chilly gust of wind shook me despite the borrowed jacket. I felt suddenly exposed again on the midnight streets alone. Never had I been out so late, and even walking the streets of another time didn't take away my shivers.

As I rounded the corner Summer's Girl came into view. She already saw me and whinnied softly upon my approach. "Shh, girl.

Don't call attention to us," I whispered while removing the tether from the hitching post. I led her down onto the road, realizing the elevation of the boardwalk would be useful for aid in hoisting myself into the saddle.

That was indeed an ordeal, especially with my sore knee, but we were away unnoticed.

The moonlight was magnificent in showing my way home but also made me feel conspicuous. It seemed a long ride, and my knee became excruciating. I was like a frightened doe cringing from shadow to shadow, wishing to avoid being seen. Though who I was hiding from I wouldn't know. I didn't encounter another soul.

At last the house was on the horizon. My knee ached as if I'd never be able to take another step. Timber stood, a sentinel at the center of the steps up to the porch, and I slowed Summer's Girl to a walk and entered the yard as silently as possible.

My sharp groan as I slipped from the saddle onto my feet disturbed the calm night so fiercely I expected the whole house to light in alarm. I would've fallen without support of Summer's Girl's side. What a loyal creature she was to stand at my aid instead of shying away at my deep complaint. I immediately wished I dismounted closer to the currier's cabin. It would test my skill to throw a stone true from where I stood.

"Excellent!" I couldn't help but whisper exclamation. I hit Master Seth's window on the first attempt.

CHAPTER TWELVE

∞∞∞∞

In Which Miss Livingstone Shares her Eccentricities
- with Some Regret

"Miss Livingstone, I'm mighty pleased you're home safe," Master Seth graciously told me upon his appearance. I'll take her from here." He gave me an odd up and down appraisal – perhaps because of my foreign short coat? "You get back to the house and get warm."

"Yes –" I bit off the end of my reply with a grit of my teeth. Pain stabbed through me upon transfer of my full weight onto my knee. "Good night." I managed to call as he retreated to the barn.

It turned out I was glad for my position so near the porch. I'd never seen Timber so attentive. He still stood at full attention by the top of the steps. But he sidled away as I heaved myself up the stairs with one unbendable knee. Strange kitty, he was curled in a ball under the topiary as if he'd been sleeping for hours by the time I cautiously opened the door to step inside.

I rushed, as best I could, up the stairs to my room under cover of the grandfather clock's chiming. My Western room was as welcome as my room in Boston. I carefully placed the key to the shop and the jacket from the future in a place where they wouldn't be discovered, and began to dress for bed at the twelfth chime of midnight exact.

∞∞∞

'Oh, I must intercept the message that Jaimeson was to deliver to Janie! Get up at once,' was my first thought when half awake. He was to take it to her as soon as it was polite in the morning. I had thought during my ride to remove it from the book but was so exhausted and shaken when I came in last night that it slipped my mind. I threw on my morning gown and hurried to retrieve it. But he'd taken it from the table and doubtless tucked it away to avoid forgetting it on his errands.

"Good morning, Camille," I greeted on my way through the parlor.

"Good morning, Miss Caprice. Are you better, dear?"

"Yes, much, thank you. Have you seen Jaimeson?"

"He left on errands early this morning. Says he has some extra stops today, though I expect him back soon. Do you require service?"

"Em, no. That is, I should like to call on the Adams household. Please send a message to ask for an appointment with Miss Mary Jane as soon as is convenient?" Perhaps I could make an excuse to see the book before she inspected it herself. "As soon as possible." I added vigorously.

"Oh, yes, Miss Caprice. I didn't understand your urgency was so great. I was going to order your breakfast." The woman turned on her heel with a sniff at, what I realized was, my barked command.

"My pardon, Camille, I wasn't trying to scold or rush you. I accidentally spoke my own impatience to see my friend. But please proceed with requesting the appointment. I'll see Cook about my breakfast, thank you."

"Yes, dear." She gave me an indulgent nod like I'd seen her give my father when she thought him impulsive or eccentric.

Perhaps I would become more refined with age. Or if I continued with such unusual adventures, perhaps no one would relate to my quirks at all. Such experiences were bound to leave one strange, even if remarkably so. Like for my father, it could be my fate to be different. It was a small price to pay to follow the mysterious stones.

I interrupted Cook as she was pumping water at the sink for tea and eggs. She looked over her shoulder with an indulgent smile, and I took it as permission to sit at the kitchen table until my food was served.

Cook was not a chatty sort, so while entwining scents of breakfast filled my senses, my mind wandered off to plans for further experiments with the stones. I elected to try the amber next. Although a part of me desired to try the emerald again to see if the same result happened. It was prudent to repeat the experiment and search for predictable patterns – the scientific and logical way. But my curiosity couldn't be contained regarding the next stone. I sought to obey my intellect and training, but oh dear, I was as full of quirks as others perceived me to be. If I couldn't follow my wit, I deserved to be considered silly.

The argument in my mind and worries about the message finding Janie were set aside as I indulged in the plates of poached eggs with truffle, dried apricot scones and a perfectly steeped cup of Mariage Frères breakfast tea that Cook provided for me. Apparently midnight escapades and traveling through time left one famished.

I was contemplating if it would be untoward to clean up the last tidbits by mashing them with my fork when Camille announced that Jaimeson had arrived home and would keep the Steamer at the ready. I was expected at the Adams home in one hour. The crumbs were abandoned for a hurried visit to my chambers to dress properly for the day.

∞∞∞

"Janie, dear," I called upon entering the front hall at the Adams' home.

Her blue eyes flicked at me and away twice as I reached to embrace her lightly in greeting. She'd read it!

"Jaimeson brought the book, then?" I continued.

"Oh yes. It was delivered to me first thing when I awoke, just as he instructed Solomon." Her look added, 'Why do you think I'm upset?'

"I'm immensely grateful you agreed to see me on such short notice. Is there somewhere we can talk together?"

The housekeeper and cook, who had come to see who arrived, disappeared through different doors at the cue.

"Please come into the parlor," Janie directed, "Mother and Father are at table for a late breakfast. We won't be disturbed." 'Any more than I already am,' she might as well have said out loud.

I'd never seen her countenance so clouded. Regret washed through me. Confiding my fears to her may have been an error. The apricot-toned wallpaper seemed a sickly yellow in the beam of sunshine that stole in through the window between the trees. Perhaps the first night's caper was the extent of her tolerance for mischief. Had I destroyed our chance at friendship?

"Janie, my dear friend. Thank you for receiving my note. I see you're upset, and that was not my intent. My thoughts were of myself without realization of how deeply this would affect you. My sincere apologies."

"Thank you, dear. I was just so afraid for you." She stopped short with a choke of emotion. "Perhaps had you confided in me about the cabinet the first night, I would've been prepared. But when I read your note about the stones and your conjectures…I had so many questions, and the thought I might never get to ask you…"

I took her hand. "I see now it was unfair to bring you into my speculation. You know how dramatic I can be."

She looked up, and her cobalt eyes were alight. "Did you really go there – all alone? I think you're the bravest woman I've ever encountered."

If only she knew. Could I tell her about it?

"So what happened?" Janie pulled at her hair mercilessly. "Did anyone see you? That dark man wasn't there, was he? I'm so glad you came over this morning. I would've been beside myself all day wondering what happened to you. It would have been excruciating."

"No one saw me in the bookshop. Nor between home and my arrival there."

"Did you find out more about the cabinet? Did the stones glow again? Did you find the source of the light?"

I decided to plunge in. "Actually, I believe they have powers."

Her brow wrinkled at me.

"You know, like what some would call magic, though it's probably some scientific principle that changes things."

"Why would you believe that?" Her eyes grew round.

I had her hooked. "On the first night, an energy emanated from them. They were enthralling, and I couldn't get them off my mind. It was as if they drew me back to discover their mystery." I withheld the part about my urge to steal them.

She was silent, gazing into my eyes as if to read the secret.

"I went back and opened the desk again. When I touched one gem with my glove, nothing happened except it slipped out of my hand. But when I took off my glove and picked up a different one –"

"What...what happened? I can see you have a story. I've never seen you look more serious. What happened, dear Caprice?"

"Please, call me Lizzie," I reacted to hearing my given name.

"Pardon me?"

I'd lost her. "Nevermind." I shook my head playfully – the curls danced on my head.

Janie laughed.

"So, no drama, and no carried away imaginings – this is what occurred..."

My friend was again rapt in her gaze, her hand stroking the ends of her hair with absent intensity. So I told the full tale of sneaking out into the night and into another time. And then I described the train ride home.

"You rode a train. On your own?!" Her face was painted with disbelief.

"That's the part of my tale that stretches your ability to believe?" I was incredulous.

Janie broke into the most delicious giggles and pulled me in along with her to a bout of full blown laughter.

"Are you girls well?" Mrs. Adams put her head into the parlor.

"Actually Mother," Janie's voice dropped from laughter to a serious tone, "can we have Viola take a look at Miss Lizzie's knee?" She winked at me with a flash of humor. "She took a bit of a fall last evening."

"Miss Lizzie?"

"My nickname, given me by a dear friend. It's my grandmother's name as well." I felt sheepish asking to be called something other than my name.

The woman skipped the name and went straight to the point. "You've been hurt? I'll get Viola immediately. Please follow me. Are you well enough to walk?"

"Yes, I..." Oh dear, I had stiffened up since I arrived.

Hobbling behind her mother, I longed to hear Janie's reaction to my story, but she was more sensible regarding my well-being than I was for myself. Gratitude filled me for the help from her housekeeper that I would dare not solicit at home. No invented explanation would've possibly satisfied Camille on this one.

CHAPTER THIRTEEN

∞∞∞∞

In Which Good Logic Bows to the Dictates of Strong Intuition

Once she considered me appropriately nursed, Viola set Janie and me up on the porch with a large pot of steaming mulled cider and a cheery blue gingham-patterned plate heaping with tea biscuits. The luscious scent filled air, and Viola's smile glowed from her honey-toned face, as gentle as the pleasantly warm afternoon. The clear view of the river running toward the mountain that towered over the spring green valley made me wonder why I would ever yearn to be anywhere else. Funny how a trip abroad made one appreciate home. And Snoqualmie was fast becoming that for me.

Hating to break the idyllic mood, I just had to know, "Janie, my indulgently kind friend, you haven't told me what you think of my tale."

"It's extraordinary, of course."

"But you do believe me?"

"Should I not?"

"I just thought..." I was expecting her to vie me with questions. It never occurred to me she'd believe with such loyal devotion and trust in my conclusions. She seemed to embrace it more than I did myself.

"I do have one question," she volunteered. "When will you try it again?"

"My dear girl, it's my greatest fortune to gain you as my friend and confidante. I'm humbled by your trust in me, and delighted you support my adventure. I'm more than pleased we can explore this mystery together."

Her blue eyes glowed with happy affection over the rim of her cider cup.

"I, of course, want to journey again, or at least attempt to do so. But I'm also wary of being caught," I confessed. "Though the future Mr. Worthington has met me, the current one has not. And I got the impression even the future Thomas was stymied by his dark partner's behavior. I wish I could've learned more about that man. But I was anxious to return to Snoqualmie. Especially with the uncertainty of how I was affecting you all waiting for me here. I was frightened of the worry I might cause."

"Worry indeed. I was heartsick from the moment I read your note – upset you'd taken a risk and pulled me in without telling me more, and then worried you'd be lost. I was flung between terror for your safety and wanting to murder you for leaving me on the edge of my seat."

"Yes, I see now that was terribly cruel. You must have nearly died of curiosity. Can you forgive my shortsightedness?"

"Don't mention it. But let's make a pact that you'll not run off without word again."

"Done." I held my glass to hers to seal the agreement, then downed the spicy-sweet treat. "So I'll take a night off to rest my knee. I promise you, no matter how the stones' enticing power calls to me. But I have plenty to ponder. Perhaps you can help me decide?"

"Oh, plotting is my specialty." She sat forward and began to worry her blonde tress.

"Yes, I've noticed that in book club. You're always quick to find the holes or anticipate the twists and turns. That expertise and your level head will probably be the best protector I could ask for. Oh! And speaking of book club, how did it go –"

"Nevermind that now. So what's the puzzle?" Her eyes lit with intrigue.

"First, I'm torn about whether to pick up the same stone or another," I began, catching her fire. "If I repeat the same one, I may learn more about the mechanism or power and how to control my future journeys. But if I pick another, I may go to another time or perhaps another place. Or perhaps nothing at all. To the point, I'll find out if the other stones have power as well and be able to compare the two."

"Do you have a reason to return to Newbury Street?"

"Not especially." I felt a wave of nostalgia to visit my Boston home, but that would keep.

"Do you have a reason to go elsewhere?"

"Oh yes! How did I neglect to tell you? I've taken a job finding books." As I sketched the details, Janie's eyes brightened with enthusiasm.

"Definitely try a new stone," she declared. "But not the rust-toned one with the sparkling stars. I don't like the sound of the bright light that you described as shining from beneath it. There's no guarantee the next one won't have that, but...I don't know I just have this feeling."

"Good logic bows to dictates of strong intuition. At least my logic does. Invention is a combination of what can be seen and a few twists of intellect or inner nudges that cannot. At some point, one must take a leap of faith. I will follow your nudge, Janie. Now the difficult part will be waiting."

"Maybe we can find a distraction together."

"Well, if you read my note, you must have also done the reading for this Saturday's book club meeting. We could discuss our understanding of *The Virginian,* chapter IX: 'The Spinster Meets the Unknown.'"

"How apropos," Janie giggled mercilessly.

I gave in and giggled too, and we laughed ourselves into tears. It was rather fitting, after all.

"Or if you're feeling up to a short walk," she continued after catching her breath, "we could deliver *The Virginian* to the Lucile Hotel for Emeline Kinsey – she'll probably be minding the counter for her brothers – and then we could see if the bookshop has opened, or at least posted a sign for Opening Day," an impish look took over her sweet features.

"I believe you're as incorrigible as I." My laugh bubbled forth. "It's possible you could persuade me to hobble alongside you."

∞∞∞∞

Janie's mother was skeptical about my walk, but I demonstrated my strength and she permitted us to go. "I'll have Solomon check on you if you're not back in an hour."

"Yes, Mother." Janie waved her off as I bit my lip and made my way down the front steps. It was a glorious afternoon and had opened up to a cloudless sky.

My knee eased as we proceeded, losing some of the stiffness. It was only a cut, after all. Everything was in working order. But Janie insisted upon lending support, and it felt wonderful walking arm-in-arm basking in the spring weather. As we completed our errand at the Lucile Hotel, I observed the heads of more than one young man swinging our way to rest on Janie's golden beauty, but she didn't notice at all.

Our arrival at the bookshop revealed a window-cleaner hard at work removing the soap from the windows. My first inclination when

I saw the open door was to run and hide, but of course this made no sense at all. It was most likely guilt for my trespass on the property that made me skittish as a deer. As if Mr. Worthington would somehow know I took advantage without his knowledge. I suppose I also dreaded encountering the man with the dark moustache. The magnetic draw he once held for me had polarized to repel me. I had embraced the discomfort Thomas displayed regarding the man.

No matter what my feeling, I knew I was destined to enter the shop and meet its proprietor. And despite the strange message about changing my fate, I very much looked forward to the event and wouldn't have changed it for all the mysterious stones in the universe. My heart began to thump in my chest. "Do you think he's here?" I whispered to Janie.

"Mr. Worthington?" she whispered back.

"Yes, should we peek inside?"

"Can you go home having done anything less?" She gave me an indulgent smile and an eager nod.

I approached the door, pulled it open and set one foot inside.

"Hello?" I called out, impressing more confidence upon my tone than I felt. "Are you in, sir?"

"Yessum, I'm here cleaning the windows," the cleaner answered.

"I can see that. Is the proprietor about?" I jumped back causing searing pain in my sore knee. My searching gaze had unearthed the dark man just inside the door near the yellow-green curtain. His imposing figure manned a tall stool about a yard from where I stood. His piercing black-brown eyes were steady on my face as he stroked his very trim moustache. He nodded with a nearly intangible duck of his head. Regaining my stance, I didn't back down, but all my confidence was gone. "Will you be opening soon?" my voice squeaked.

"Yessum, they're opening tomorrow. I've got this here sign to post after I'm done with the windows. Mr. Manush doesn't speak English, so I'm letting you know, if you'll pardon my forwardness, ma'am."

"Em...th-thank you. We'll return some other time." I nearly ran from the gaping doorway – without even pulling it back to its cracked open position. I felt chased, and Janie followed my lead to put plenty of space between ourselves and the bookshop.

"Let's take a bench, Janie." I was out of breath and my knee was in agony from my near-run across the street. The sun was scorching rather than pleasant, and I wasn't satisfied of our safety until we'd reached the train depot.

"What did he say? I couldn't hear from outside. Did he threaten you? Why the mad dash?" Janie's questions tumbled out in alarm.

"The dark man, was there, not Mr. Worthington. Mr. Manush – he said nothing. Or at least nothing you would've heard. But I felt threatened, in the same way I feel the stones' call. Whatever power is in the stones is known to that man. And I'm certain he knows I'm aware of it too."

"Oh, Cap... Lizzie! I've changed my mind. I can't bear the risk if you return." Janie's golden brow folded with worry.

"I can't bear life without going – whatever the consequences. And we have assurance I'll survive for some time. I have a daughter, remember?" Confirming this brought a strange satisfaction.

"But if Mr. Worthington's put in a twist by getting to know you sooner instead of leaving that to fate, couldn't everything be different now?"

"Can one ever know what the future holds?" I had a strange pang as I realized perhaps I could – but not surely. "We do know that when I went to 1941 Boston this time, many of the same things happened. I stayed at Newbury Manor, which Thomas believed I did when I was there in 1941 the first time. But in that scenario I stayed there before we met. I still took a job as Mr. Worthington's book-finder, and I even still hurt my knee."

"True…" Janie pulled at her hair, lost in thought.

"The important thing that changed is Thomas has revealed our friendship to me upfront this time in Boston. Apparently we had only a brief encounter in that time period before, and we didn't yet know each other. He wanted to make sure I truly knew him before I met him at the bookshop on Opening Day here in Snoqualmie."

"Yes, I see. Perhaps it would create a predisposition to relate to him with more depth?"

"Perhaps. I don't know what it is he wants to change – something that made him sad. But feeling as if I know him already, and the other things I learned…it's possible my knowledge and my reaction to it could change things for good or bad. Nevertheless, I must move forward with this. Please don't abandon me to it, Janie. Your support is my lifeline. If I don't return, you'll know to ask Thomas – Mr. Worthington – about Mr. Manush."

"Yes, alright. I suppose you must continue. I won't abandon you now." Her dear voice was shaken with emotion – fear?

Any fear I had was overwhelmed by my curiosity. My encounter with the imposing Mr. Manush was like facing my enemy. I was ready to rise to his, or any challenge if it meant I could learn more. My heart felt Thomas needed me to do it, and I'd be abandoning myself if I didn't try.

CHAPTER FOURTEEN

∞∞∞∞

In Which Even Sneaking Becomes Easier with Practice

Coming face to face with Mr. Manush, gave me urgency to continue my quest to discover the stones' secrets before the shop was open to the public. As we walked the long way around, past the Reinig Bros. store, back to her home, I suggested another visit to Janie.

"Would you release me from my promise not to return tonight?" I begged.

"It's a shame you couldn't just gain entry once and bring the whole set back to my house with you. You could dispose of this frightening cat and mouse game each night – trying to get in and out without being discovered. But I suppose that would be stealing."

"Yes." I had to shake off the memory of the intense temptation to do just that. "I know I'm borrowing some of them without permission, but I can't steal all of them outright."

"No, but – well are you sure you can ride your horse? I wish you would wait."

"I feel that something will change tomorrow and I'll miss my future opportunities unless I attempt to travel again tonight. I can't explain it, but I just know."

"You trusted my intuition. I'll trust yours. But only if you'll stay with me so you won't have so far to travel."

"Oh, could I?"

Her smile glowed at me in reply as we reached her front step. She helped me limp up to wait on the porch while she spoke with her mother. The leather-cushioned chair felt divine.

Janie obtained permission for an overnight for me at her home and arranged for Solomon to get my things from Jaimeson and Camille for my stay. Her parents were too kind, and thankfully my father would be away for another couple of days. But this time, I planned to leave her home on my own in secret rather than she and I creating a ruse.

∞∞∞

After a hearty dinner of venison and trout with her parents, Janie and I tolerated a few stories in the parlor and then made our excuses and retired up the interminable narrow staircase to her bedchamber. Had it been any other night I would have longed to linger. Her father told tales of hauling goods by wagon for the Snoqualmie Hop Ranch, and had many anecdotes regarding well-known guests from Seattle. Mr. A.A. Denny, Mr. Dexter Horton, Mr. Henry Yesler, and even Dr. Maynard came up for Tally Ho parties at the Meadowbrook Inn where Janie's father was a guide for such adventures. Janie's parents, while showing their frontier strength on their sleeves, also hid a high intelligence and spoke of many things I hadn't learned at Miss Preston's School for Girls. Now that I faced time travels and adventures into the unknown, I was hungry for more practical knowledge. A flawless recitation of Kipling would not be much help if I was caught in the start of a snowstorm without shelter, except to give me a noble passing.

Janie and I tried to read but were too restless. Eventually our conversation faded and we doubtless would've been fast asleep if it were any other night. Instead I sat at the ready watching the moonrise out the window, and she lounged in yawning attendance watching the time until near ten of the clock. Since that hour proved the street clear last night, we'd decided it was my best hope for success again. She would send Solomon to retrieve me if I hadn't returned by eleven of the clock, as a caution.

At last the time came, and Janie waved me off at the door of her bedchamber. We'd decided I could slip out of the house undetected with greater probability if only one set of feet risked squeaky floorboards. I'd learned the danger spots on the staircase, though it was extra labor to avoid them as well as nurse my knee.

I gained the yard, and quickly left the looming dark brush behind. Fortunately, the clear weather held. Breaking into the moonlight, my spirit soared. My secretive path to the shop was a margin less frightening with routine. Even sneaking got easier with practice. The lock turned with a vigorous snap, the bells signaled my entry, and as the door clicked closed behind me. The change with the windows clear of soap was visceral. The boardwalk and open lot on the far side of the street were visible in minute detail. I imagined someone passing by could spy me with the same precision. Pressed up against the wall closest to the door, I was unwilling to move.

So, I was in or I was out. I couldn't bring myself to leave, so quickly pulled over the table and wasted no time in climbing up – with care not to stress my knee. I pushed left to release the mechanism beneath the strange symbol. As the cabinet swung open, the outpouring of the stones' glow filled me with trepidation. It was like a sea beacon calling everyone still awake to the window of the shop – from my point of view, in any case. Mastering my fear, and with bared hand, I picked up the large piece of amber.

Oh my! That was disconcerting – being there and then somewhere else entirely. I was unsure where I'd arrived. It was an old city with stone architecture, and I could hear...French. It was French. Was it possibly Paris? Oh yes, it was! I stood near the *Fontaine Molière*. I recognized the monument that my literature instructor always praised since it honored the first non-military hero in Paris' history – a playwright, she noted. That meant I was on the rue de Richelieu, I happened to know – painfully near the Bibliothèque nationale de France. So close to such a library, the excitement was hardly containable, and I was agonized there was no time to visit. But my objective was to find books for purchase.

Fortunately, I had learned some French, and my gratitude to Miss Preston's School for Girls resurged. Even so, I felt inexplicably anxious. Time pressed upon me, like there was only so much allowed to achieve my purpose and return. Dropping the amber into my deep pocket for safe-keeping, I confirmed its position with a surreptitious rub near my stomach. I could feel its bulk alongside the key to the bookshop.

A *pshshshsh* confirmed a steam engine nearby, I was close to the station. But what was the year? I walked along the posh stone way under striped awnings trying to gain my bearings. The streets were not yet crowded, and the shopkeepers were setting out signs with specialties of the day or indicating they were open for commerce.

An exquisite pastry shop caught my nose and eye – so tempting, especially the palmier on the third shelf. I could almost taste its flaky crunch. The aroma was heavenly. Judging by their full window-shelves it was early in the day. I brought money this time – dollars not francs – but feeding myself patisserie was not the intent for these funds. I left the dainties with a wistful glance over my shoulder, and returned to more pertinent observations.

The people on the street were dressed with similarity to home. Their fashion was more avant-garde, but it was Paris not Snoqualmie, after all. I saw no bustles and almost no corsets – a few of the s-curve style. It was contemporary to 1910. The amber had taken me across the world in the same time period, was a valid working assumption.

"Excellent!" I declared rather too loudly, "a bookshop."

I had a job to do! There was no doorbell to delight like the one at Thomas' future bookshop on Newbury, but the brass bell that rang upon my entry was pleasing in an old-world way. I think my grandmother had one like it. I wonder if my father brought it to her from Paris. He traveled to the City of Light when I was an infant.

The cluttered shop was filled to the ceiling with tomes. I had no doubt there were treasures beyond imagining within its walls. I was lured to my right between the awe-inspiring wooden shelves and was soon lost in the volume of volumes. So many to choose from. I considered what would enhance Thomas' shop? What fun it would be to give him one when we met tomorrow. For I would certainly attempt to see him on his opening day in Snoqualmie.

Perfect. I found the one! A first printing of *Bel Ami*, Guy de Maupassant's second novel. I recalled there were thirty-seven printings in four months when it was published. It was a dream to own a first printing. I just hoped I had enough funds. And I needed to choose a couple to offer for his purchase. The 1903 English translation of *Bel Ami* was a good choice, and two French classics would be a good balance.

I brought my selections to the front of the shop for purchase from the proprietor. How rude I was upon entry not to acknowledge her. And when I saw the woman sitting behind the high counter, it was a wonder to me that I'd dismissed her so easily. She wore a crochet shawl, again like my grandmother's, but that's where the similarity ended. She was of darker and much rougher complexion – as if long baked in the sun – and had nearly jet black hair.

I suddenly realized she'd risen and spoken, but missed her words while so taken with her intricate and striking amber and gold earrings. I'd never seen anything like them. On top of being oblivious to the conversation I was staring. I raised my eyes to hers and flinched under the intensity of her gaze.

"Excusez-moi," I stumbled. "Je voudrais acheter ces livres s'il vous plaît." I quickly recovered remembering to ask to purchase the books in French. I set them in a stack upon the counter between us.

She continued to regard me without reply. I worried she was waiting for a response to her first utterance, and then decided perhaps she was calculating a price. She definitely appeared to be appraising something – though it was as if she measured my worth rather than noting the volumes I'd chosen.

I held out a handful of money hoping she would name her price or at least drop her nearly black eyes from my face. And she immediately chose two coins from my palm and pushed my fingers closed over the rest with a wrinkled brown hand. Her touch was soft but electric, and my breath caught as I looked up again and saw an equally soft spark in her eye.

She turned and lifted some paper to wrap my purchases, and I turned away toward the window to shake off the strange feeling her meaningful glance had bestowed upon me. I nearly threw myself to the floor in fright at what I saw outside. I grabbed the stack of books and jumped back between the shelves in self-preservation.

CHAPTER FIFTEEN

∞∞∞∞

In Which Miss Livingstone Stumbles upon the Supernatural

The brass bell announced another entrance. It was Mr. Manush! Or a man so like him, I avoided him even so. I had the same feeling of apprehension he'd sparked for me in Snoqualmie.

I wove without a clear plan through the shelves to the back of the store, farthest from where we'd entered. A small door presented itself, just when I would've been trapped. Without hesitation I turned knob, but it was locked. I threw myself against the door in desperation then noticed a metallic shine. What luck! A key was lodged in its keyhole. My heart was beating out of my chest as I re-balanced the books and turned the key.

"Oh!" A fierce wind blew up, and I closed my eyes against a blinding flash of light. When they were opened, the sight was unbelievable – I was outside in a narrow stone alley with a door firmly closed at my back. I hadn't moved my feet at all. I twisted quickly and confirmed the locked knob. My instant response was to break into as much of a run as I could manage through the cluttered passage. Though it was uncanny, I felt certain Mr. Manush was here in my pursuit. And my remarkable exit made me sure there was something larger afoot.

I came out to the street near the pastry shop and conquered the pain of my aching knee to run toward where I'd heard that release of steam upon my arrival in Paris. I labored to avoid tripping on the cobblestone walkway and became quickly overheated by the sun. When about to lose my breath, signs appeared indicating the way to the train depot, and I struggled on to arrive at last. Even in my hurry I had a moment of aesthetic wonder as I beheld the ironwork and overall grandeur of the station. It rivaled and perhaps eclipsed Boston's Park Square.

"Aargh." How humiliating to moan as I stepped upon the platform. But there was no help for it. I needed to climb up to reach the ticket booth and didn't dare to slow my pace – not even to wonder at the flash of light and gust of wind that seemed to blow me right through the bookshop's back door.

"Je voudrais acheter un billet a Nice?" I requested a ticket to the first city that came to mind.

"Aller simple ou aller retour?" the agent asked.

"Aller simple," One way, indeed. If only he knew.

"Merci, mademoiselle, le prochaine train departs dix-huit heure..."

I shaded my eyes and looked up. The station's clock approached noon. Four hours? I forgot my French in my urgency, "Em...sooner?"

"Non mademoiselle."

"I mean anywhere... em, Il n'y a rien plus tôt? N'import ou?"

"Oui, il y a un train à Lyon qui part dans cinq minutes."

"Merci, un billet à Lyon, s'il vous plaît." I tried to control my demanding tone, but the man's firmly pinched lips as he changed my dollar indicated I'd missed the mark.

Having secured my ticket, I followed signs to the correct platform. The train was stopped but not yet boarding. It was behind schedule, and the delay was maddening. My urgency to leave was overwhelming. It was illogical, of course, he couldn't possibly have known I left the bookshop as I did. He may not have even known I was there. In fact, the man looked like Manush but I didn't stay to be sure. But no, my intuition was sure it was him and he was after me. I couldn't let him catch me.

"Tous à bord," the conductor called.

Ah, I would evermore consider those the most beautiful words in the French language. When I limped visibly to the entrance, the porter all but hoisted me onto the train. Most undignified, but at least I boarded and found a seat without sign of being followed.

The amber was a burning weight in my bodice, or at least on my mind. I longed to take it out and hold it. But since the train wasn't yet in motion, I feared it wouldn't transport me yet. Of course there was no way to be certain it would work at all. But it's always best scientific method to repeat the same factors when seeking the same result. By necessity several details were different, but I planned to be as faithful as possible in duplicating the others – no matter how much it pained me to wait. Anything to reduce the chances of being whisked back to the place from which I'd just escaped.

Looking for distraction, I noticed for the first time that the key I'd found in the back door of the shop stayed with me. I hadn't noticed after I was moved outside the store, but it was gripped against my bodice along with the books as I dashed from the scene. It was a smaller key than the one to the bookshop in Snoqualmie – rather squatty and made of silver. As I looked closer I made out letters which had been nearly rubbed away. *Journey,* it said, in English not French. How curious. I dropped it in my pocket with the other pieces of mystery, and waited fumbling the books into a more secure bundle without patience.

"Oh!" Heads swung toward my cry.

I saw Mr. Manush – with certainty this time – weaving through the crowd near the side of the train. My heart jumped to my throat.

Woooot, Woooot, the train's whistle signaled to depart the station and my heart raced along with the time left before we proceeded. The doors closed on our car. And after what seemed an eternity the coach began to move.

Mr. Manush was not on my car, but anxiety convinced me he'd made the train and would soon pinpoint my location. With a quick glance around at those in the crowded coach, I spared no indignity to pull the amber from my bodice into my hand at once. I wished with all my might for Snoqualmie.

Gratefully, I moved to disembark and suddenly stood on the table in Thomas' shop, just after stepping from the train toward the depot platform in Snoqualmie once again. The arrival in Snoqualmie had been instantaneous with my wish. But I didn't feel safe yet. I set the amber into its place, shifted the books to my hip, and stepped down and closed the cabinet in one knee-wrenching motion. Gritting my teeth against the pain, I managed to heft the books, replace the table and run from the shop, struggling to snap the lock to behind me.

I limped along in the lamplight at remarkable speed and took a right around the corner toward Janie's. I looked up to measure the moon's placement. I hadn't been gone long it seemed.

"Aareek!" I ran smack dab into Solomon in the half-darkness. The books scattered on the ground. The poor man was quite undone by the impact of my body and perhaps even more by my distressed scream.

"Take me home, quickly!" I demanded, and it sparked him into action. He gathered my books and then clipped my hand into his elbow. I was able to move even faster, leaping along with his support.

As we turned left to cross the street after our two block run, I glanced back toward the spot I'd collided with Solomon. A figure disturbed the shadow by the corner of the street that held the bookshop. Its head broke into the moonlight briefly and peered along the road in our direction, and then disappeared again around the corner.

Solomon brought me in through the back of the house, weaving a path around squeaky boards with expertise. He sent me up the stairway to wait in Janie's bedchamber while he woke his wife Viola to see to my knee. Blood had come right through my stockings.

I woke Janie – how she could fall asleep while I was gone, I'll never know – and told her my latest adventures while we were waiting for Viola to come in. "I'm not sure I'll have the nerve to return again," I concluded. But her attention had transferred to the fascinating books I brought – as soon as she was assured I wasn't in danger anymore tonight.

"First edition Guy de Maupassant," Janie mumbled as she reverently turned the pages. She softly stroked the tips of her loosened hair.

Viola arrived and cleaned and dressed my wound again. I studied her focused hazel eyes and mass of tiny brown braids as she administered aid toward healing with admirable skill. She gave only the smallest *tsk* when she saw what I'd done by stressing my wound. I owed her and Solomon a debt of gratitude.

Janie and I settled into our beds, but I couldn't sleep. My mind kept running and I shivered with a chill that defied the layers of wool and quilting so generously heaped upon me by my new friends.

Janie had met my tale with wide though sleepy eyes, but when I saw her attention so taken by the books, I couldn't help but wonder if my story was one of many to her. Did she even believe me? But I was being silly, of course, why would she send Solomon after me if she doubted my word? And she had hard evidence in her hands. All this slinking about creating ruses and deceiving my loved ones was bending my character to paranoia. Was it possible the urgency to go tonight was part of the same type of impulse?

"Janie!" I caught my shout just in time to squeal only half as loudly as I sat up within the covers. Poor Janie shot upright as well, but I cut off her confused grunt, "what if the reason I was so urgent to go tonight was due to some spell the stones have cast upon me, or even worse, some power of the dark man, Manush? I felt certain he was chasing me down – at the shop across the world at the same time as my visit there, and then appearing here at the corner when I returned. But what if he was directing me? The wind and flash of light that transported me from the back of the shop to the alley– it was uncanny – was magical or invoked a science I can't explain." Perhaps these things weren't due to my pattern of deceit at all. "I didn't tell you when I described my first encounter with him, but I felt...well...mesmerized. Do you suppose Manush has been guiding me all along – in some kind of hypnotic state?"

She took my erratic interruption to her doze with grace. "Oh, my sweet, Lizzie, calm yourself. I know it's been a most eventful evening, and all of these changes to how we'd imagined things to be, are causing me wild speculation as well. They're difficult to grasp. But you sound hysterical. Think about it carefully. If he was manipulating you, he could have easily caught you. Why would he follow?" She sat up and lit a candle.

"You're right of course." My keen mind seized her logic. But my intuition was not set to rest.

"What I'm wondering is why you bought this blank book with the strange symbol on the front." She picked it up off the nightstand. "Are you planning to write about your adventures? What a strange paper it has."

The book in her hand was foreign to me, but the symbol was not. Or at least I had seen it before – in two other places in these few days – this image like a striped parasol atop a fence. It suddenly clicked that the fascinating gold and amber earrings of the woman behind the counter in the bookstore in France held the same symbol as the one high atop the carved cabinet in Mr. Thomas Worthington's Most

Excellent Bookshop right here at home. It was tapping that symbol that opened the desk doors and set this whole adventure in motion. And here it was again on a book that followed me home.

"I didn't purchase this book, Janie. I didn't see it at all. I must've gathered it up from the counter in my haste." I shivered again with a sudden chill.

I took it from her and looked through its pages. "But these aren't blank at all...or at least not the first section. Look."

I held it up so Janie could see the description on the first few pages. It showed the names, Emerald and then Amber – the stones I had used. It also had drawings of their exact shapes and descriptions of their properties. Emerald – Love, often called the Traveler's Stone. Amber – Life, Energy, Ties to Ancient times. Then I turned it back and leafed through the next few pages which displayed the names and drawings of the other stones, but no properties.

"Emerald, Amber, Blue Star Sapphire, Amethyst...Oh! And look here! It shows the two that are missing. A Crystal Quartz and – oh my, a Ruby." I turned the book toward Janie again. "And the strange sparkling one is a Goldstone. How can I rest? This is our best clue yet. Look, it outlines thoroughly the properties of the stones I've tried but only has illustrations and titles for the ones I haven't yet touched. And it shows the exact shape and tells the type of those that are missing. Aren't you thrilled?"

Janie's brow scrunched down further than I'd ever seen. Any trace of thrill was expunged from her face. "Caprice, dear...I mean, Lizzie. The pages are blank." Her fearfully drear face whitened as if entombed.

I felt my face flush in stark contrast. There was something more than strange happening here. I'd stumbled on the supernatural. It was possible Mr. Manush wasn't manipulating me, but it certainly seemed something was.

CHAPTER SIXTEEN

∞∞∞∞

In Which Miss Livingstone Giggles Like a Schoolgirl

The sunny Spring morning gave promise of an ideal day. After a late awakening, Janie and I breakfasted on her porch, full of anticipation for opening day of Mr. Thomas Worthington's Most Excellent Bookshop. When I first imagined this day, my spinnings were full of new literature and my intent to educate the townsfolk of Snoqualmie. What a turn life had taken, and all starting with the turn of a key.

In my narrative to Janie last night, I left out the part about keeping the Journey key found in my moment of peril in Paris. I implied it stayed behind in the door – though I didn't say it directly. It was disturbing that I'd again hidden something, when prior to these experiences I'd prided myself on being forthright. Clarity is part of intelligence. Had I given over my wit to fancy?

I would not let strange behavior or the oddity of the unexpected book cloud the immensity of this day, however. I tucked the book deep within my bag. It was time to meet Mr. Worthington. Hereafter, I would no longer call him Thomas until the day he asked me to do so. According to his theory of twists, that day might never come, but I was longing for it already. I intended to befriend him, and I'd begin with the gift and offerings of enchanting tomes. What bookseller could resist that charm – even if he found mine dubious?

"What?" Janie flashed me a quizzical look when my burst of laughter broke into our meditation while enjoying a peaceful view of the river and imbibing perfectly splendid Twining's tea.

Perhaps her kitchen had a thing or two to teach me about fine tea after all. I may have been presumptuous in assuming the ignorance of the inhabitants of this town with such a grand view of my own education. I was mistaken about the whole shape of time, and therefore feeling less inclined to set myself up as an authority on anything at all.

"Well?" Janie's firm brows were propped high above her sharp eyes.

"I'm sorry, my dear. I let my mind wander away downriver instead of paying proper attention to you. Forgive me."

"I will if you tell me what caused you to give such a hearty laugh."

After a focused backtrack, "Oh, yes, I was imagining meeting Mr. Worthington and how charmed he'll be with these unique books, especially when one is presented as a gift."

The firm brow furrowed. "I fail to see the humor."

"I was just thinking that he'd find the books much more charming than me."

Janie let out a most satisfying giggle. "You're being silly, of course. Though the books are fascinating, I'm sure he shan't be able to take his eyes off of you."

"Oh, you tease."

"No, truly. You don't know the magnitude of your own charm, my dear."

For all the world, she looked completely sincere. I guffawed again, and she laughed merrily at my side.

∞∞∞

After all that talk of charm, I was quite nervous to leave the house for town. I was grateful Camille had sent Jaimeson over with my fine wool emerald green tailor made suit for my day's attire. While a little warm for the weather, it was perfect for representing my dignity while showing my feminine curves to their best advantage. And apparently it was to be memorable for my dear, Thom...Mr. Worthington. That boost of confidence also unnerved me in its predestination.

"My word Lizzie, you're as fidgety as a school girl dressing for her first recitation." Janie observed as we readied ourselves in her chambers. "You're really taken with this Mr. Worthington, aren't you?"

"No, of course not." My face flushed, despite my protest. "I merely want to make a good impression. After all, he's taken me into his employ. Even if he doesn't yet know it."

Janie looked at me in momentary puzzlement. I must confess, it was an odd thing to comprehend.

We made it through what felt like a long descent from her chambers and left the house on foot, at last. I refused Mrs. Adam's offer of Solomon to give us a ride although my knee pained me. It was only three blocks away, and I'd not arrive in a motor vehicle like royalty. How would that appear for a woman of independence and strength? Viola's ministrations eased the stiffness somewhat, and Janie set our pace at a gentle stroll. She truly was a compassionate friend.

My pain dissolved into excitement. A series of painted placards announced the opening in a line along the walk. And there was music! What a stout fellow to provide entertainment – as if any additional enticement was required.

As we drew closer, the wisps of melody took shape into rich and exotic strains of accordion music that whisked my imagination to another part of the world. It gave me a strange foreboding, but carried mystery I couldn't resist.

At the end of the stream of song, handing out handbills by the invitingly open shop door, was Mr. Thomas Worthington himself. I pulled back abruptly, and Janie looked at me in shock as she halted her own step. Mr. Worthington hadn't noticed us yet. He was occupied with a rather fat overdressed woman and her peaked looking daughter.

I didn't budge.

"What's the matter?" Janie whispered.

She gazed at my face, intent in her concern, and so followed my eyes to the tall dark gentleman playing accordion on the other side of the threshold. To enter the shop, we'd have to pass by his touch. I felt terribly ill at the thought. I'd never felt such revulsion in all my days.

"Mr. Manush…" she guessed correctly. "He can't harm you here – even if he is such a man. Look, there are children, and he's occupied playing his tune. What can he do to you?"

Her whispered reasoning was sound. I worked to master my emotions. I determined to look only at Mr. Worthington. Once I passed his inspection, we'd be in before I could balk.

"Good morning, ladies." Mr. Worthington gave us an open smile, and I saw a hint of that light in his eyes I'd already come to like.

I was mute. I, the woman of words overflowing!

"G-Good morning," Janie supplied on our behalf.

"I'm Thomas Worthington, and I thank you for attending the opening of my bookshop." He touched his hat politely.

Janie paused, likely expecting my usual exuberance to bubble forth.

"Our pleasure," she filled into the too long silence.

I managed a nod as I met and dodged his eye, but approaching the accordion strains so closely demanded my full attention and all courtesy was lost.

When we passed through the doorway, painfully close to the dark man's countenance, a breeze suddenly wafted at my skirts. I jumped, causing a startling jingle of the mass of little brass bells attached to the door. Manush also nodded, though I only saw it from the corner of my eye. I couldn't begin to look him in the face. He said nothing.

"What's wrong with you?" Janie whispered after we pulled to the left into a removed part of the shop.

"I don't know. I just...froze."

"You're the boldest woman I've ever met. What could possibly intimidate you so? Is there something you haven't told me?"

Yes, and yet, nothing that explained my sudden reticence. "I'm not sure." The truth. "I've never felt this way before." Also the truth.

"He looks perfectly wonderful and kind. Are you disgusted by his beard?"

I let out a strange bark but mastered my inappropriately loud laughter. Janie joined me in silent giggles, and the two of us were shaking like perfect fools. We lost all dignity and showed an embarrassing level of immaturity. Though I recently left Miss Preston's School for Girls, I was no little schoolgirl.

Thankfully, the laughter brought me back to myself. My usual confidence surged through me, and whatever strange fears had overtaken me were dispelled into the ether.

We separated and spent the morning looking through volume after volume of the books, that were neatly placed on shelves and new side tables, that had apparently been brought in early that morning.
The books I brought began to weigh heavily in their bag on my shoulder.

"May I relieve your burden?" Mr. Worthington's reedy voice inquired. It hadn't yet developed the richness it would have in his older age.

"Pardon?" I responded absently. I had been deep in thought while sampling a passage from *An Enquiry Concerning Human Understanding,* by David Hume.

"Your bag appears a wee bit heavy. May I take it for you while you browse the collection, Miss...?"

"Yes...oh, Livingstone, Miss Livingstone...Thank you."

"Pleasure to make your acquaintance."

He hoisted the bag from me, and it brought remarkable relief.

"Likewise, I'm sure." Our eyes met, and I realized I'd never spoken truer words. I didn't notice the depth of his attractiveness when I met him on Newbury. He wasn't classically handsome. *Winning* was more the term I'd use. But, oh dear, I kept staring. "Em...actually the contents of the bag are for you. Or at least potentially...if you'd like."

Thomas moved eagerly to an open table just off to the right of the imposing carved desk. He set down the bag and stepped aside to allow me to empty its contents. The mark of a gentleman that he didn't dig inside, even when I'd implied they could be his property. I admired his patience. I'm not sure I could've appeared a lady given such directives.

I gave him the first printing of *Bel Ami* first, careful to leave the blank book in the bottom. "This one, I'd like to present to you as a gift for your opening day. I've looked forward to welcoming new literature to this town, and I thank you for being its proprietor."

My smile was beaming as I held it out to him, but he only admired the book. A man after my own heart. The book was far more charming to him than any person could ever be, it seemed.

I found it endearing. But I was forgetting myself. We were to only have just met.

I expunged the affection from my demeanor. "And these tomes I offer for consideration of purchase or trade. If you're open to barter, I'm sure I could find many things here that I'd love to own."

"You're shrewd to guess I would give up treasures more easily in trade for others than for mere money, Miss Livingstone." Was it my imagination, or had he held his stare at my face a bit longer than was customary? "Please take your time in locating and building your proposed bargain. There's no hurry, and I'd be pleased if you return several times while making your decision. Since you've welcomed me to town, I'm supposing you're local to Snoqualmie?"

"Newly so, but yes, it is my home."

"Ah, then we are both strangers finding our way in the West."

"So it seems."

He gave me an enigmatic smile.

CHAPTER SEVENTEEN

∞∞∞∞

In Which Miss Livingstone Resolves to Jump in Heartily

More townsfolk crowded around the store as it built toward noon, and Mr. Worthington's attentions were removed elsewhere. Janie's appetite for literature really was inexhaustible it seemed, but I felt the distraction and weariness of my past nights' journeys. I turned over books and pages aimlessly without attention to detail. And as I became more aware of the environment I realized an odd triangle between myself and the desk and Mr. Worthington's partner, who no longer played the accordion but still lingered near the door. When I directly studied him, I had to drop my gaze, for each time he immediately took notice of me. It was as if he marked my every move. And when I neared the desk, his presence imposed on me and I moved off again.

My thoughts were consumed with the tension surrounding the desk until I couldn't enjoy the literature at all. And the weight of the book that held images only visible to me pulled at my bag with greater gravity. Perhaps it was all rubbish, but something had changed in me. I was not the carefree girl of a few days ago, lamenting the ever-present mud or the quality of the tea.

"Janie, are you ready to depart?" Giving in to my discomfort, I pressed my will upon my friend. At least I regretted the imposition.

"Oh...I'm sorry Lizzie, I've lost all track of time. Must we go so soon?"

"I'm sorry, my dear, but I feel compelled to move along. We can of course come back in the future." A cloud of resistance seemed to push against my words.

"You're so right, Miss... Livingstone isn't it? You are always welcome." Mr. Worthington's smile pushed through the cloud like sunshine in the mist. "And you too, Miss...?"

"Adams," Janie supplied. "I certainly will, sir. It's an admirable collection. I'd like to purchase this manuscript of E. M. Forster, please. My cousin wrote from England to tell me of *Room with a View* but this looks to have more depth."

"*Howard's End*, a superb and shrewd choice. Mr. Forster's a personal friend of mine and sent this advance copy for my opening. The publication is slated for November."

"How generous of you to share it." I was pulled out of my morose concern. His gift was magnanimous.

"My pleasure. He asked that I share it. He hopes to get folks jazzed about its release, and I have the pleasure to oblige and work to get him his big break. I'm constantly adding rare finds and the newest releases I can bring to the West. I love helping authors and readers alike." He beamed with pride, but somehow avoided arrogance. A comely trait. And he processed Janie's purchase with perfect efficiency.

"What will be your expected hours, if you please?" Practical strategy returned to me, I nearly missed my chance to ask, so preoccupied was I by my thoughts.

"Afternoons mostly, though you can look for me some mornings."

"Will you open evenings?"

"No, I'm afraid I live too far from the shop to risk travel at or after dusk. Over in North Bend near Mr. James & Mrs. Viola Allen, if you know of them. I hope it will be no inconvenience."

"Yes, I know the Allens," Janie answered absently.

"None at all, thank you." I acknowledged to save our manners. Oh dear, Janie was pulling at her hair and poking at another book. "Come, dear." I hated to command her so, but it was awkward demanding so much of Mr. Worthington's attentions. And when it came to it, I was urgent to get out of range of the dark man's scrutiny.

I ushered Janie gently before me and managed to slip out the shop's door without incident. My tailor made suit was smart, but I had wilted given the bustling shop and my nervousness during escape. The sun shone warmer than it had for months. I required a rest in the shade.

"Janie, would you mind terribly if we stopped at a bench by the depot? I feel as if I'll perish if we continue to your home presently."

"I thought Jaimeson planned to meet you here anyway?" Her brow came down.

She was undoubtedly worried I'd missed such a detail. Out of character and a sign of just how flustered I'd become. "Oh yes. All the better then," was my attempt to comfort her.

I beelined for the nearest open bench – the one overlooking the intersection on Railroad Avenue, the main street of town. Nearly everyone crossed there going to and from the train. The train had pulled into the station a short time before our arrival, so there were many folks about greeting those who'd arrived or seeing off those preparing to speed away.

"Trains are curious things," I observed aloud. "They're so steady and time seems to slow down when you ride across country on one.

And yet destinations fly by and mark progress more quickly than seems natural. I always feel so free when I board, and before I know it, I'm in a travel trance where everything becomes part of a scene beyond reality. I wonder if such feelings exist when one rides upon a dirigible? I'm so intrigued to take flight. I must remember to ask Mr. Worthington if he has books about flight or the workings of dirigibles."

"Mmmhm." Janie replied – amiably but with divided attention.

Bless her, she was consumed with her new purchase. She had been setting aside savings for the big day, and who could blame her. Books always set me to dreaming as well. It was a shame that part of Mr. Worthington's shop brought me nightmares. Fear surrounded my thoughts of returning to the cabinet, and yet I could think of little else. At least I confirmed that Mr. Worthington was outside of town in the evenings, but what about his partner? He appeared to slink in the shadows as a rule, and would likely be happier working at midnight. But I succeeded twice by night and ought to try again before sunrise.

"Janie, thank you for sitting with me," my voice raised just enough to pull her out of her tome. "I believe I'm myself again. Although, I do have a favor to request – if it's not an imposition. May I release Jaimeson when he arrives and continue on at your home for one more night? You needn't fear I'll stay forever since Father is to return on Friday. I'll need to be home tomorrow night to prepare to greet him."

"Oh, Lizzie, you are incorrigible. May I assume that means you plan to return to your midnight hijinks?"

"Yes, quite." I stifled a yawn.

"But I thought you had misgivings about Manush? And what about the book. Aren't you worried that you can see the content and I can't?"

"They've made me all the more determined to decide my own destiny. I want to see if the book continues to reveal more. And if the dark man has made me afraid to return, I must confront my fear and jump in heartily."

"You are a paragon of feminine courage, my dear!" Janie cheered.

"Or quite mad."

"Or both!"

Our laughter gained the attention of passersby. I waved. My mother would have been appalled. My face flushed with the realization of my impertinence.

"You're impossible. I'm so glad I met you!" Janie whispered between her teeth through fits of laughter.

CHAPTER EIGHTEEN

∞∞∞

In Which Miss Livingstone Flirts with Infinite Fantastical Possibilities

When I arrived at the shop, I was breathing hard with exertion through my pain and anxiety from dodging every shadow. Clouds had come in and hidden the moon. The darkness was oppressive. My insistent urge to sleep was gone, but I was left with a nightmarish foreboding. The spirit of Manush seemed to be lurking nearby, though I didn't see anything materialize from the shapes imagined behind every tree and lamppost.

When I pulled the key from the pouch of the tea dress I'd borrowed from Janie and bent forward to insert it into the lock, I was flabbergasted. The keyhole was gone – or rather it had moved and changed shape. In fact, the entire assembly of knob, latch and plate was new – or old, but different. Someone removed the one I knew and replaced it with an antique latch. While it was quite unique and would intrigue me under usual circumstances, it did nothing but confound me now. The opportune key, given to me by a small boy's hand of fate, sat useless. Standing on this side of the door just wouldn't do. I had found a new destiny and couldn't turn back now.

Although it didn't appear the type of keyhole to match, I decided to try the Journey key. It had pulled me out of a jam before. Or would that be a jamb? I snickered.

Reaching again into the deep pouch-like pocket, I took out the squatty weathered silver key. It was worth a try. I put its small form into the over-sized slot with little hope of result. But nevertheless I turned the key, which wobbled in the gap.

A blast of wind and flash of light and I was inside the shop as though I'd been there all along. I rubbed the key, perhaps looking to confirm its substance, and placed it far down in the pouch for safe keeping. Such odd circumstance brought it to me, and I was moved from a tight place to freedom. And now it brought me in when I was out and granted the opportunity my heart desired.

"I'm in!" I remarked with glee.

I wasted no more time and soon stood with the stones before me once again. The emerald had taken me to another time. If I chose it again, would I go back to Thomas in 1941 or to another time altogether? Or would it work at all, for that matter? And the amber took me to another place in the same time when I first used it. Would it do so again? The same place or different? I wondered. The new book gave some detail, but not beyond what I had discovered myself.

I was also fascinated by the other stones – and those that were missing. I gazed at the spaces. Were they here and then borrowed out, or was the owner still collecting them? It was all speculation, and my mind followed the mystery. The empty slots were not mere grooves but had unique shapes which presumably would conform to the missing stones. They were perfectly known – just as in the book.

I was filled with desire to find the missing ones. Instead of repeating my experiment with either of the first two, I decided to choose yet another.

The one that continually drew my attention was the one colored an alluring dark blue. I remembered the book's description – blue star sapphire. Deep within its rounded form, there was a shimmer that resembled a six-rayed star. I inspected it more fully with a gloved hand – being careful not to let it slip, of course. Fascinating. The shimmer moved each time I turned the stone so it couldn't be pinpointed exactly where it lay within. It was magnetic yet elusive – much like Manush – only this felt pure and light, rather than a thing of shadow. Like it held infinite fantastical possibilities.

I removed my glove, reaching down to touch the sapphire's lovely blue surface. "Oh!" My finger pulled back in shock as I watched a ripple run outward in every direction from where it touched, and broke, what was now a wide blue water surface. I nearly overbalanced, but righted myself in a tipping boat. A vast pond rolled out around me. I stabilized in the simple rowboat, crude but soundly made of weathered wood. Its color had retreated into nothingness. Cool grey, as though the life had been leached out over time.

The pond wasn't the stagnant kind. It was more of a lake truly, and bluer than blue, like the stone. The sun shimmered upon its surface, sending rays out into the depths in the shape of a star as elusive as the one in the center of the stone. It was idyllic, like a journey of the mind. Since I could see no one, no structures, no shore, I took up the oars and began to row.

The ripples spread from the oars as I dipped and pulled. Leaning with all my might, I gained some momentum. But in this empty, peaceful place, my mind traveled faster than my body. Like a dream. I always thought it strange about rowing that as you progressed, you watched where you had been. The wake spread before my feet like a path to might-have-beens, heralding my passing to those I'd left behind.

I tired of rowing, both physically and mentally, and nothing seemed to change, so I rested.

The monotony was mind-numbing so I turned to face the bow. The change of perspective was inspiring. Light spilled out over the lake in a rich golden hue that lapped around the front of the boat and dissipated in swirling tendrils from the sides in wide angles. Looking back, all I could see was blue descending to darkness. Looking ahead again, it appeared I was floating on light into the light. I watched it come.

The waves lapping against the boat were gentle. Time stretched without measure and it seemed the moment would be forevermore.

"No," I whispered.

As if in response, a wind blew over the surface of the pond and broke the glass-like surface into thousands of points of light dancing every which way. The pattern was intricately busy and yet uniform in its chaos – mesmerizing.

In my musing, I leaned toward one side of the boat, but just in time thrust my backside awkwardly in the opposite direction to keep from capsizing. When I regained balance, I stuck a finger in the water again. "Amazing!" It returned to the placid surface from which all the pattern had come. Like a dream before awakening. Deep, deep blue.

CHAPTER NINETEEN

∞∞∞∞

In Which Miss Livingstone Goes Flying

There was no measure of how long I'd been floating. The boat rocked so gently I dozed. Poor Janie! I hoped I hadn't worried her to death. But one thing I learned in all of this – time passes as it will – different in every place and subject to the whim and mood of something not yet defined. I needed to get out of this limbo and find my way back to the shop.

"Oh!" I no sooner had that thought, than I was back on the table in the shop, poised before the palette of stones. The dazzling blue one remained cradled in my hand. I replaced it into its custom-formed space.

Strange, that journey. I couldn't help but wonder if it was all in my mind. And yet...My finger was wet. Perhaps it made thought reality?

I decided to choose another since the bookshop clock showed no time had escaped at all.

The rust colored one with the sparkling stars tempted me again, but I remembered Janie's warning and had my own discomfort with the beam of light that came out beneath it when dislodged. I had no reason to risk myself against her wishes.

Perhaps the amethyst? It had the most beautiful purple hue. Purple often symbolized serenity, spirituality or royalty. "What is purple to you, oh great stone?"

Replacing my gloves, I pried the gem from its place. It carried a resistance that exceeded its size – a disproportionate gravity weighing it down.

I slipped out of one glove and set the purple stone on my bare hand. It was suddenly weightless...and so was I as I sailed through the sky rather more quickly than I liked. "Oh my!" I cried as my feet touched down with a jarring shock to my knee, and I grabbed for the railing that presented itself to my glad hand.

"Oh!" I couldn't stifle my cry. It was one shock after another. I realized the detail of the ground over the edge and comprehended how high I must be... "Flying! I'm flying!"

"Yes, indeed, or rather we are riding and the *Dame Fortuna* is flying, to be exact." A young boy addressed me with a self-important air. He seemed quite pleased with his grasp of the workings of the situation. "But pardon my asking, who are you?" His brows sat up high and mighty awaiting my answer.

"The *Dame Fortuna?* But..."

"Aw Miss, don't tease me. I know that's the ship's name, I just said so. And –"

"But that must make you the young Master Matthew Fisher-Swift."

"Yes ma'am, ship's boy and gun monkey. You've heard of me?" Matthew's face beamed brightly beneath his light brown hair.

"Well only in stories – accounts, I should say. Remarkable!" I took another peek over the side and looked upward at the open sky. Without a doubt, I stood upon the deck of a dirigible. I had achieved my dream of flight, though not with the fine young Mr. Chesterton of Chesterton Air, but on the very vessel that birthed my hopes of air travel – the *Dame Fortuna*.

The accounts of this crew's conquering of the American west were released the year I was born, and I cut my literary teeth while reading them. How thrilling! But that would mean I was back in time…about 1815-17, perhaps? Could Miss Harriett Wright and the Coltranes and the infamous… "Sam Bowe! Pardon me, is Miss Samantha Bowe on this craft?"

"Oh yes, ma'am, I reckon Miss Bowe is about. Do you know her?"

"In a manner of speaking yes, but we haven't…Oh, do you think I could meet her?"

"Now how did you get aboard this craft without meeting the…You still haven't told me who you are." The boy crooked his brow and pulled his shoulders back fiercely.

"Livingstone. I'm Miss Livingstone from Boston, and the far west. And the ornithopter? Is it here as well?"

"Yes, though it's still not quite itself after the storm and all. Not to fault Miss Wright's handwork on repairs. I'm still on the mend as well, they say. I've got this here binding on my leg. But as you can see, I'm perfectly capable of keeping watch. I found you, after all."

"You certainly did, sir. And I think it's about time you reported it so."

"Should I report you to my Aunt Ruth or take you straight to Eddy?"

"Oh my, I'm feeling a bit faint." I dropped the amethyst down into the pocket just in time to use both hands to keep myself from pitching over the edge as things went black of a sudden. I recovered my sight quickly, but had the shakes.

"Are you ill, Miss? Now that you mention it, you do look like you're dressed for resting. I don't normally see woman in dressing gowns or clothes without all of those contraptions and coats and all, except for Miss Bowe, of course, but she's got her own reasons. Can't hardly knife-fight in those confining stays. Don't tell Aunt Ruth I'm talking of such things."

"Knives or lady's undergarments"

"Either... or I mean, neither would be best."

"I would guess you're right. Now have you decided where to take me, I really think I best get away from this edge." I'm afraid I was not adjusting well to flight, and the adventure I'd always dreamed of was leaving me rather woozy and upset at the stomach. Perhaps I could adjust if I went inside the structure.

"Alright, Miss Livingstone, you can follow me." The boy left me and struck out across the deck as if striding along the beach at low tide, even with his leg splinted. He finally looked back. "But you'll have to loosen your grip on the rail...Miss Livingstone?"

I fully intended to follow, but my hand wouldn't let go. "Alright, Caprice, one finger at a time..." Oh, dear, I was talking to myself and telling myself what to do. Had it come to that?

I took a deep breath and looked away from the edge. Now if I could just focus on Master Matthew about ten or twelve steps away.

Freeing the rail, I flailed slightly when leaning too far forward, but lurched into a walk. The glide of the magnificent ship was actually quite smooth, and once I set my mind to believe I was walking on a boardwalk – and I couldn't see over the edge – I moved along with dignity.

"Madam," a deep voice surprised me and pulled my focus from my feet. As I wobbled and caught my balance, the tall slim, well-muscled man swept his hat from his head and gave me a nodded bow.

"Oh...oh dear. I..." gathered my wits enough to give a small curtsy, but was flabbergasted. Before my eyes was Mr. Eddy McBride the famous rifleman and war hero. I was walking in legends. "Em...Sir." I curtsied again.

"This is Miss Livingstone," Master Matthew thankfully supplied. "I found her while on watch near the bow."

"Eddy McBride at your service." His eye twinkled in a most unsettling way. "And where might you be from?"

"Boston...er, Snoqualmie. Do you mean now?" I was ridiculous – an utter fool.

He regarded me with a raised brow and pulled a pipe from his jacket pocket – a jacket from an era past.

"I believe you ought to take Miss Livingstone here to your Aunt, Master Fisher-Swift. She'll know how to get to the bottom of it."

He puffed smoke and moved off toward the terrifying rail. I had a momentary feeling of dizziness just thinking about it.

CHAPTER TWENTY

∞∞∞∞

In Which Miss Livingstone Finds Avoiding Capture a Difficult Trick

Master Matthew's Aunt Ruth, otherwise known as Mrs. Fisher, the captain's wife, eyed me with suspicion as I inspected the ship's interior with fascination. The compact room where we stood had one wooden wall with, thankfully, a small port hole and an open hatch. I gulped at the perceived fresh air, trying to quell my nausea and nerves and dispel the claustrophobic feeling of the cramped area crowded with goods needed for the journey. The other three walls were mere partitions constructed from light frames covered with hemp canvas. There was a constant creaking and slight sway which did its best to toss me on my posterior.

To my delight, Matthew returned with the Coltranes – the greatly renowned Sir James and Miss Jillian. The bizarre realization of truly being in the past made my head spin again.

"Good afternoon...Miss Livingstone, is it?" I was expecting Sir James to interrogate me, but was instead treated to the grace of Miss Jillian's questioning.

I nodded and did my best to curtsy. "Yes, Miss Caprice Livingstone, at your service."

My knee complained with a pain that blackened my vision and shot stars at the edges as sight returned. It must have shown on my face.

"Are you well?"

"Yes, I…well no, not exactly. I'm a bit nauseous and I…seem to have lost my memory. I don't know how I got here. And I've apparently wandered off in my dressing gown. I was under the care of…of…I'm not certain now. But I was sent away to rest after…after…Oh!" I gave my best rendition of an overwrought swoon. The cover of nervous illness jumped to mind thanks to Master Fisher-Swift's innocent questioning of my health at our first encounter.

I blinked slowly several times and opened my eyes to see Sir James' face remarkably close to my own. I had felt arms surround me as I fell, but the realization I was enfolded in Sir Coltrane's embrace nearly made me swoon in earnest.

"I…em, oh…" I struggled awkwardly, and he set me gently back on my feet.

It was as if the room held its breath. I noticed a man and a woman near my own age had joined us. It must have been Mr. Gregory Watts, the famed photographer of this journey. Such remarkable documentation he would provide for the future. And the woman was Miss Harriet Wright, the American. I would recognize her awkward demeanor anywhere, bless her eager heart. I turned my head from side to side to get my bearings while deciding what was next. Sir James still stood in close proximity – perhaps to catch me again, if required. Mr. Eddy McBride, the rifleman, was propped in the doorway, watching with interest.

"So you can tell us nothing of yourself?" Miss Jillian tried again.

"I know I'm from Boston," my voice said rather desperately. "Nothing else, no." Truth. She didn't ask what I recalled, but rather what I could tell them. Any more could have been devastating.

"We won't be setting down for quite some time," Sir James was decisive, "so whatever her past, she will remain aboard until then. I'd like her to be accompanied whenever possible, but we'll allow her free movement about the ship." He turned to me. "Miss Wright will be charged with your orientation and will make space in her quarters for your berth."

"And what of her dress," 'Aunt' Ruth Fisher insisted. Her expression hadn't softened in the least.

"You may come with me, Miss Caprice Livingstone," Miss Jillian offered, along with her outstretched hand.

The elegant Miss Jillian Coltrane led me to her makeshift chambers and looked through her own wardrobe to give me appropriate attire – stays and all – and in the long dark blue pelisse coat and multiple petticoats, I looked a proper lady again. The fashion was a good deal warmer as well, for which I was grateful.

∞∞∞∞∞

As a prisoner of fate, on my trip of dreams, I abandoned myself to adventure and learning from the well-known explorers. The crew remained disturbed that I got aboard without notice but accepted my presence – not that they had much choice unless willing to throw me over the side.

Because of my dizziness the adventurers readily believed I was nervously unstable. It occurred to me that malady might earn me the thrilling chance to pilot the craft. I all but hounded the captain for an opportunity to take the wheel.

On the second day of begging, the captain hesitated to cross my enthusiastic insistence that he teach me to steer.

"Please sir, it's been a lifelong dream of mine to pilot an airship. I'm not sure I can endure –"

Mr. Eddy – or Eddy, as he insisted I call him – came along as I raised my entreaty to a fevered pitch – seeming unstable indeed. He gave the captain a nod with eyebrows raised.

"Oh," I groaned with ecstatic desire, hoping to push the man over the edge. To teach me to steer, of course, not over the terrifying rail. "I don't know whatever I shall do if I can't fulfill this dream."

Eddy cinched my opportunity with a tip of his head when the man nearly balked at my wishes. Eddy then gave me that glittering-eyed crooked grin of his. I took it as confirmation of his conspiring to raise my independence. But perhaps he also enjoyed a joke at the captain's expense.

"Alrighty then, Miss. Ye put your hands here, just so, and…well, we'll save the more complex workings till after you're steering," the man turned over the wheel with a pointed glare at Eddy.

The moment the craft came under my direction, I soared in spirit as well as the air. It was marvelous! The feel of the rough wheel gave me a sense of smooth sailing, and I was captain of my own destiny in a way I had never been before. It was a dream indeed, and I'd never felt more real.

Eddy took in my wonder, staring without shame while I learned more from the captain and settled into steering with confidence. I don't think Eddy believed my illness ruse, but then most everyone suffered his shrewd inspection. Only Miss Harriet Wright was given a slightly softer eye. His penetrating gaze made me squirm in my deceit. Whenever he regarded me, I also thought of the gem I'd stolen. What strange choices I had made in recent days. But I couldn't imagine living without knowing these adventures and more of the stones' power. The drive to continue was unrelenting. And I planned to return the amethyst in time, of course.

∞∞∞

The compulsion to stay and follow the entire expedition was nigh irresistible. But I had constant concern for my dear friend Janie and my family. And I longed to get back to my new vocation as book collector. When no one was watching I tried wishing upon the purple stone many times with no result. So lacking other means, I sought a steam train.

Sir James Coltrane – our charming leader – assured me our flight over Ohio Territory toward St. Louis would bring us near a station, or at least a whistle stop eventually. Indeed, the railway often snaked across our westward landscape, which was much less settled than when I rode the train across country in the early months of 1910.

Avoiding capture in Mr. Gregory Conan Watts' photographs was a difficult trick. He insisted he should document every encounter no matter how unintentional. But I didn't want to unravel the tales I loved so well with my meddling, for of course it was his letters and journals that would survive to be published. As such, I ducked him at every turn, and on the third day I jumped through a door that proved to be the portal to the large ship's bay where Miss Harriet Wright was feverishly working to repair Sir James' mechanized battle suit after the damage it received in recent battles and in the terrible September Gale of 1815.

"Oh! It's remarkable!" I shouted upon beholding the great suit for the first time.

A great clattering of metal met the end of my exclamation, as the startled mechanic dropped her wrench, and let go an abundance of small metal parts and the largest spring I had seen to date.

"Oh!" Miss Harriet sounded bewildered rather than angry.

"My apologies," I tried to pick up the scattered pieces. "I just –"

Her delicious down-home laughter relieved my embarrassment. "It's no matter. I'm always dropping things." She reminded me of

Janie in her practical and accepting demeanor. And she was kind to me as her ward aboard ship. She'd even taken to calling me Lizzie.

We commenced working together to replace the spring and make further adjustments. Our conversation fell naturally into mechanical cooperation, and we made great headway as a team. After a few hours passed in what seemed like moments, we stepped back to admire our handiwork.

"You've remarkable talent for repair," I told her.

"Just something I picked up helping Daddy on the farm." She inspected her hands and then flashed a winning grin.

"If only I could see the suit in action. It's massive – and marvelous," I enthused. The armor-like exterior coupled with the visible gears, springs and weapons were as formidable as its reputation.

"Yes, it's kind of intricate, but having the plans handy made it easy to fix. It's Bubsy I'm having trouble with. That takes more ingenuity, and I'm no inventor, just a tinkerer."

"Bubsy the ornithopter? How exciting. My father's an inventor, and though I haven't his skill, I'd be honored to lend what analysis and innovation I can, if you think I could be of assistance."

"Oh, would you?" The girl's face lit with open delight. "We can begin tomorrow just after breakfast."

∞∞∞∞∞

On my way to retire for the night, I again ran into Mr. Gregory Watts and his camera. I needed to shake his persistence, so pressed how devastatingly it would shame my family if my presence here was discovered. Then I lamented my father's weakened condition and how the shock could be too much for him. Mr. Gregory took that to heart, it seemed, and finally eased his mission for my portrait.

A strange puzzle this thing of time travel. Would my visit here necessarily change the past, and therefore the future, in my own time? In this case I prayed not, though I would treasure the journal I kept here – for I did keep my own – more than the jewels I had found thus far...with the exception of the emerald that took me to Thomas and Newbury Street.

CHAPTER TWENTY-ONE

∞∞∞∞

In Which an Unforeseen Connection Casts Dark Foreshadows

In the morning, Harriet – Miss Wright –showed me her tinkering on their beloved ornithopter, and explained how she was stuck. I was able to suggest a creative solution, and we began work to help the poor fellow get on better. The strange amalgamation of flying machine and dog was truly a wonder. The span of his mechanical wings straightened and began to beat more smoothly as we worked, but the gears that drove his wheels upon the axel were still jittering.

"Might I ask about Miss Sam Bowe?" I pressed upon Harriet while we affected our plans on Bubsy's mechanisms. As my hero, Miss Bowe was not what I expected, and I jumped at the chance to find out more about her.

"I don't know that I'll have answers. She's a conundrum. But you can surely ask."

"I hope to count her among my friends, but it's hard to strike up conversation beyond, 'could you please pass the salt,' or a simple compliment regarding her boots."

"Yes, I have the same trouble. She's one of a kind– talented and daring, impossible to tame."

Indeed, uniqueness was exactly what defined her. But I'd always imagined she'd be something like me – or I like her, since she came first. I'm fairly unique, after all. But she was unfathomable.

Harriet continued, "I'd bet she'd protect me to her dying breath – and she'd protect you too. I'm sure of it. But I've never detected one speck of affection. Unless perhaps toward Miss Penn."

"Miss Penn?" My heart beat raced inexplicably as I remembered accounts of the dark gypsy fortune-teller who had been on the expedition. I had completely forgotten she would be aboard. There had been no sign of her.

My attention returned to Harriet, "…She's been abed these many days since the big storm. Though she's nearly well enough to –"

"Rise? So have I done." A rich voice of mixed European accent cut in. The captivating, though diminished in health, Miss Julietta Penn propped herself up on the edge of our workbench. Her vivid green eyes burned from the olive-toned skin of her still-bruised face.

I felt as if I should say something, but words wouldn't come. I couldn't quit staring at her too-exposed bosom and commanding countenance. Her black hair was a loose and disheveled mane, though it's silkiness evidenced vigilant care. She was quite as daunting as history remembered.

"Come with me," her voice was deep with persuasion.

I gave a helpless shrug over my shoulder to Harriet while leaving with the dark woman who had apparently exerted herself to fetch me. The gypsy led me down an interior passage, tight with storage, to her small berth.

Miss Penn heaved a coarse-sounding groan as she reclined against the propped up pillows on her bed. The tiny, hemp-walled room closed in further as I occupied the chair wedged into the open spot of floor. Her eyes closed and remained so until I thought she may have fainted away. I leaned in to determine her condition, and her optic flames of emerald suddenly popped open and burned through me. My guard was like tinder under her discerning gaze and I felt my identity and purpose laid bare like a hillside after a wildfire.

"Manush," she stated.

The word shook what was left of my composure, and I babbled like the mad woman I'd purported to be. "He's following me and I don't know his motive, and he knocked me down but won't speak to me. He lurks there, and Thomas seems to support him in part, but he's full of secrets as well. No one will tell me who Manush really is and what he wants with me. Do you know?" It suddenly occurred to me how odd it was she even knew his name.

"I can tell you he is my relation."

In looking for resemblance, I rather saw her likeness to the woman in the bookshop in Paris.

"I recognize your name as a Traveler he mentioned. You are not from this time."

"Please don't give me away. I –"

"I am unconcerned with this. No fear. As long as you answer what I ask of you."

"Yes, anything," I heard myself promise.

"What are you seeking here?"

"I didn't mean to come. It was just curiosity. I mean, I wanted to travel, but when I picked it up I didn't know where it would take me…" I trailed off realizing more was revealed than intended. The woman had a way with inquiry.

"Which stone."

I challenged her green scrutiny briefly and then dropped my eyes. "Amethyst."

"Mmm. It's too early. You can't tell me of him then. And if I advise you, it will not dissuade him from his path. You won't understand how to deliver what I wish to tell him. Pity. I hope our travels will cross again – when it will do you both good. There is time. You will have a long road together."

The fortune-teller sat forward slightly and plunged her hand into her bosom. She pulled something from her revealing dressing gown. I was unable to see the small token, but was grateful it wasn't the bodice knife she was reputed to carry. She held it out toward me, and I extended my tremoring hand. The tiny tile of mud-clay that fell into my palm was stamped with the now familiar symbol of the striped-parasol and fence.

"Speak of this to no one, not even your best friend. Keep it always with you. Give this to Niccolò – Manush – when you come to know his purpose, and tell him of our meeting in this time. Tell him I wish to see him again. Keep it well." She slumped back to her pillows with another loud groan and waved dismissal with a flick of her hand toward the room's exit.

I could do nothing more than nod and retreat. Clearly there was much that was beyond me. I had dabbled with the mysteries of time and so was now put at the whim of those who had mastered its workings in ways I couldn't yet imagine. Though the gypsy's charge implied that someday I would know more.

∞∞∞∞

I stumbled down the narrow corridor, feeling as woozy as I had during my first hours aboard the *Dame Fortuna*. I glanced at the rather ancient-looking tile and secured it in my own bosom. I worked to gather my wits. It was best that I hid this whole scenario rather than inadvertently expose my real identity or anything of my travels through time – even to Harriet. Though I would try to be as truthful as possible with my friend.

"Hello, dear," I called gustily as I returned to the shop.

Only a small clatter this time, and Harriet's face turned to me and clouded slightly. "What did she want with you? Are you alright?"

"Oh, she's an odd one to be sure. She wanted to discuss my future, but concluded it wasn't the right time for me to understand. I'm just fine. There was no harm in humoring her when she was feeling poorly."

"Mighty kind of you. I wonder why she'd pull herself up from her rest and single you out just to —"

"Yes, strange. Well, back to work, eh? Where were we?"

Thankfully, Harriet dropped the subject and we returned to work on the ornithopter in earnest. The repairs we completed gave Bubsy a good deal more facility. His gears lost their jitters and both wings and wheels moved freely. He zoomed around the work area like — well, like a dog in an open field on the first day of spring. Miss Wright was thrilled, and threw her arms around me in an unexpected embrace. "He's quite himself again. Let's go to tea," she enthused when she loosed me.

When I regained my equilibrium, I had another idea. "Will you indulge me, dear? If you can wait to eat, that is. I could use some help to understand a mechanism of my own."

"Certainly. I'm not that hungry, and it's such fun to work with you, Lizzie. What is it?"

I held up the mysterious Journey key. "This small key has some uncanny properties and I'd like to discover more about it." A twinge of guilt ran through me as I remembered I hadn't even told my dear Janie that I kept this key. But with Harriet and my minds together, there was hope we might find a way for the key to take me back to my own place and time. I needed to share it with her.

I dropped the key in Harriet's hand and suggested she put it into any slot and turn it. She put it into a small crevice on an interior wall joining the bay to the rest of the ship, and with a flash and gust of wind she was gone. She came in breathless from the passage outside the work bay.

"Remarkable!" she exclaimed. "Where did you get such a thing?"

"Nevermind that now, let's try some other configurations, such as what happens if I hold the key and you hold my hand – or the hem of my skirt."

"How exciting," she beamed.

We spent the afternoon trying the key in different spaces in various ways for experiment – careful to avoid anything near the exterior of the dirigible of course. As before, there was always a gust of wind and a flash of light. We would be inside if we started outside, or outside if we started inside, and not far from where we turned the key. Any contact between us would bring us both along – even the petticoat. Harriet was duly impressed, but had no explanation. We concluded it would be handy for quick entrances or exits. But I resigned to the fact it wouldn't get me home.

∞∞∞∞

Over the next couple days, Bubsy the ornithopter took to following Miss Bowe again as he had used to do, and everyone was greatly relieved. Her glad approval of his companionship was the first spark of connection I'd seen in Miss Bowe. And his loyalty to her was touching. I quickly became attached to him as well, dear Bubsy. Though the discomfort many felt in observing so much personality in what appeared to be a completely mechanical construct was certainly understandable.

Harriet wanted to give me credit for Bubsy's repair, but I insisted on not being mentioned in logs or letters – again appealing to how it might shame my family when I'd wandered off so.

As much as Miss Wright and I enjoyed each other's company, it was the young Master Matthew Fisher-Swift who captured my heart. He was quite an amiable companion. Perhaps because he was less busy than the others – unless on the hunt for an absolutely horrid-sounding rat. He was perfectly pleased to accompany me on deck to watch the countryside slide by below. And once I became accustomed to flight, it was my favorite pastime of all.

My excellent adventure was tainted only by my fear for Janie. She was constantly on my mind. Each time I had a moment to myself, I prayed that, as before, it would be as if I was gone for almost no time, though I'd been aboard the airship for over a week.

CHAPTER TWENTY-TWO

∞∞∞∞

In Which Miss Livingstone Thrills to Her Heroes' Heroics

Ever since my clandestine conversation with Miss Penn I was plagued by nightmares that painted many scenes I couldn't grasp. Her piercing green eyes haunted my thoughts. My anxiety was heightened by the secrecy I promised, and I pulled out the tiny tile often when alone and contemplated what it all could mean – without conclusion. One morning I sat up abruptly from a disturbing dream. It was as if I witnessed great peril from a remote place and was helpless to intervene, but at the same time my decisions were bound to the final fate.

When I was fully awake, I couldn't shake the melancholy of it. I asked Mr. Gregory for the date, thinking my dream could be a portent of things to come. I recalled October 8, 1815 was the date of the most compelling letter from the collection on the *Dame Fortuna*, published by Dr. Cordelia Bentham-Watts, Mr. Gregory's fiancé currently – and his amazing wife, eventually. This very day, the crew of the *Dame Fortuna* was – or would be – part of a great and frightening rescue. I was as nervous as I was on my first day of boarding school. Imagine being a part of what I'd read so much about!

I lurked near the railing, hoping to see events unfold. True to the text the wind had fallen and the cold weather warmed in the afternoon. The incomparable Miss Samantha Bowe and the sharpshooter, Eddy, were on the deck taking air. Right on cue.

Oh, I could see it! A train in the distance. I couldn't give it away. What if it changed the outcome?

"Miss Livingstone, is something the matter?"

Oh dear, Eddy noticed my attention to the ground.

"Look there!" Gregory came forward at Eddy's alarm and sighted them off the bow. The train, and some still undefined specks converging on it at galloping speed.

"We're headed right for them!" I couldn't help but chime in.

Miss Bowe jumped to alert.

"Matthew, prepare and bring my guns," Eddy shouted.

"Oh!" I nearly spilled over onto the deck as Master Matthew rushed by me into the hold.

While the others scrambled to prepare, the Captain brought our elevation down some, but our approach hadn't yet been spotted. I could see them clearly below – a group of well-armed bandits on horseback, fast approaching the train in open country. The train was laboring, headed for a water station. The bandits were going to overtake it.

They still hadn't seen us when Master Matthew arrived with Eddy's guns. Eddy stationed himself along the rail and pulled his googles on. He expertly tinkered with his custom-made lenses to hone in on the range, but held his fire. It would be key to maintain surprise.

"Yes!" I cried out in fear and excitement. My heart beat out of my chest, it seemed. We were just behind them now and Miss Bowe whistled for the ornithopter. She balanced remarkably, standing on the railing and then jumped! Bubsy, ever at her side, unfolded his wings and sprung aloft. She caught his axle in mid-flight to glide toward the train below. I'd always thought that part of the story exaggerated, but there it was before my eyes.

The bandits mostly boarded the train at the middle cars but split into groups. Miss Bowe was almost down, guiding Bubsy to land at the thick of the action.

There were startling *cracks* as Eddy finally commenced gunfire and shot two men climbing onto a car. Unbelievably, my heart raced even faster.

"They've seen us now!" Mr. Gregory hollered by my side.

"Gregory! Your camera...quickly you must document the scene!" I woke him into a run for the hold. I hadn't meant to be so familiar, but without my interjection the silly man may have missed the whole thing. But he would succeed in recording photos of the day. I'd seen the article preserved from the Missouri Gazette. How strange to know the future in printed images frozen in time.

"Oh my!" Mr. Gregory was back, and Miss Bowe was fighting three men on the train below. They fired their shots, and she dodged butts of guns and threatening knives. She wrestled intensely and threw one from a boxcar. With deft movements she escaped the others.

Master Matthew was following Eddy's commands and kept him shooting steadily. Many men fell from horseback but others continued to board the train. They worked their way toward the engine on top of the cars – presumably to stop the train short of the water station. It was excruciating to see them crawling along bringing danger nearer to the passengers and crew on the locomotive. Eddy was swearing like the soldier he was, without regard for his young powder monkey's sensibilities.

"Oh!" I almost swore myself. Miss Bowe was progressing but things looked dire. I wished I could jump to her aid.

"Yes!" A great grinding and whir of gears arose behind me, and with a startlingly loud rush of released steam, the Coltrane's mechanized battle suit jumped out from the *Dame Fortuna* in mid-air! She...em, he crashed through the roof of the storage car, but remarkably, didn't derail the train. I would've been devastated, but I knew the suit was made to protect the one housed within it. The car where it was lodged would be where the safe was kept. The mission to protect it was clear.

The powerful metal arms threw one bandit out the hole created by the crash landing, and the other crooks were falling back as the way was effectively blocked by debris. Men popped out like ants from a stirred up hill, and the battle suit came up out of the wreckage. The bandits on horseback were scattering, and I could see others surrendering to folks on the train.

The last three crooks, intent on stopping the engine, were oblivious to what had occurred – although it was hard to imagine how they ignored the crashing battle behind them. Miss Bowe miraculously persisted in her race to stop them. One enormous fellow seemed about to cut her off, but she was more nimble through the coal car and maintained her progress unscathed. He continued forward on her heels. The second man fell, and the *crack* of gunfire reached our ears marking what downed him.

"Hooray for Eddy!" I shouted without thought.

But the hulking man engaged Miss Bowe at last. Their grappling felt like a strangle hold on my own throat. Surely his greater size would overcome her. She disappeared behind his frame, and I thought I would faint with suspense. But suddenly he toppled backward, losing his footing, and she was up and knocked him toward the open part of the car – throwing him from the train! Only one more remained.

"Ohhh!" How terrible and thrilling! A well thrown knife, and she took him down, just before he could stop the train.

"Hooray!" I cried. It was clear the robbery failed, and we were low enough that my own cheer joined the sound of the cheers coming up from the train. They realized they were saved. The soldiers had it all under control, and I happened to know that the railway payroll and property deeds were protected. There would be great fame for the heroic acts of this day. And I was there to see it all unfold! Thankfully, the dread left by my dream did not apply to this day, and all was as it should have been.

Oh, but wait, now that the train was saved – there was my ride home. I started to rush to the captain, and then remembered we'd surely need to stop to collect Miss Bowe, the ornithopter, and em...Sir James and his battle suit.

"Will we be touching down?" I asked Mr. Gregory as I came to his side.

He was stowing part of his photographic gear, now that the majority of the images were captured. "Likely we'll make contact with the train at the water station just ahead."

"Of course. I must prepare to depart then." I hurried into the hold to get the precious treasure of my diary from aboard ship and to freshen up for the crowd below.

CHAPTER TWENTY-THREE

∞∞∞∞

In Which Miss Livingstone Tests Her Mettle

We shadowed the train from above, slowing our progress to match their arrested speed as they approached the water station. We could see their destination, and our captain confirmed Mr. Gregory's conjecture that the station would be a good place to tether and reload the ornithopter with Miss Bowe and the Coltrane-filled battle suit.

We were still hovering airborne, and the moment we were tied off, there was an enormous rush of steam again and the battle suit sprung into the air. It was expertly piloted into the bay of the dirigible. I made my way there hoping to find the Coltranes. Their repeated expressions of gratitude for my aid with repairs to the battle suit had given us considerable social time together during my days of adventuring. We'd developed mutual appreciation and, dare I say, affection for one another, and I couldn't bear the thought of leaving without wishing them farewell.

To my delight, Miss Wright was there assisting Sir James and Miss Jillian Coltrane in securing the suit. As I exchanged an embrace with my dear friend and colleague in invention, Harriet, another large cheer came up from below.

"Come, Miss Livingstone," Mr. Gregory brought the news, "the train is awaiting your arrival and has granted you free passage as far along the line as you wish to go. But you must hurry."

"Farewell, Sir James," I called to where he stood with Miss Jillian.

He rushed to me and bowed over my hand. "It's a pleasure to know you, Miss Caprice. Farewell."

His sister left her task and came to my side offering a light embrace.

"Oh, but my dear Miss Jillian. I must get changed and leave you the..."

"Nonsense, my dear. Please keep your attire. My gift to you at our parting," she insisted as she set a gentle kiss on my cheek.

I suspected she was removing the embarrassment for everyone, by avoiding my arrival below in my bedclothes – as she described my tea dress – but she delivered the gift with her usual impeccable grace.

"My eternal gratitude to you. And to you all." I called into the hold while following Mr. Gregory out to the deck. I had a momentary feeling that Miss Penn's green-eyed flames were upon me, but a glance around showed her to be as hidden as she had remained since our first encounter.

The captain waited at mid-ship. "Are ye certain she can climb in that get-up?" he addressed to Mr. Gregory with a tightly squinted eye running over my long white skirts and back up to my tied on hat.

Master Matthew let go a capital giggle near the captain's elbow.

"Climb?!" I interrupted with a most inappropriate outburst, "but surely you can't expect..." I looked over the edge, and though we were much closer to the ground, being tethered to the station's guard tower, I couldn't imagine... "Oh!" I spied the swinging ladder.

At least I had opted for the short rosy Spencer jacket rather than the blue pelisse, thanks to the warmer weather. But I still carried the weight of one flannel petticoat and pantaloons, and my knee was better but still sore…Oh dear.

Mr. Gregory was discomfited as well. "There's another way, is there not Captain? She's a lady, after all."

"Miss Bowe is a lady." He cocked his teeth around his pipe stubbornly.

"But she's no regular…"

"And neither am I," I interrupted Mr. Gregory boldly – appropriate or not. The challenge had been issued, and at last I would test my mettle against something of Miss Bowe's feisty accomplishment. After all, I was evolved almost 100 years beyond her time. My independence should measure up accordingly.

"But…" Mr. Gregory began. My look silenced him. Perhaps I had something of his remarkable Dr. Cordelia Bentham-Watts in me as well.

With great verve I turned just slightly from him and stuffed my cherished journal securely down my bodice to free my hands for the task.

As they readied the ladder for – "Oh my!" – departure, I laid a quick kiss on the cheek of Master Matthew while no one was looking. I squeezed his shoulder with a whispered, "good-bye, my young friend."

He blushed profusely but did not wipe it from his warmed face. A duck of his head hid a wide grin.

I regretted missing the chance to wish farewell to Eddy – as he'd still insisted I address him. He was missing from deck and undoubtedly was resting after the afternoon's taxing duty. I'd never seen anyone fire so many shots so well. And despite his gruff exterior, he was quite compelling – though he couldn't displace my affection for Thomas. Perhaps it was his skill or the fact he respected skill where he found it – even in a woman. "Please give my regards to your mentor sharp-shooter."

Master Matthew recovered and nodded at the charge.

"Alrighty then, Miss, it's over the edge for ye," Captain Fisher announced to me remarkably gently. "Yer sure it's not overmuch for ye now." Concern etched itself into his deeply weathered features.

I opened my mouth to decry my doubt, but couldn't possibly betray the shining admiration in young Master Fisher-Swift's eyes. A shake of my head agreed to the feat. The rest of me trembled so intensely I couldn't speak.

Captain Fisher took my gloved hand to steady me up onto a box and over the rail. "Don't look down except at your next foothold," he advised.

My knee complained some at the tall step, but the shot of pain was nothing compared with the spike in the beat of my heart.

"Look!" Master Matthew pointed just before I lowered over the side to put my foot on the top of the rope and rung ladder.

Bubsy, the dear ornithopter, had risen from below and was hovering next to us, presumably to comfort my descent with his companionship. It was steadying, indeed.

My last glimpse of topside of the ship included Eddy upon the bow. He didn't miss my departure after all. I gave him a bright smile, which he returned with an almost imperceptible nod. The glint in his eye buoyed my courage.

"Now, I'll just think of this as stepping down from the stirrups, one after another after another," I mumbled to myself.

The sound of the ornithopter wings and gears was soothing by my side. "Oh!" I almost lost my footing and my knee pained me again when I was startled by a fresh round of cheers from below. But my hands gripped so tightly I don't think they could've been pried from the ropes had I tried. "One, two, three, four.... Oh my!" I stumbled off the bottom rung, right into the arms of the conductor. And the roaring cheers of those nearby warmed my cheeks to what I'm sure was the scarlet of the reddest rose ever grown.

"Many of the passengers were allowed to disembark from the train to greet you," the conductor said. "You're a hero." He set me on my unsteady feet.

I broke into victorious laughter and indulged the cheers by waving to the crowd. I forgot my knee, and all my jitters turned to mirth – I had done it – petticoat and all!

"Oh, but what of Miss Bowe?" I called to him above the din.

"She has already ascended," he assured, pointing at the dirigible still tethered and hovering above.

And sure enough, Bubsy the ornithopter was up at the side of the *Dame Fortuna*, and I saw a tiny figure swing from where she gripped him to leap upon the rail. She quickly disappeared onto the deck.

I had hoped to have one more encounter with the incomparable Miss Bowe, proud as I was of my ladder descent. But I trusted she saw me go, since in my own observation, as well as the accounts I'd read, she'd never missed a thing.

"Miss Livingstone." I heard my name as if through a clearing mist. As if I was waking from a dream. "Miss..."

"Oh yes, pardon me," I replied.

"I'd like to thank you on behalf of the Symonds Jeffrey Railway[1] for your bravery and for your part in the protection of the passengers

---

[1] In 1815 there were no railways, you're quite correct. In *Dawn of Steam: First Light's* alternate history, railways were added to the era, and this adventure is built upon that reference. The name *Symonds Jeffrey Railway* is in homage to author Jeffrey Cook who wrote *Dawn of Steam* with Sarah Symonds.

and the railway's livelihood. Captain George Thurman, at your service," the leader of the soldiers gave a slight bow.

"It was nothing; I assure..." I was drowned out by the demonstrative crowd.

"We'd like to award you with some token of our esteem. Please name your desire, and we'll do our best to grant it," he spoke for them.

I could hear the wind over the plains in the attentive pause for my answer. "I... I'd like to go home."

"Yes, yes, your passage is assured, but what can we give as reward in memory of this day? What is it you value the most?"

"Well, books, of course!" I spoke without thinking. "I mean you don't have to..." The crowd roared with laughter. I cringed, hoping I hadn't been ungracious, but they appeared jovial enough.

"Then books you will have. Any particular kind that suit your fancy?" He had a rakish flash in his eye, this soldier. He may have been making light of me.

"Something classic...no, most contemporary would do the trick," I answered and raised my brow in defiance. If he planned to play me as foolish, I would play along and gain my demands.

"I have a most special publication, Miss." A young woman, of apparent means stepped forward. She dropped her eyes along with a perfect curtsy. "I was bringing it as a gift to my Aunt, but I wouldn't be there to deliver it if it wasn't for your Miss Bowe. She...well she..." the woman broke off and dissolved into tears.

"She saved all our lives is what she did. Never seen a woman wield a blade like —" The man was cut off by gasps from the crowd. He pulled the brim of his weather-worn hat and stepped back.

The young woman stepped forward and placed a lovely package in my hands, tied with real French ribbon, a luxury from the East.

"It's lovely. You really don't have to…"

With a shrug of her grand puffed sleeves, she turned tail and disappeared with a barrage of sobs into the crowd.

"All abooooooard!" the conductor called.

"Even with the justifiable delay, we must do our best to keep to schedule. Please be timely in the return to your appointed places," Captain Thurman instructed.

The crowd dispersed with some scattered applause.

CHAPTER TWENTY-FOUR

∞∞∞∞

In Which Miss Livingstone Flees Forthwith

Captain Thurman escorted me through one train coach to my seat at the front of the next car, and I could hardly follow when so overwhelmed by curiosity of what publication was within the beautiful wrappings. I tried to wave him off with propriety. My manners were questionable when I unwrapped it before those that bestowed it upon me, but I couldn't endure another moment without knowing what the package contained. I untied the lovely ribbon.

"Perfection!" I'd earned a treasure beyond compare for Mr. Worthington's store. It was so pristine; folks would wonder at his ability to preserve such an immaculate collection. For of course, it was recently published. Imagine, Jane Austen's *Pride and Prejudice* only two years from release. I truly couldn't believe I held the three volume set of its first edition. I feared to touch it. Although, I reasoned, it would be a more believable collectible if I broke it in by reading, just a little. What an honor.

"Oh!" I glanced back over my shoulder feeling a bit guilty for opening such a rare book, and stared when I saw Mr. Manush! He was there, trim black moustache and all, sitting near the back of the same passenger coach in which I was seated. I couldn't tear my eyes away as he finished rubbing the fine green jewel on his striking gold watch and then snapped it shut and stowed it in his vest pocket. When I saw it more closely, it seemed rather large for a watch. Could it be his device for finding my place in time? I felt quite sure he was on my trail. How else could he be in 1815 aboard the same train? Although he looked completely absorbed in thought and unconcerned with me.

I gathered the Austen volumes and quickly pulled my *Dame Fortuna* journal from my bodice to stack with them. In a jiffy all were secured in the wrappings with a not-so-pretty bow. I moved myself side-saddle on the seat, so to speak, to keep Mr. Manush in my peripheral view.

Since I knew from Thomas that the desk belonged to that man, it was a reasonable assumption that his jeweled timepiece could have uncanny properties as well. He still wore an immaculate dark suit, but adapted it to this time period with a double-breasted coat and waistcoat cut short and straight. His dark trousers stood out as slightly out of favor but held the fashion in their close fit. So he was either here for some time or was dressed for where he'd purposely arrived. His face held the same weathered look – of similar age. I was now fully convinced he was manipulating my journeys, or at least privy to them.

He still didn't look up or acknowledge my scrutiny. I wondered what he could be after? The tiny clay tile was secured in my bodice, but he could know nothing of that. In my mind's eye I saw the two spaces in the tray of stones, molded to the shape of the crystal and ruby that were missing. Perhaps he used those two in some way – or, of course! He was trying to find them as well. I would most certainly keep watch for the two stones along the way, with more vigor than I had when first noticing their absence.

I longed for the train to leave soon. I wasn't sure I could endure the suspense much longer.

Oh! He stood up! Mr. Manush was moving toward the front of the car – toward me!

Woooot woooot. We were under way, and just in time.

Without thinking I gathered the bundle of books close and pushed my hand down my bodice to find the amethyst hidden next to my stays, held firm by the high waistline. I wished for home and withdrew my hand as soon as it grasped the prize, wary of attracting notice on the crowded train – now pulling into the station in Snoqualmie midday. Folks were standing, and I jumped in among them to disembark first, hoping against hope that Manush couldn't make his way through the jammed aisle to catch me. I checked over my shoulder for him constantly, but was unable to see around those protecting me from behind.

Just as I stepped down to meet the platform, the woman behind me stumbled on the step above and bumped me from behind. I caught my balance on my good knee, but the amethyst jumped from my hand and then fell back down my bodice. I hardly had time for relief. When my foot met the boards, the daylight remained, and I wasn't back in the shop, but rather walked among those leaving the train. Apparently my arrival was now on the usual train schedule at noon. I was sparked to flee forthwith.

Such a strange image I must have presented in my hobbling run from the station garbed in my old-fashioned blush-toned velvet Spencer and flowing empire waist gown. It was kind of Miss Coltrane to be concerned for my propriety and supply me with proper foundation, but I looked quite silly dressed in the fashion of ninety years ago. Whatever would people think? I squeezed my package tight and rushed toward the Adams' home, hoping to vanish before someone I was acquainted with saw me. I would have to replace the stone into the cabinet later. Mr. Manush was not visibly in pursuit, so there were some mercies.

I was surely missed at breakfast and likely luncheon – assuming it was the first day since my departure. My dear Janie would have used my headaches as an excuse for my staying abed, but Mrs. Adams with her kind soul, would be clamoring to go in and comfort me.

"Oh heavens!" I ran smack dab into the standing sign outside of Mr. Worthington's bookshop and took a nasty fall – thanks to my flowing bundle of skirts. I managed to preserve the precious package of books unharmed, but my dignity was completely lost. My aggravated knee flared with pain and I couldn't right myself. I had to lay upon the boardwalk waiting for aid. At least my face was partly hidden by my tied-on hat, knocked askew.

"Are you alright Miss? Here, let me help you." Mr. Worthington's reedy voice full of concern turned my cheeks hot with humiliation. I couldn't even answer. How very embarrassing!

"Oh...oh no," I cried, trying to duck further into my hat to hide my face.

"Are you hurt? Please let me help you up. Are you able to stand?"

"I... oh dear...I," had to look up at last.

Recognition jumped to his eyes. "Miss Livingstone! Oh, Lass, whatever are you doing on the ground? Here, please take my hand."

No matter the humiliation, I was forced to allow his help. When his offered hand touched mine, a strange rush of pleasure and further embarrassment filled me, which intensified as my bare skin locked against his in a firm grasp. I'd forgotten to replace my glove as I hurried away to escape the dreaded Mr. Manush. I hardly felt the awkward yanking and teetering that put me upright, so taken were my senses with the feeling of his hand around mine.

I forgot to let go for a moment. But when I did, my eyes flicked to his and saw there a warm smile. There was nothing accusatory or amused in them. My embarrassment was needless.

I bumbled my hat back into position and fumbled for words. "I... I have brought a publication." A pull at the ribbon produced the three volumes, and I held out the offering with my gloved hand. My bare one clutched the paper around my prized journal.

His face kindled with interest as he examined the three volumes of Jane Austen's *Pride and Prejudice*. "It's in remarkably fine condition," he observed, "even the paper is pristine. It's like it was just printed, but appears to be the first edition around about 1813?" He opened the first volume again and check the publishing marks and date.

"You know your business well, sir, for this is indeed a first edition copy." I smiled at him, and we relished the mutual enjoyment of two bibliophiles.

"You are most remarkable, Miss Livingstone." His thick brows dropped as he continued inspection of the crisp paper that was to be nearly 100 years old.

A nervous giggle slipped from me, but it did the trick of pulling his attention from the uncanny perfection.

"Perhaps it is you who has a collection of books worthy of presenting to this town rather than I," he suggested.

"I have brought it for your collection, Mr. Worthington, and I trust you'll compensate me in an appropriate manner." I took a step back when met with the amber fire in his eye. Mine were also alight and I dropped them quickly.

"But do you generally dress in the fashion of the era of publication of a book you plan to sell, Miss Livingstone? Your garments are impeccably correct for that time period, am I right? And it seems you suffered for your authenticity by taking that fall over my sign. I shall move its location to prevent any further mishaps."

"I, em...yes," I answered feebly. The embarrassment was gone but replaced with awkwardness over the many apparent things that begged for explanation. No wonder I had told him of my journeys eventually. It was time to go, before further questioning became too difficult for response. "I will take my leave then, and you may keep the books and settle on...em...compensation at a later date. I really must be getting on."

"Yes, of course, but please come in, and I'll post receipt with terms to be settled later. I wouldn't feel right to take possession of such a valuable item with no guaranty to you."

With all the events of the day, my quick wit failed the invention of an escape from his nobly suggested delay. I mutely followed him into the shop, causing a ruckus by upsetting the bells in the doorway with my skirts.

As he directly took care of the receipt at the sales counter, I noticed the desk was securely closed and the small table that I'd stood upon was back in its place. Had Mr. Worthington moved it or was it returned to position some other way? Perhaps Mr. Manush...

"...then?" is all I heard. I had no idea what he'd asked me.

"Please pardon me, could you repeat the question?"

"Will you be returning on further adventures then?"

Why would he ask that? Perhaps I missed something? "I'll be back soon, yes," I tried – mortified with fear that he knew of the jewel I held.

"I'll look forward to the pleasure of your return." He displayed an unassuming smile.

"Thank you, and good day." My mind raced, wondering if he meant the return of the missing gem, but he appeared oblivious.

I retreated from the shop and heard the brass bells clang as I shut the door rather too hard. I focused on watching my step, and would be more careful until I shed the cumbersome ensemble. I clenched my teeth against the revived pain in my knee and limped my way back to Janie.

CHAPTER TWENTY-FIVE

∞∞∞∞

In Which Miss Livingstone Exposes Flim-flam Fare

When I rounded the corner toward the Adams' home, I jumped with anticipation and nearly called out loud. Jaimeson was returning to the car from their house, and Father was aboard his Steamer automobile with all his luggage. He was a day early! I longed to run and embrace him, knowing he would have missed me as well. But good sense ruled I must be discreet. Undoubtedly poor Janie had just managed to keep them from her room. Oh, and they would be terribly worried. She'd have invented a horridly dramatic story indeed to excuse my refusal to greet Father's return and sensibly ride home while Jaimeson had brought the car.

I hesitated with regret, not wanting Father to suffer concern. A movement caught my eye, and I recognized Solomon and Viola's boy through a break in the trees. He held up a hand toward me in signal and disappeared in the brush. I slipped back around the corner presuming he would meet me after the Steamer departed.

In a few minutes the boy materialized from the shadows of the wood with barely a snapped stick, crossed the street, and whisper to me conspiratorially, "Miss Mary Jane told everyone yer in the throes of a terrible migraine and couldn't be disturbed. If you follow me, I'll show you a less visible way to enter the house. We can't be seen by anyone. Even my ma believes yer inside. She's been preparing sustenance for you and fretting that Miss Mary Jane won't let her in to check on your well-bein'. Here Miss, I'll take yer package to carry."

With an eye toward the woods, I reluctantly gave up my journal to his care. As we proceeded I did my best to invent explanation of why I was out walking with the boy, just in case we were discovered. But with my sore knee and bulky skirts it was difficult to think of more than the placement of my feet. How inconvenient to arrive during the day! We crept through evergreens and brush at the edge of the property, and the light lawn of my dress was constantly caught on branches and blackberry brambles, causing delay. It was a terrible shame to soil and tear the dress which was a beautiful piece from a bygone era. I would still treasure it as a memento of my time on the *Dame Fortuna*, and the gift's being bestowed upon me by Miss Coltrane was dear as well. They were a bonny crew, to be sure.

Feeling footsore and ragtag we arrived at the back entrance. The young boy cautioned me to silence with a finger raised to his lips. This would be the most dangerous part of our journey together. We needed to escape notice by the household. I didn't want to undermine Janie's kindness by revealing our treachery.

Trying to keep my excessive fabric from rustling in the stairwell was the largest challenge. Especially with my labored movements due to my knee. It sounded like an army of shuffling leaves to my ears, but at last we neared Janie's bedchamber, where I was to be taken abed. Solomon's boy returned my package and silently withdrew with the flash of a grin.

"Oh!" Janie's exclamation nearly made me jump from my stays it startled me so. She spied me through the cracked open bedchamber door. A girl after my own heart to cry out so when we were supposed to be sneaking. Our chorus of laughter posed even more danger, but I couldn't help it. Our embrace was a dear reunion, and it was obvious she'd been on the edge of her seat trying to keep my secret.

"Wherever have you been?" She whispered fiercely.

"I'm so sorry. What a bother I've been."

"Bother? There was no bother other than my fear for you. Are you well?"

"Just fine, I – yes"

"Let's get you out of...oh my, what a dress it is, too. And is that another book? I can see there's plenty of adventure to tell. But what are you doing back during the day?"

"I... I'm not sure, but I lost my grip on the stone when I was stepping off the train, and instead of being in the shop at night, I arrived on the regular train. It was fortunate the amethyst fell back down my dress and not onto the platform. I could have lost it."

"It must have stopped your heart. How long were you gone from your point of view?" Her words gushed with excitement.

"About ten days. What span of time passed here?"

"Just night to day, though you've missed breakfast and luncheon...Oh! And your Father –"

"Yes, I nearly cried out to him on the street and ruined everything. But Solomon's boy waved at me to wait until they departed."

"I have some tasty treats set aside for you by Viola. But you simply must tell the tale! Oh, and can I see the book in your package? I can hardly wait. It is a book, isn't it?"

"Of sorts, yes, but I believe your first thought's correct, to start with getting me out of these contraptions and into bed. We're likely to make noise as the telling unfolds and attract someone to check on us. It'll be much easier to convince them I'm feeling better if I look as if I was once feeling worse."

"Right you are, as always," Janie agreed. "But I'm simply bursting with curiosity."

"As am I, with excitement, to share my adventures with you. For this one was beyond glorious!"

"Oh, you are cruel to tease me so. Let's get you into your sickbed, posthaste. If such can be achieved with these archaic bindings. I'm so glad we don't wear such stays anymore. And how many petticoats are you wearing anyway? Getting out of this will take all day."

"Just get on with it, please my dear. It's almost time for tea."

∞∞∞

"I can hardly believe you witnessed the train chase as told in the annals of the *Dame Fortuna!* Had I not already come to respect your integrity, I'd have difficulty giving verity to your words." Janie's beautiful blue eyes danced with admiration.

"I must admit I can hardly believe it myself. But I wrote my own account of the days there as well." I finally pulled the journal from its well-traveled package for her perusal. "And if it hadn't been for my fright in running from Mr. Manush upon my return – and the embarrassment of my fall in front of Mr. Worthington – it would've been pure elation." I didn't mention the elation I felt at the memory of my hand in Mr. Worthington's. Some things just couldn't be spoken of, even to one's confidante. The encounter held an entirely different quality than the relentless flirtations of Mr. Eddy McBride. I could hardly admit it to myself.

I changed the subject abruptly. "There is one thing I was puzzling on, and I could use a second opinion." Janie's brow rose with interest at my words. "What could Mr. Manush want with following or chasing me. Do you suppose it has to do with the two gems missing from the cabinet of stones? Oh wait! Right now there are three."

I showed Janie the amethyst gem which I'd concealed in my glove on the dressing table as she helped me disrobe, though I didn't bring out the mysterious clay token I'd promised to keep hidden. I'd been reluctant to reveal even the stone, but realized I couldn't expect her to aid me in the puzzle without every clue I was able to share.

Janie's right hand pulled at her hair and her left reached toward the stone with a sigh of wonder. My hand snapped the glove shut over the amethyst.

"No!" I cried out, much too loudly.

She looked stricken. I opened my hand with an effort, hoping to ease her. My behavior surprised me too.

"I'm sorry, dear. Please don't touch it."

"Oh, it's alright. I was going to take the glove from you too. I know not to contact –"

"No,' I controlled my voice this time, but was unable to master my emotion. "I don't mean to be cruel. I..."

"Don't give it another thought. We've determined their hold on you is strange. Do you suppose he could be looking to complete the set?" She jumped right in with her suggestion. I loved that about the girl – tight to the mystery with little regard for petty turmoil.

"I had thought he was looking for them too." I tucked the stone, and the glove with the tile, into a bag beneath the bed. A deep groan that reminded me of the chilling Miss Penn, escaped me at the pain in my knee when I did so.

Janie hopped up from her seat. "Oh you poor dear. I'll get Viola to check your knee again –"

"I'm fine, truly."

"If you're sure."

"Certainly."

"Well then, in books I've read on magic, sets of amulets often have a power beyond each single one. Perhaps the stones are such amulets."

"That's brilliant. But if Mr. Manush covets the set, why doesn't he just travel on his own? And he obviously knows I'm traveling. It seems he could stop me in a moment, but he hasn't. I don't understand why he would allow me to travel and risk my getting to the final stones before he does."

"Yes, that is a puzzle."

"Although," I needed to tell her I still carried the Journey key. I didn't know why I'd been hesitant in the first place, "I've forgotten to mention that when I arrived last night, I was locked out. The latch and lock on the door were changed. I would presume it was before the grand opening. So perhaps Manush is trying to stop me."

"Yes, he may have noticed the missing key. Although the old one was sticky. I remember that horribly suspended moment on the first night when the key didn't immediately turn. Maybe Mr. Worthington wanted a latch that would work smoothly for himself and his patrons, and it wasn't Mr. Manush at all."

"You're correct, of course, there's no way to know."

"But if the key didn't work, how did you get in?"

I looked down at my hands, "I'm sorry I left this out of my former account, my friend. I'm not sure why I didn't tell you. But I hold another key." With an effort I met her eyes. They were full of interest – not chastisement.

"Of course, they've hidden the new key near the door jamb as they did the old," she concluded sensibly.

"No, this is a different sort of key. You may remember, I found it in Paris when in dire necessity of escape. It helped me then, and I've discovered more of its properties since." I wrapped my hand in a blanket and pulled the key from under the pillow where I'd hidden it as I settled upon the bed. "Be careful not to touch it, my dear. I'm not cagey with it like the stones, but you may cause its power to throw you out into the hall."

"Journey," she read aloud as she leaned in close. "It looks so old."

"Yes, and I can't explain it, but I have the feeling it was there for me to find when needed. Like I called it or...someone put it there for me as they knew it would be of help."

"It's so exciting you've kept it. I recall how it got you out of the bookshop in Paris, but what else do you know of it?"

I had a nostalgic vision of my experiments with Harriet, which I didn't share. "From what I can observe, it doesn't need to fit a lock, it can be inserted into any slot, gap or keyhole. When I turn it, if I'm inside, I am instantly out, and if I'm outside, I'm immediately in."

"How interesting...and useful."

"Indeed. And there's always wind and a flash of light when I turn it."

"Like a magician's trick."

"Yes, regular flimflam fare. It's part of what made it — awkward to talk to you about it. It's difficult for me to admit such absurd happenings, and that I clung to them. But I assure you it has helped me."

"I can forgive your concealing it, dear. Though I don't understand your reservation on talking about the key's powers when you so readily discussed the stones. They're both beyond the realm of usual experience. Although I've heard of travel amulets in stories, especially from other lands, and the key's power is more like...well...magic."

"Yes, travel with the stones could work with a scientific principle — like an affinity between the substance and the place, perhaps. But the key works anywhere in the same flamboyant manner. But there must be something more than magic."

"I don't see why there need be more. Your strange book regarding the stones doesn't seem very scientific."

"My book! I'd almost forgotten." I left our debate on the supernatural behind.

CHAPTER TWENTY-SIX

∞∞∞

In Which Things Become Rather Tangled

I hid the pain in my knee this time and retrieved the strange book, with the parasol-like symbol on its front, from the bag I'd tucked neatly under the edge of the bed. I put my *Dame Fortuna* journal in the bag and dropped the amethyst stone deeper into the bag's depths.

The blue star sapphire was now outlined within the book's pages as providing a journey of the mind, within another dimension, like a memory. No wonder it took no time at all. And there was a rather lovely illustration of a rowboat on a lake. But I had never been on such a lake. It was more like I lost my memory of what was. Not like a memory of what had been.

"It worked. There's more," I nearly shouted and turned the book toward Janie.

"Shhh," she giggled quietly. "You're only to be feeling better, not gloriously well. Viola will be here any time now with our tea."

"Oh yes," I whispered as I turned further pages to the illustration of the amethyst stone. The full description was there as well. It was a stone of change – of dreams.

"Look here." I turned the book toward Janie again. "The purple stone is one of dreams. That certainly fits with my desire to soar through the skies, and I even learned to pilot a dirigible."

"I'm afraid I still see nothing. But I believe you, of course. Like I said...magic."

"Well, tricks, spells, magic, mystery – call it what you like for now, I was most certainly there." I pondered the closed book on my lap, and the repeated symbol on the small tile I was given on the journey. "My gown attests to the time period I visited, as does the book I delivered to Mr. Worthington."

"Oh, I do hope he'll let me touch it. I'd love to see it in first edition. My father has the third edition, and it's wonderful, but the thought of seeing it brand new! How intriguing and utterly thrilling."

"Assuming he'll let either of us do anything at all near his books. I have stolen the amethyst after all. It wasn't my intent. I was standing in the shop but was too flustered to come up with a way to get it into the desk midday."

"Right in front of the proprietor? That would have been magical, indeed." Janie laughed. "But you're certainly correct that we must get it back there soon."

"The book collecting part of these adventures is still enticing, but the rest is becoming rather tangled. Now I'm a sneak thief – a regular creep – and I may be seeking powers for a man with motives we don't understand. If we assume Mr. Manush knows I can get into the shop and that I might travel again, and if he doesn't stop me, then he must want me to go. Why?"

"That is the question, for certain. But maybe he's looking for the stones on his own and is just behind you, and your sightings of him are coincidental."

"It's possible, but I don't feel it captures the truth." Miss Penn's revelation that Manush and I would have a long road together hung eerily in my mind. "For one thing, the stones that caused travel to each place were in my possession when I saw him."

"So he must be getting there by some other means."

"Exactly, that's my bright girl. Perhaps it has something to do with the green jewel on his watch. Or rather the contraption in that beautiful gold fob. I was able to see it more closely, and it is larger than most watches by a good margin. Do you suppose it could direct him through time?"

"Oh, that's a whole other wrinkle then, isn't it? Perhaps his travel has nothing to do with the stones at all." Janie's hand drifted to the ends of her hair.

"But I feel he's lurking there waiting for me. And I definitely feel pursued."

"Let's assume it is the stones then. The missing ones may do things beyond the abilities of the current ones, and beyond his abilities as well. Or we're back to the power of the set. There could be some reason he can't get the others on his own and needs you to find them."

"Yes, that makes perfect sense. But what could the reason possibly be? And why me?"

"Thank you, Viola." Janie thanked her rather loudly to drown out my final comment. I'd almost given us away as the housekeeper entered the bedchamber.

"The tea is lovely. Thank you, indeed." My compliment solicited a smile from the kind caretaker. "And I'm feeling much better."

"Yes, Viola, can you please take the pot back with you and deliver some scones to the front porch. I believe she's well enough to take some air now before returning home, and please have Solomon let Jaimeson know he can bring the car." Janie's report on my health had the woman beaming at me.

"I confess to feeling some guilt at the trouble caused to your household," I told Janie as Viola retreated. "You're all so caring, and I've been nothing but injured and ill."

"Nonsense. It's no trouble. Let's get out to the porch. We can watch for Jaimeson from there."

"Oh yes, he will be here soon, no doubt." Disappointment took root. I'd grown very fond of my new friend. "Ow, oh!" I couldn't help but cry out as I stood.

"Lizzie, dear..." Janie cried grabbing my elbow to steady me.

"I'm afraid I've torn my wound a bit. But it's mostly just stiff. I can manage."

"I can have –"

I shook off the kind shower of aid with a wave of the book in my hand and a labored movement toward the door. "Just get me dressed," I allowed.

"Oh my! I've lost your lovely tea dress, and I think the lace was even finer than on my own," I lamented.

"You must accept use of this second tea dress," she insisted. "Your green tailor made is much too difficult for your short trip home. She accomplished my adornment with efficiency and kind ease of my pain. There now, don't you look keen? In fact, the dress is a gift to you. It was poorly fitted to me, and flatters you swimmingly."

I smiled, mute of excuses to deny her given such praise. "But now that I have more guesses at the real workings behind these things, I'm weighing the adventure of looking around the next bend, against dangers or consequences. They may be larger than first imagined," I picked up the strange book and continued quietly as we entered the hall. "Oh wait! My bag."

Janie generously retrieved it for me, and I set the book in its folds next to the journal, nudging the amethyst with the binding to assure myself of its presence. I removed the gloves and put them on, securing the small tile inside them to keep it on my person, as I'd promised Miss Penn.

"I'll send Solomon up to retrieve this valise filled with your green suit from Opening Day," Janie assured as she buckled it up.

My cheeks warmed as I thought of how the elder Thomas remembered that fine green tailor made, as he first met me when he was a young man – and with so many patrons that first day.

"I'll have to pick up the clothing gifted to me by Miss Coltrane some other day," I whispered. "We'll need to scheme to hide it from Jaimeson."

Janie shrugged a smile, and we began the arduous journey down the stairs. We were enticed to gain speed as we approached the front porch and the delicious-smelling scones.

∞∞∞∞∞

"Yes, I'm terribly curious about what else you'll find," Janie agreed when we'd settled in, "but caution is wise. Perhaps you should take a break from experimentation with the stones and take time to get to know Mr. Worthington a little better. We can also both attempt to find out more about the mysterious Mr. Manush."

"But I need to return the stone to the cabinet, and what of my agreement with the future Mr. Worthington to procure books for the shop? It's not merely the excitement of collecting them – which is considerable, I assure you – but also the good fortune it will bring him. I don't want to slouch on the job or get in the way of his success." I was quite drawn to the young Mr. Worthington, and also valued his opinion of me.

"You're right, of course my dear, Lizzie. It's not simple to decide upon." She pulled on her long blonde tress. "Perhaps we can ruminate on it while apart. It's time for Jaimeson to arrive with your car.

"Yes, splendid." I'd decided to look for the bright side, "and I can't wait to see Father. Perhaps I'll find a way to get his advice on the matter without revealing all. He has such a way of knowing just what I need. But you and I should speak on it again tomorrow, Janie. Would you be available to visit my home in the afternoon?"

"I'd be honored." She smiled, and her blue eyes shone.

"Say about two of the clock then?" I suggested.

Solomon approached through the yard. "Pardon me, Miss Mary Jane, but Miss Livingstone's car has arrived." He climbed the porch steps and carried down the valise from where he'd stowed it for the ready.

I could just see the Steamer through the evergreens. Its quiet approach had managed to elude me. I was distracted indeed.

"Perfect, she'll be right down," Janie confirmed.

She reached out to me with a most comforting embrace. I do believe the demonstrative nature of the West was growing on me.

"I'll speak with my father and let you know what I decide," I confided.

She squeezed my hand and nodded, her eyes rich in sincerity.

CHAPTER TWENTY-SEVEN

∞∞∞

In Which Father Listens with Heart and Mind

The ride home gave me some much needed time to think. I hardly noticed Mount Si as we passed, though the puffs of clouds around its top were majestic. My vision was turned inwards. In the past, before Mr. Worthington added the twist of meeting me upon my first journey, we had become friends. But he told me a twist can change things, and I could certainly comprehend why. My consciousness of our future relationship had already colored my caring, and therefore my actions toward him.

It may have been one of my great flights of fancy, but I couldn't help but wonder – did Mr. Worthington have romantic feelings for me the first time around? He didn't say as much, and he gave no indication of being father to my daughter, but there was something in his eyes.

∞∞∞

"Are you quite well?" Camille's intense stare indicated she disapproved of my missing Father's arrival, but I knew he would understand my independence. "Your Father has requested your presence in his shop."

"Can you please let him know I'll join him shortly, Camille. I'd just like to freshen up first." I needed to stow away the stone, journal and, well... magical book. That was the most scientific name I could apply to it given current observation. I also wanted to get my mother's locket from my jewelry box. Its size would be perfect to hold the small clay tile, and no one would question my wearing it at all times since it was clearly sentimental.

"Yes, Miss Caprice." She gave me a rather smug nod of approval.

I suppose she thought I looked a mess. If she only knew what I'd been through. She gave me the most terrible glare at the guffaw I released. I could hardly contain another! I had to hurry off to the stairs.

∞∞∞∞

My hand was one of the few allowed to push open the wide green-painted wooden doors to Father's shop whenever I pleased. Of course I knew to be quiet until addressed, even though welcome. Father always thought it laughable that a woman would be any less capable of problem-solving and invention than a man. He delighted in imparting to me anything and everything I was willing to learn, and I'd helped him puzzle things into place more than once.

"Oh!" The brass knocker with Father's initials was on the door. That wasn't there before. He must've brought it back from Seattle and mounted it today. How strange that I noticed it was gone from our home in Newbury Street just three days ago, and now I see it was gone from there for a very long time.

"My Caprice, come in and look at this for me, will you?" He went straight to the point, pushing up his shirtsleeves and bustling to the far side of the cluttered shop.

"Father, it's so good to have you home!" I chased him down and clutched him in a tight embrace full of affection.

"You're well then?" He glanced at the locket and then smiled into my eyes.

167

"Very."

"Good then." His expression traveled back to his prior train of thought. "This is the Colossal Clock, the time-keeper I've been working on for the railway. They're all about precision, as you well know. Well, that and notoriety. They not only want to arrive on time, they want everyone to know they've arrived on time. It's a matter of pride and good advertisement, don't you know." His bushy moustache twitched, and I suddenly noticed it was laced with grey that matched his eyes.

I laughed, but other than a slight glow to his round cheek that showed pleasure in my amusement, he continued right along. A hand ran through his wild brown-grey curls absent of his attention.

"It's beautiful!" I was unable to withhold my enthusiasm. It was truly grand enough to adorn a station aimed to be the pride of the spirited city of Seattle. It filled his multi-story workshop from floor to ceiling, and I finally understood why he'd demanded construction that would open its side upon the yard beyond.

"Yes, and enormous – to be seen from great distance," he muttered as if it were no great feat. "Where I'm stymied is in finding a material to create the tension to wind it for enough duration to be practical in running. I'd prefer it to run more than twenty minutes."

"It's a marvelous machine, Father."

"Just wait until you see it work – even if the duration is a little short at the moment. Ha, I made a pun."

It warmed my heart, and I couldn't help but giggle to see him so tickled by his own humor. A little short at the *moment*. Not one to entertain the masses.

"Wait while I wind it." And he was off.

He climbed feverishly up to an intricately built platform and used a series of levers – attached to assorted gears and pulleys – to move the crank and wind the timepiece. His rust colored damask vest looked about to burst with his efforts. I lost interest in his repetitive process, and my attention wandered across the lovely etched face of the machine. I gasped in wonder as the brass trains began to move across its wide expanse. The sounds and unbelievably accurate details of the trains were a delight to observe. I could have watched them all evening.

"Unfortunately in twenty minutes it will stop," he lamented again as he stepped back down to my side.

"Father, it's enchanting!" Most girls would have kissed his dear cheek in comfort, but I stepped up to his challenge. "I do see your dilemma. It's not practical to require such complex winding so many times a day. But a solution will come. It always does."

He plunked down upon a leather ottoman – his favorite perch. "With you and I together it will."

I went to his side and set my hand upon his shoulder. "You're right of course. You and I seem to be charmed with the answers." I offered my form of comfort.

"Quite right my dear, indeed."

With this mundane agreement, my curiosity suddenly sparked. "Do you really think so, Father?"

"Yes, I'm sure I'll figure it out."

"No, I mean that we're charmed. Do you believe in such things? That there may be more than what science has defined?"

"Undoubtedly there's more to the world than meets the eye – as they say. If I didn't believe so, I couldn't invent. It naturally takes a leap of imagination and a little faith to go beyond the tried and true. And sometimes inspiration comes from mysterious places."

"So you believe in magic?" My heart beat with anticipation.

"Magic? No, not magic," He raised himself from the ottoman with a bit of an *oof*. "Just the unexplained. Everything has mechanism and follows rules. It's just a matter of rules yet unknown when we label something uncanny."

"*What is now proved was once, only imagin'd,*" I quoted.

"Ah yes, William Blake, that's my girl. If we continue to observe, the pattern will emerge."

I thought over my recent experiences as he disappeared behind the large white face. There did seem to be patterns. Although I hadn't yet repeated many of the processes, I had tried to discover rules. The Journey key was about inside and out – of that I was certain.

"Do you believe it's possible to skip across space without travel time?" I called to him.

"Ow," he expressed in reply, along with a loud crash of a metal tool on the hardwood floor. "You mean to be in one place and then another without seeming to be in between?"

"Oh, Father, it's always such a pleasure to talk with you." I was unruffled by his familiar fumbling. "You follow my mind's wanderings so much faster than most. Yes, that's the sort of thing I mean."

"I can conceive of it being possible, but haven't worked out the details." He popped out from behind the machine and eyed me intensely. "Why do you ask?"

"What about travel across time? Like into the future or the past?"

"Mmm..." He disappeared again. "There's been much conjecture on that subject. The theory to explain it hasn't been formulated in scientific writings to my satisfaction." He reappeared and pulled the ottoman closer to me and sat, intent on his point. "I think it's about pinpointing a moment and a place in the cosmos and finding a means to arrive there. I haven't figured out how to do that yet. But I think I solved the puzzle on how to measure one's location in such a paradigm"

"Oh Father! You cracked the code without me? Have you finished your chronospacometer?"

"Not quite, just a small adjustment, but I believe I found the key so it can synchronize with its position in time and space and then reset itself. And, of course, it still sticks occasionally. It will indicate location, and time – like the railroad's standard chronometer, but it will have the added feature of knowing the date in any space in history, and adjusting automatically. It will be a marvelous tool for the rails...and perhaps for..." His words trailed off as he stood and scurried over to shuffle through a box on his overcrowded workbench. To anyone else it would have been a place of ultimate chaos, but he knew the order to locate a given item at need. He produced the device contained in a gold watch fob that looked like any other, except for its greater size.

"So you don't think instant travel across space and time is impossible?" I almost dropped the chronospacometer with my startling epiphany as he set it in my hand, but Father was oblivious. Short of the green jewel, it looked exactly like Mr. Manush's strange instrument. I felt I would burst with the knowledge.

"Hardly impossible. It's...not in the papers," Father continued as he snatched the mechanical piece from me and began to tinker inside its casing. "And I would call it improbable that we'll provide explanation for its workings any time soon with current scientific progress. But you already know, Caprice, I consider the human mind infinitely creative. And there are marvels of the universe's versatility around every turn."

He snapped it shut and placed the timespace locator back in my hand, missing what was surely my feverishly flushed face. My heart was about to beat out of my chest. I popped the case open again and the letter and number wheels on its face began to spin with a whirring of gears. It settled on 05:23 PM APRIL 21 1910 AD SNOQUALMIE NORTH AMERICA.

"That's got it, I believe," he declared. "Oh, and did you see the comet last night?" His mind jumped again.

With all our anticipation, how could I admit I'd missed the first night of Halley's Comet visible to the eye? "Em...I'm afraid my mind was somewhere else," I tried, hoping not to disappoint him too much.

"Splendid, it was. Reflected in the waters of Elliott Bay. But there will be plenty of more nights to observe it now that it's come so near," he excused graciously. "Perhaps you and I can take a look tonight together."

"I'd be delighted!" And happy for the distraction on this first night without a plan to travel with the stones.

"Now where was I?" Father searched for the thread he'd left behind. "Oh yes, yes, when so many consider an idea – well the imagination is a powerful thing. Especially when combined with determination. I'll not declare the ability to travel through time impossible nor even improbable if you press me for my feelings on the matter."

He looked shocked and pleased when I threw my arms around him and kissed his cheek.

"Oh thank you, Father. It means so much to me that you listen to your heart as well as your mind. Your wisdom and faith encourage me to carry on with my journeys."

I tucked the promising chronospacometer into my bag, certain he wouldn't miss it now that he'd solved its last adjustment. Especially while absorbed with the railway clock. If he was aware of my quest, he'd most definitely wish me to have its aid.

"The journey for knowledge and experience of the heart is a path worth pursuing, my dear. All the mechanisms in the world can't replace what you know and feel."

Father's mindset on these things filled me with a new fire to continue my journeys. I'd uncovered what made my father so successful and yet eccentric to most. So many thinking people are taken with mere mechanism and dry observation. I would be ever grateful that he brought me to be with him in the West – for education and affection.

CHAPTER TWENTY-EIGHT

∞∞∞∞

In Which Janie is Cast for the Perfect Role

Janie arrived in the mid-afternoon as scheduled. I had slept long, glad that my invented illness had allowed the indulgence without need of explanation. A small part of me pined to go back to the workshop with Father after luncheon, but it was far overshadowed by the one that begged to know more of Mr. Manush, Mr. Worthington and the mysteries that surrounded the bookshop. Since I'd decided to stay in the game, I was set to build my strategy. Janie would be the perfect partner.

After Camille was persuaded I was well enough for company and a visit to the bookshop, she wouldn't hear of my seeing Janie again without providing a splendid tea. I suppose she was correct the generosity of the Adams' was put upon in large measure and should be repaid. And although I doubted my hosts' favors had been ravaged, it was good to return the kindness. I wore the locket and gathered the amethyst gem and stowed it within the bosom of my bodice, careful not to contact my skin. I would hope for opportunity to remove my label of thief.

Another lovely spring day. We enjoyed it on the porch with Timber in lazy attendance – napping in his favored spot by the railing. Large bumblebees traversed our table as we talked, making me curious what patch they sought in this wide world.

"So you've decided to proceed! Have you decided what to ask Mr. Worthington today?" Janie tugged her golden hair, and her eager blue eyes set upon me with expectation of a plan.

"Father and I spent much time solving other quandaries, I'm afraid," I offered up to stall, "but perhaps it's time to get a measure more personal with him."

Her eyes grew wide. "You're going to speak to Mr. Worthington directly? I mean about other than books? How will you be so bold?"

"Well, I've already ascertained we become friends, so I can't go too wrong." My teacup was lifted to hide the flush I felt hot on my cheeks. For of course I knew of an intimacy she was unaware of. I fully expected his appreciation of any advances I encouraged. "It's a great advantage to have met in the future and already know another's intention."

"Yes, but perhaps that can only be applied when you're with him in the future. Maybe you should try to return and ask him questions there?"

"I've thought the same, but what I do here affects how it will be there. So I'll still be required to relate to young Mr. Worthington before he'll properly know me as an older man. It's a bit difficult to get one's mind around."

"So what shall be my role?" She appeared ready for assignment – so serious.

"As always, to be my companion and to look after me if I go missing. And to browse many wonderful books with great attention so I may have time with Mr. Worthington under the guise of indulging you. And please choose a better book to introduce at Miss Mabel's book club tomorrow or I'll skip it again, on purpose this time!"

Janie joined me in a round of knowing laughter.

"You'll be both my escort for propriety and entirely absent in practicality. You may become as absorbed in story as you wish, my friend, "I assured her. "The less attentive you are, the less chance we have of being pulled away too soon."

"I've never had a more appealing task on a friend's behalf. But then you're no ordinary friend."

I was unsure whether she meant to reprimand me, chide me playfully, or compliment me. A non-committal smile sufficed – with hopes she'd go on.

"Jaimeson will take you to town now," Camille came out to announce. She took away the decimated biscuit plate and the one that held lemon tarts – now quite empty. A definite favorite of us both.

As I eased my way down the steps from the porch with Janie, Timber followed. The silly thing hopped upon the automobile, even with the boiler at full tilt. A truly strange feline. As if he wanted to know what I was up to. He settled his large fluffy grey form into the seat between Janie and myself. I tried to oust him.

"Oh no," Janie protested, "don't make him go. Can't he ride down and back with us? He made all that effort to settle in."

"If you'd like his company, my dear, who am I to deny it?" A rumbling laugh came from me like a purr. I was glad for the diversion. Now that it came to it, I was quivering at the aching knees to speak so directly to Mr. Thomas Worthington.

∞∞∞∞∞

"It really is a beautiful automobile, Miss Livingstone," Thomas said as he glanced out the window at Jaimeson waiting for us outside of the bookshop. Janie was already lost in the stacks.

I was embarrassed of Mr. Worthington's potential perception of opulence. "It belongs to my father, of course."

"I assumed as much. My father admired excellent machines as well. He had two automobiles as soon as they became available and was given much harassment for spending the fortune of his heirs. Though my brother and I were nothing but encouraging on the expenditures."

"Father was awarded his by the Stanley twins," I inserted.

Mr. Worthington looked at me curiously mid-sentence, but continued, "I enjoy all things mechanical very nearly as much as literature, though I've shown little talent in fixing them. Actually you'll soon be able to meet my brother. He's traveled from Scotland and is crossing the country to stay here with me for a time. He came to aid in establishing the bookshop. He insisted on traveling by means other than train – for the adventure – and should arrive any day. That is, if he's not further delayed." Mr. Thomas' brow furrowed, and his pleasant face presented something like a scowl. "I expected him three weeks before the grand opening."

So his family was wealthy. I should have surmised it from his collection at such a young age.

"It will be my pleasure to meet your brother. My father is a very talented mechanic, and in fact, a well-known inventor. He..." The man's captivating amber eyes were shining with amusement. "You already know of him, don't you?"

"It's a small town, Miss Livingstone."

Ah, he evaded my eye. Had he been asking after details of my family?

"So you've decided upon our bargain, or do you require more time to search the collection?"

And he changed the subject. Yes, he'd been checking on me. I couldn't hide my wide smile, but gave a demur cough to help reduce its over-brilliance. There should've been no humor or joy in his remarks. But certainly they held both for me.

CHAPTER TWENTY-NINE

∞∞∞

In Which Miss Livingstone Gains an Unexpected Audience

"Actually, I have decided upon my trade agreement, if you're amicable." It was time to return Thomas to business before I revealed all of my affection. "I would like to call upon your expertise and knowledge of your collection to recommend a trade, both fair by your reckoning, and which you believe will enrich my learning or enjoyment."

My loud laugh was hardly stifled at the look of shock on his face. He apparently didn't expect such trust – or perhaps responsibility – to be given so bluntly. I suppose it is unusual in such a short acquaintance.

A warm smile enlivened his features and shone golden in his eyes. "It's an honor." He bowed his head slightly, "I will choose carefully. But I shall require an interview such that I can correctly gauge what's fitting."

I nodded my assent to the sound of the ringing brass bells at the door announcing a new arrival. Mr. Worthington kept his focus on me. I was poised ready to rise to the challenge of his questioning.

The expected inventory of what classics I'd read and missed was not forthcoming. Instead he asked, "What's your favorite meal? From beginning through dessert, and tell me why on each element, if you please."

I quickly recovered from the surprise. "Let's see, I'd start with a browned onion soup, cooked down sweet."

"Very practical," Mr. Worthington remarked.

"For a start," I emphasized. "Then, a roast goose with herbed dressing – though I've no appreciation for sage, and it must be lavished with gravy. I've developed a taste for sweet potatoes, smothered in butter, if you please, and perhaps the table should hold a fricassee with rice. Then add in every vegetable in season, prepared simply – steamed fresh, with a dash of salt, to bring out their unique characters. The flakiest and lightest of pan biscuits for bread will do, made like only Cook can manage – with salted butter. I think a lemon ice is best...or no, perhaps a lime ice with fresh mint garnish and save the lemon for tarts..." I went on.

As I spoke, his eyes twinkled more and more, and I became ever more passionate in my descriptions of things I loved the best. He gave me further encouragement, and when I was about to burst with excitement, I stopped suddenly. I'd risen to his bait and openly shown my full enthusiasm! His brows went up which made his beard twitch comically. The indignant phrase I was about to unleash caught in my throat and came out as a terrifying guffaw. Rather than looking appropriately horrified, my dear Mr. Worthington gave a deep belly laugh that warmed me from the tips of my toes to my hot scarlet cheeks.

"I thought you were going to give me a tongue-lashing, Lass. I've never been so relieved to hear laughter in all my life. You get a fierce look when you discover a man's game."

"You're correct in reading my ire. You were jesting all along and only wanted to hear me carry on as a fool. It was no interview at all.

How would you learn what literature I lack by a description of food? Only your twitching beard saved you from my tirade."

"So, by the hair on my chinny chin chin, was it?" We shared a chorus of laughter that carried the harmony of too many voices.

"Oh!" I cried in my impulsive way. We had an audience to our forthright flirting. Janie, some other gent, the man who had come in the door and the mysterious Mr. Manush – appearing from behind the yellow-green silk veil – were amused in concert. I'd never before been the subject of such attentions, and I went quite silent. The lump of amethyst felt suddenly heavy at my chest.

"Please pardon me, Miss Livingstone, I assure you I was not attempting to make you look foolish," Mr. Thomas appealed. "It's a technique of mine to match taste in literature to other tastes. The kinds of things people like to eat – lavish and complex or Spartan and for nourishment – and the way they describe them – simply and clearly or with color and passion – this gives me an understanding of their leanings and preferred mode of expression and consumption. It's a test of communication tastes and styles."

"If that's so, then tell me what literature will suit. I've certainly given you more than enough to work with." I delivered my best *huff*.

"You enjoy Dickens for detail and Hawthorne for richness. But you will have read them extensively already. Although you savor your tried and true, your appreciation of the exotic and unexpected twist leads me to offer trade of something new. My suggestion is for you to take my newest acquisitions from the East and from England. I will then ask you to wait until I can add two more volumes that have not even arrived yet, but will be in your hands first when they do. Genre is not important. Quality – as it will be entering my shop – is guaranteed."

I was unable to speak; I was so perfectly pleased. This man could be wittier than I. But I struggled to say *something*.

Clap, clap, clap, clap, clap. How frightfully strange. The onlookers were applauding his gain. I had to make this stop. "Yes, yes, the bargain is good. Very perceptive. Done." I stepped away from him and brushed my glove along the surface of the carved desk. With a jump back, I realized what I'd done. Mr. Manush stared at me openly with his usual straight-lipped expression. Again I felt the burden of the stolen stone, and I was terribly conscious of the tiny clay tile within my necklace.

Teetering back a couple more steps, I almost fell, but steadied myself by grabbing hold of the desk. I looked up at the high top of the carved cabinet above the desk's back and gasped, recovering in haste with a genteel cough. My eye had discerned letters in the intricate design that disappeared as quickly as they came.

The way to understanding is understanding the way.

Janie missed my discreet signal as she and the first gent returned to their browsing. The other man, who apparently enjoyed my humiliating show, still stood by the door expectantly. With a quick nod to Mr. Worthington, I moved toward Janie. I truly hoped he'd drop me from his attention. It was time to gather my dear confidante and get out of this place. This had all become too much.

"Scott!" Mr. Worthington's reedy voice exclaimed.

I vaguely heard the hearty slap of the men's embrace as I reached Janie. With great effort, she was nudged away from the section on natural history. "Let's go," I whispered.

"Miss Livingstone and Miss Adams," Mr. Thomas Worthington addressed us as we came away from the shelves.

I tugged on Janie's arm, desperate to escape before further conversation, but supposed we must offer reply. "Yes, Mr. Worthington," I conceded, mumbling with downcast eyes to discourage anything more than necessary.

"May I present my brother, Mr. Scott Worthington."

My eyes snapped to the man's face.

"Charmed." The handsome second Mr. Worthington leaned over Janie's extended hand with a quick bow, and then took my hardly offered hand. He bowed over it with a deep and extended bow. Then he tipped his head and his devilish green eyes stared up at me. I could see he was charmed indeed.

CHAPTER THIRTY

∞∞∞∞

In Which Miss Livingstone Slips Away from Unwelcome Pursuit

"What's the rush?" Janie asked as we settled back into the car.

I heaved a huge sigh. Timber curled his tail around my arm, but his comfort was in vain. I'd hurried us out as quickly as we could disengage from the ritual of the introductions. Jaimeson had insisted on waiting for us, and I was grateful, ready to be away as soon as possible. I felt exposed in the afternoon sun.

"I think we were quite done. Or I suppose I shouldn't speak for you, but I discovered something new."

"Yes, he's charming, isn't he?" Janie dropped her voice to avoid being overheard by Jaimeson who had stepped from the auto to make some kind of adjustment to the boiler.

I kept my voice low as well, "Mr. Scott Worthington?" I could see how she'd be drawn to his crisply trimmed auburn hair and fine features. And though a bit devilish in his flirtation, he had an air of adventure.

"No, silly. I mean, he's handsome, but I'm speaking of Mr. Thomas Worthington. It's exciting news that he's so fond of you?"

"That's not the discovery I mean." Drat my cheeks for flushing. I would need to learn to control that to be a proper adventurer. "I saw a new message in the carving of the desk. A sort of directive, I think. It said, 'The way to understanding is understanding the way.'" The amethyst weighed heavily as I spoke. How ever would I get it back into the cabinet? If only I could take it there immediately.

"Ready to go, Miss?" Jaimeson startled me with his question that seemed to accommodate my thought. I hadn't even seen him climb into the driver's seat.

"Yes, em, we'll stop at the Adams' to drop Miss Mary Jane at her home."

He levered us into motion but then stopped again and stepped back out of the car.

"A further delay?" I worried.

"Do you know what it means?" Janie's serious tone confused me.

"What?"

"The saying on the desk." She brought us back to the point.

"Oh yes, well, not exactly, of course. It's rather enigmatic. But I think I should travel again. To the same place. I want further understanding of the workings of the mechanism or magic and where it takes me. I should like to repeat the gem that took me to Newbury Street."

"I see." Janie's blue eyes shone at me knowingly.

What was I missing? "Oh! You think I'm going to see Mr. Worthington there." Some nerve she had in jumping to that conclusion.

"Well, aren't you?" She smiled and nodded maddeningly.

"No! Well, yes. I imagine I'll see him, but I'm not going to see him directly... or mostly."

"You're just mostly going to see him."

Now she was straight up teasing me. Infuriating! "I am not the kind of woman..."

"He is charming, isn't he?" She tried again.

I rolled my eyes at her. "I shall go back to the shop and once again try the emerald. My hope is to repeat the experiment and find similar results. And besides I need to replace the amethyst as soon as possible."

"Oh yes, I'd almost forgotten."

How clear she didn't live in my skin. I could think of nothing else.

"It's true you haven't allowed for repetition," she continued. "It's just been assumed that a similar thing would happen if you were to pick up the same stone. I'm surprised you haven't done this before with your bent for science and logic."

"Ah, but you've forgotten my even more overwhelming bent toward curiosity. I intended to pick up a stone I had chosen already, but the temptation to try another was just too great. And you encouraged it, remember? But now I have a directive that's made me curious in another manner. Even in repeating a stone I can venture in a new way. I'm ready for the next journey."

"We'll be off now, Miss," Jaimeson called from the front, as if in answer once again.

"Finally," I couldn't help but say. Fortunately, my tone was still conspiratorial, so Jaimeson needn't feel offended.

Janie giggled as the Steamer rolled down the block. "Shall we make excuse for you to visit me tonight?"

"I appreciate your generous invitation, of course, but I believe I'll be missed less if I leave my own home," I decided. "I don't want your family – or mine – to worry I'm truly ill. I'll take one of the horses."

"The horses? Will you manage?"

"My knee is repaired enough, I believe, and the currier's son smiles sweetly on me. I persuaded him to help the last time without giving me away."

"Oh, so you *are* the kind of woman..." We both laughed uproariously at this one, and I realized the reason I was unable to find humor before is that the tease was not silly and had run too near the mark.

I had succumbed to Mr. Worthington's game much too readily and publicly. I would be more careful in future. It would be refreshing to spend time with the older Thomas Worthington who was not such a playful cad.

∞∞∞∞

"And you remember to hitch her securely and..."

"Yes, and near other horses. Once again, you have my gratitude, Master Seth. I shall let you know immediately when I return." I gave him a hearty smile and reeled away into the clear night.

I felt much more secure on the road this time, and my only bother was the dull ache of my knee. It was thrilling to not only have my independence but to gain confidence in it. The countryside slipped by smoothly with the whistling of the wind in the twilight of the moonlit night. Now that Father and I had observed it, even with the moon nearing the full, it was easy to pick out Halley's comet amongst the stars. I rode across the town as it rode across the sky.

The smooth rhythm of Summer's Girl's gait helped me clarify my thoughts, and I decided upon another point that Janie and I debated. I'd use the emerald stone, but also take the amber stone on my journey. I don't know why I didn't think of it before. Being caught with one would be devastating, so what more would it be to risk two? Perhaps I could go from one adventure to another without need of return. If I had time or need, that is. My hand checked the locket at my throat.

First and foremost, I wanted to find out what I could from Thomas – for so I could call him again in the future.

∞∞∞∞

Excellent, there was no one outside the saloon. I struggled – oh dear – to dismount. And then I secured Summer's Girl to the hitch and checked for extra security. It wouldn't do to have her escape before I returned. A cool breeze disturbed my riding scarf as I loosened my hat and stowed the wrap in my bag.

"Miss Livingstone?"

Oh, this was not good. "Yes, good evening." That was, good evening as in good night.

"I didn't know you frequent the saloon." It was the same gent who was browsing books near Janie after my embarrassment earlier in the afternoon. He was getting much the wrong impression of my character. I was sure he thought me highly inappropriate and – well, I had become rather unconstrained.

"I don't really. Em...in fact I'm not going in."

"Oh, but you've just hitched your horse." He looked up and down the block for who I was meeting and where I might be going. And yes, just where might that have been?

"I'm just leaving the horse here for my, em, currier's son. He'll need it going home, and my car will be by for me in a few minutes." Oh, that was good, if I do say so myself.

"Well, I can wait to go back inside. I wouldn't want you to wait without escort by the saloon, Ma'am."

"That's kind of you." Kind of difficult, actually. "Jaimeson may take a while, however, and I don't want you to miss out on your evening. Besides, I am to meet him by the bookshop, so I'll just be going along now."

"I can walk..."

"Well, goodnight." I assumed if I could just get around the corner before he finished his sentence, perhaps I wouldn't have to turn and acknowledge his request with an answer. I was thankful to be wearing riding boots. And I discovered my knee had definitely improved.

"Dio, Miss Perry is asking after you." A gentleman informed my unwelcome pursuer from the doorway of the saloon with a jeer.

Yes! Someone was after him. I hoped it would take care of everything.

"But...Miss Livingstone...I..."

Good, he was dropping off. As long as I didn't look back. I was out of sight. Free!

Quickly now, Journey key and a twist. I was in. I hoped no one saw the flash – and drat the gust of wind, my hat was askew. Nevermind that, I climbed up and opened the desk.

At last I was relieved of the burning amethyst, safely returned to its space. Amber into my riding pouch, and emerald – wait. I wanted to look more closely at the spaces for those that were missing. It would be important to recognize them if I encountered the stones on my journeys. And though the book showed a sketch of each, the spaces gave more concrete understanding of their scale.

Being once again in such close proximity to the stones was intoxicating. I'd forgotten the intensity of their spell. Giving up this quest would be nearly impossible, even if Thomas told me something new that was so chilling I'd be risking death itself. I felt fated to follow this magic. For magic it seemed to be. But I had to know more of Mr. Manush and whether or not I needed to fear him.

I slipped off my glove, touched the emerald and was whisked away.

"Oh, that's a surprise," I said right out loud. My arrival was on the platform by the train in Boston, just where I'd left from when last here. I shivered as I met the cold wind. People were scurrying about with heads down and dull coats and hats pulled tight against the chill. Interesting, if I could always come back to the railway station, it would be like legitimately arriving – not to mention the convenience of Thomas' shop so near the station.

The clock over the platform displayed 2:23, but what day? Oh, and what year? A season that was cold, and rather dreary, that much was obvious. But though it was the same place, it was a grandiose supposition to claim it was the same year. Shame on me, a strict student of logic. It was time to see if my father's special device delivered the time and place correctly. How strange!

When removed from my riding pouch, the chronospacometer engaged immediately upon popping open the fob. There was a loud buzzing of gears as the hands, and numbered and lettered wheels moved at remarkable speed. The noise calmed and the dials slowed until it settled on 02:24 PM DECEMBER 16 1941 AD BOSTON NORTH AMERICA. No wonder I'm freezing. I pulled my riding scarf from my bag and wrapped it around my throat.

I was terribly anxious to see Thomas, but science first. A stop at the newsstand was just the thing to verify the reading on the chronospacometer.

Bill of Rights Day Observed Solemnly... I continued to read the New York World Telegram article wondering why it would be solemn. "Oh my!" I remembered Thomas mentioning war, but now America was fully involved. "Oh, this is terrible!" I cried out as I noticed the headlines on the other publications. Japanese ships were sunk and Germany – a dictatorship. What had the world come to?

"Yes, ma'am." The proprietor's breath showed in the cold as he displayed the palm of his thick wool glove for my nickel.

"Oh I..." Taking note of the date, I waved him off, dropped the paper and left the stand, mastering my shock.

The date matched Father's ingenious device! The papers were mostly from Boston with a couple from New York with yesterday's news. And of course I recognized the city sights here in Boston. But how did Manush acquire a chronospacometer? This prototype was just perfected.

"Oh!" A woman nearly knocked me from my feet with the swing of her case. The hustle and bustle of the station was remarkable after being out west. I needed to move on. All of the automobiles – I guess I was very nearly killed by one last time. But I was swept away just in time by the kind attentions of Mr. Worthington. What a fond memory that made.

And speaking of memories, I was taken with the differences in the street as well when I looked more closely. This part of town was built when I was young – in my own time – but the details of repair and update, the style of advertisement, and of course the many differences in clothing were remarkable. "Oh!" There was a huge and startling beast-thing on the advertisement at the theatre. *The Wolfman.* I should say. What strange entertainment. But how thrilling to see what was over the horizon. My heart raced. I had great privilege in being able to travel not only across the world but across time. I would endeavor to do it justice.

Thomas' shop was just ahead. The already familiar sign, *Please Come In,* made my heartbeat rise even higher with anticipation. I rubbed my icy gloved fingertips together. I would see Thomas again at last.

CHAPTER THIRTY-ONE

∞∞∞

In Which Miss Livingstone is Certain There is More to the Story

"Oh!" The suspense created with anticipation of seeing Thomas made the presence of someone else startling. A shudder ran through me from surprise and from shaking off the chill of the street. The tiny pipes' special tune assured me things were somewhat as I had left them last.

"May I help you Miss?" the kind-looking fellow addressed from near the front counter. His oddly fashioned dark hair and spotted large-framed spectacles made him look very bookish indeed. I could hardly tear my eyes away from the strange bars that held the glass in place by attaching at the top of his ears. Brilliant!

I didn't see Thomas about the shop at all. "I... well, yes. I have brought two books for T- for Mr. Worthington to consider. Will he be in?"

"I'll be happy to evaluate their worth. I'm trusted to make trades or purchases on behalf of the proprietor. I —"

"Oh, I'm grateful, truly, but I'd like to wait for Mr. Worthington, if I may. Will he be in?" While repeating my question I realized it was quite rude to have interrupted. I tried a smile.

"Oh, yes Miss, he'll be back presently. He just stepped down the way to get a daily paper. He's wanting to keep apprised of the war. Shame we had to enter a second world war."

World war! – and second, but when was the first? I couldn't possibly ask without exposing my secret. The future was a hard burden to bear at times, apparently. So much for privilege. But how could I have missed Mr. Worthington between the newsstand and the shop? These streets really were busier than was best.

The boy's magnified eyes still rested on me expectantly. "Em...thank you kindly. I'll just browse the collection until his return." Thankfully he nodded and withdrew, though his eyes continued to stray to my unusual dress. I tried to attire myself to blend more readily this time, but was unable to research the future of course. Riding dress tended to stay more to tradition than general fashion, so that was helpful. I also remembered the colors and tailoring were subdued and sleek. Perhaps due to war times – imagine, a world war. Horrifying. I must say the tailoring was smart. Admirably sensible to make the best of the materials you can spare by spending more time on fitting and design. Though in the grey of a winter day, the palette on the streets was rather bleak.

On top of blending, in full riding gear I was much more prepared for whatever came. It would have been splendid to have breeches beneath my skirts on the *Dame Fortuna*. What ever would I have done without the petticoats of the kind, Miss Jillian.

"Oh!" A burst of noise and cold wind from the street startled me yet again, but it was accompanied by the joyous sound of those tiny brass steam pipes that sang again, 'I'm in Thomas Worthington's bookshop.' He had arrived! I was quiet to see how long it took him to notice me – if he hadn't heard my exclamation upon his entry.

"Anything interesting while I was away, Edward? There's nothing so urgent in the news as there was last week, though I'm looking forward to catching up on the latest. I have so much more concern now that America has joined the war. The first war was so...difficult..."

"It would be difficult to top the surprise attack on American ships at Pearl Harbor for headlines, sir. You do have a patron waiting for you, before you delve more deeply into the news. I believe she's in the history section presently."

I heard him coming and had the overwhelming urge to hide and jump out at him. But I calmed myself in an attempt at some dignity. Was it dignified to wear a glowing smile? I couldn't hold it back.

"Miss Livingstone! What a wonderful surprise," his amber eyes danced above his filled out cheeks that aged in a day from my perspective. The crinkles around his eyes changed from care to laughter.

"Thomas, I... it's so good to see you again," Oddly I couldn't go on, and found tears at the ready.

Although I saw the younger man earlier in the day, I felt a keen sense of separation eased with reunion – like it actually had been thirty years between meetings. I met his eye, and my emotion seemed to spark his own.

His voice was thick, "It's truly a pleasure to see you again, Lizzie."

The name cleared my tears like a passing rain and the sunshine of my joy shone from my face again – so brightly I felt it in my own eyes.

"Edward, can you please deliver the wrapped package near the counter to be posted right away?" Thomas called.

"Yes sir, right away." The steam bells rang out his compliance as he left.

Thomas continued when we were alone. "Although you told me the date of your first visit, and I was able to anticipate your arrival that special day, ever after I only know that you are likely to return. I don't know when or how often. It feels like a miracle." He smiled.

I could only nod.

"Is there a reason for your visit? Are you in need?" The concern returned to his features.

"Well, I brought a couple books, though I confess, I've been working harder to find good volumes for your collection as a young man in Snoqualmie. We're just getting acquainted, and I'd like to win your affection." I blushed profusely at my unintended openness. His caring was disarming.

"I don't believe you'll need to bribe me to fancy your company, lass." His warm laugh, even richer with age, filled me with happiness.

"Yes, I'm beginning to see that." Drat, my cheeks flushed furiously once more. I felt their flame push the last thought of chill from me.

"So where are we in our history there, if I may ask?"

"I brought you the first edition Austen, and we've...em...encountered each other a couple of times. I must say you're a bold young gent."

"Bold? I always considered myself withdrawn. My brother, Scott..."

"Well, today I was quite flustered. You even received a round of applause for your witty repartee and my resulting embarrassment."

"Em, I don't recall that scenario from when we first met. I was terribly tongue-tied and constantly reprimanding myself for being so reticent each time you left the shop."

I recalled the touch of our skin and my reflection on knowing our future. "Perhaps it's unraveling differently. For knowing I shall become friends with you, I may have behaved with more familiarity in our interactions than I would have otherwise."

"Yes, you were difficult to approach as a young woman, and I a reserved young man. If it weren't for your exuberance carrying you away from time to time, I may never have known you beyond our excellent intellectual debates. While that's something that I treasure, it was your affection that I sought."

"The twist you created upon my last visit may have achieved that determination. When I met you in Snoqualmie I already carried affection for you. I missed you when I last left this space in time." To my surprise my face didn't flush at this declaration. It was an easy statement like one long understood.

"And I you, my dear friend." His smile carried none of the impish edge that the young Mr. Worthington sported toward me. I immediately wished it did – scandalous!

"What are the circumstances of our acquaintance beyond the shop? Do we know more?" His eyes fastened upon me in expectation.

"You've seen me arrive by automobile with Jaimeson and understand my father is wealthy, but we haven't had an engagement outside of the shop. The only things I know of you and your family are that your father also admires machines and you live near the Allen's in North Bend."

"I see, so – "

"Oh, and you have just introduced me to your brother. He arrived today – from Scotland." I smiled brightly, expecting his pleasure, but his face dropped into its pensive lines. "Do you not care for your brother? You seemed so excited for his arrival."

Thomas paused, and seemed to choose his words. "I anticipated his arrival with great excitement, and we were always close growing up." He stopped suddenly. "He arrived today you say? After the opening?"

"Yes, why?" Thomas gave no answer, and I was sure there was more to this but had already learned he would only tell me so much. There was no point in pressing him. Yet, I couldn't suppress my curiosity. "Do he and I get along well?"

"Why would you not?" His expression was inscrutable.

There was absolutely much more to this story. Of course, there was bound to be in thirty years.

"What about with your partner, Mr. Manush – do we get along?"

"Ah, so you have properly met him now?"

"In a manner of speaking – or rather without speaking. Why does he remain silent?"

"For starters, he speaks only French."

"But I speak French fluently. It was part of my education, of course. Is he from Paris? He doesn't look French, but I saw him in Paris."

"You've been to Paris?" His brows rose in surprise.

"Briefly."

"And you saw Mr. Manush?" The creases in his face became serious folds.

"Yes, but I'm not completely certain he saw me. Although he was after me – or I believed he was. I... escaped."

"Why would he be after you?"

The tile came to mind and I wished to tell Thomas of Miss Penn and ask his opinion of its meaning, but I'd given my promise. It was my turn to work at words. "I'm not sure if I should reveal everything. Just as you need to keep things from me. You said before that I hadn't told you how I traveled. Did I tell you why I kept it secret?"

"No, you just said you were concerned for my well-being. Which of course leaves me terribly concerned for yours."

His protective look made me sorry for the risks I'd decided to take. Did I not tell him about the stones for fear he would stop me?

"I assure you I'll be careful in my travels. In fact, that's why I'm here now. I need to know if you trust your partner. How did he become your partner to begin with?"

The tiny steam pipes sang their tune, and Thomas held up a finger indicating I should suspend our conversation. He led me out to the counter near the door.

"Edward, Miss Livingstone and I will be out for some time. Can you please close the shop for me this evening?"

"Certainly, sir. Have you settled on the bargain for the books she brought?"

"Please, just add them to the collection. They're a gift," I told him.

As Edward looked at the age of the editions, his eyes grew round in his spectacles. He glanced an appraisal of my clothing and opened his mouth with a full breath.

"I'll see you tomorrow, Edward." Thomas quelled any chance for questions, and the pipes sang our departure.

CHAPTER THIRTY-TWO

∞∞∞∞

In Which Miss Livingstone Understands How to Move Forward
- Or is that Backward?

"Will you join me for a brandy at MacGinty's, Miss Lizzie?"

"It would be my pleasure, indeed, Mr. Thomas."

I folded my gloved hand into his extended elbow and we strolled down the walk. For the first time in weeks I felt secure, and I no longer felt the sharpness of the cold.

Angus' face broke into a hearty welcome when he came out to answer the ring of the merry brass bells on his green door. He nodded at Thomas with his eyebrows raised. And I couldn't help but laugh at his rakish approval of our return together.

After serving, Angus left us to ourselves at our same table. It was still foreign to my world to be alone with a man, but with this man it seemed the most natural thing in the world.

"So, you asked how I met Mr. Manush – Niccolò Manush to be specific," Thomas began.

Hearing his full name again chilled me as deeply as Miss Penn's glare had burned through me. I shivered it off.

"I, too, met him in Paris," he continued, "in a marvelous old bookshop there. It –"

"Was there a pastry shop nearby?" I blurted in my impatient way. "Excuse me, please. Do go on."

"A pastry shop is hardly a landmark in Paris, my dear." He smiled upon me with what I recognized as fondness. "More notable is the famous monument outside, between it and the railway station."

I caught my breath. "The *Fontaine Molière?*"

"Mm, on the rue de Richelieu." Thomas showed no surprise.

"So you knew I would go there?"

"No, you told me little detail of your travels. I learned bits by need. Just as now, we both understood the concern of potentially changing things if too much of the future was known."

Perhaps what I read as lack of surprise was resignation to how little he knew of my journeys. But his knowledge of Paris monuments was impressive – to know the location so readily. "So Mr. Manush was there by coincidence then?" If only it were so.

"Not necessarily – but possibly. That shop is owned by a relative of his. He had reason to travel there often and sometimes brought items from that collection for my purchase or to consign. Was it in a different time?"

"It was 1910, the same as my time in Snoqualmie. And the thing that's uncanny – and it makes me wonder if he's pursuing me – is I'd just seen him in Snoqualmie. And –"

"So he traveled, or perhaps still travels, as you do. That could explain a great many things." Thomas' brows went up, and we both laughed. He'd interrupted just as impetuously as I.

"Yes, and that's why I need to know if you trust him. Whatever my purpose in traveling through time and space, he's an involuntary companion. And I don't feel safe. Should I?"

"So I've told you I met him at Librairie d'Occasion Curiosità and that it belonged to his family. But they're not French. They're what you and I would term gypsies."

Like Miss Penn – of course. That's why the woman at the Paris bookshop resembled her too.

"Mr. Manush was a collector of more than books." Thomas paused in thought. "And now that I know he could travel as you do, it explains the variety of things he was able to produce as offerings in trade for items of mine that he desired. He was valuable to me from the beginning as a companion, and helped me through a dangerous scrape with ruffians on the street of Paris. It was my first time there, and he saved me from financial ruin as well as defending me bodily."

"So he's a good man?"

"In his way, yes, I believe so, though he is full of secrets. I made him a partner for a few reasons. One, it guaranteed he wouldn't liquidate my collection without my knowledge, since he had a stake in the success of its future growth and gain on investment. Two, it kept him somewhat within my view. And three, his skills were invaluable. He was quite savvy in many things. He was extremely shrewd. And he was one of few who could drive a tougher bargain than you, Lizzie."

I laughed. "So two of your three – or four – reasons do not imply a lot of trust."

"I trusted he'd look for advantage. Making my interest his interest was the way I protected myself from his more aggressive qualities while benefiting from his evident talents."

"Useful strategy." He'd given me the advice I needed. Now to discern what was in this for Mr. Manush. Though I suspected he was looking for the stones, I just didn't understand why he needed me – or them, for that matter. "Does he have any enemies? You keep speaking of him in the past tense. What happened to him?"

A wave of shadow crossed Thomas' features. "He was my friend. He's been gone now for many years, and I'm not sure why he left or where he has gone. He left just after my brother –" He stopped abruptly.

"Yes…your brother?"

"Suffice it to say Manush was a good man when I knew him, but he was always removed. Quiet – preoccupied, as if he sat upon the cusp of something more. I didn't understand him, and I don't mean because he spoke only French. I'm fluent. But he carried a wisdom or shadow of the future. As if he was farsighted. Perhaps he knew too much."

This was another layer, indeed. But I couldn't shake my fear. "Did anything in your time together cause you misgivings?"

"Once… I was visited by a strange character who chilled me to the bone. A woman entered the bookshop in Snoqualmie that was dark of complexion and countenance. Her skin was aged like leather, and her long hair fell loose around her shoulders – scandalous for the mores of our time and place. She wore a crocheted shawl and the most striking gold earrings. But more than her visage, it was her focus that spooked me. She was fixated on that strange carved desk that I still have at the shop. She asked if I could open it for her. To be honest, I was a wee bit intimidated and saw nothing to lose by complying with her request. I opened all the little doors and drawers, but she hardly took notice. She just stood there, staring at the top like she was seeing a message from beyond. When I had returned them all to their closed position she said, 'You're not the one. It must be a pure one,' and then she asked, 'Where is he?' I was quiet while I tried to guess her meaning, and she shouted in a voice that all but shook the walls, 'Where has he gone?' Even had I understood, I wouldn't have answered, so shocked was I by her manner. Fortunately, she made no further demands just then."

Could it have been Miss Penn? Maybe she could travel too? But this woman sounded more weathered – and had gold earrings, like the woman in Paris. "So she was looking for Mr. Manush?" My voice quivered.

"I can't know for certain, but he had gone missing just then. And just as you feel he's pursuing you, I felt that she was after him."

I tried asking you about it since you were already showing signs of mysterious behavior along with my – well, I thought you might know something of who she was or where she'd come from."

"Was I helpful?" I hoped so, for then I would find my answers – or at least the answers before the twist.

"You told me nothing of her, but you said if Manush didn't return it was likely for the best. I trusted you."

Thomas' sincerity gave me pause. "You said she made no more demands just then. Did she come back?"

"Yes – years later."

"How long had we known each other?"

"Long enough you'd already confessed you had met me here. You had been away, and I was so glad to see you again."

"How long was I gone? And where?" He looked as if I struck him.

"That's too much detail on your life, Lizzie. I want you to maintain your unencumbered choices. But it had been some time since we'd seen each other. You returned to me and said you wanted to make sure I was safe, and that I needed to know my partner would likely not be back. I was cheered that you cared, but after the strange way that woman had acted, I was worried about you too. You gave me a glimpse of your travels so I'd understand your strength and knowledge. Your compassionate revelation did set things somewhat to rest for me at the time, and honestly gave me hope, since I knew I would see you again someday – well, on a specific day in the future.

That's when you told me about meeting me briefly here in 1941. Since I had already lived for a time not knowing if I would ever see you again, it was energizing to have that reassurance and work toward it. It gave me something to live for."

I reached out to squeeze Thomas' hand. "I don't know what to say."

He gave me the dignity of some quiet time to think.

While he didn't give away my future, he certainly gave away much of his own. I realized he had been alone. How could I have left him? It should have been evident when he didn't claim young Elizabeth as his own. Certainly Mrs. Carrington didn't show any sign she knew him. But were they just hiding things?

Thomas gave a great sigh.

"I was thinking of my daughter. The housekeeper, Mrs. Carrington, thought I was here from Scotland when I was playing as Lizzie at Newbury Manor, and it has occurred to me I may have settled there?"

"You...have connections there. That's all I can say." It appeared that he would choke if he kept speaking.

But I set aside my worry of that future. Perhaps it would never come. My wariness of this woman was intensely present, and I would take the warnings from Thomas' descriptions onward in my journeys. But I was also intensely curious about her and suspected the shop in Paris might reveal more about the lost stones. I wanted to talk to Janie about it all, and soon. But I decided to try the amber stone immediately instead of returning to the station.

"Thank you so much, Thomas." I smiled into his sad eyes, and they brightened. "You've helped me understand how to move forward from here. Or is that backward?"

We shared a much needed laugh. "And you've shown me there can be a new future. Already things are unfolding differently, and yet here you are. I have hope that you won't forget me."

"There may be many potential futures, or alternate past futures, but one where I forget you is not possible." His soft caress of my hand, though stimulating, had no power over me in comparison to the remarkable affection in his eyes. I felt magically transported to a place beyond dreams.

∞∞∞

I watched the fantastic amber light fade to twilight in Thomas' eyes. "You're going, aren't you," he stated.

"Yes, I must move on for a time. But what gave me away?"

"I've seen the look many times – when your sense of adventure is sparked and your mind travels away from the place we sit together."

"I'm sorry, my dear friend. If I could stay I would."

"And I wouldn't have you stay unless your heart and mind are aligned for your contentment. It's been wonderful to see you, Lizzie, my bonny lass."

"I pray that I'll see you again soon. I will undoubtedly see the young Mr. Worthington, which is quite a pleasure as well." I pulled from him the warm smile I was reaching for.

"It would be my pleasure to escort you to the station."

"My thanks, but not just now. I have a different destination and must go alone. Please stay in the kind company of your friend.

"Angus," I called out for him.

The burly man came in through the doorway from the back room.

"Please pour Mr. Worthington another drink on my tab."

The men laughed heartily.

"Right away, Miss!" he complied. "Your credit is granted and worth the risk in looking forward to your gracing of my humble tavern again – *a dh'aithghearr* – in the near future, I hope."

"Haste ye back," Thomas added.

I gave him a wave over my shoulder and walked alone to the door.

"Fare-thee-well, Thomas, until we meet again." I turned and dropped a dramatic curtsy on my good knee, made awkward by my riding breeches. Then I burst into laughter. The vision of his full cheeks pushing up with a wide grin and a sideways twitch of his beard followed me onto the street.

CHAPTER THIRTY-THREE

∞∞∞

In Which Miss Livingstone Receives an Exotic Gift

The frigid wind had risen again in earnest. Moving toward the station, I scanned for an alcove in which to travel from this time and place to another without being seen. It was the first time I'd considered how it would appear from an observer's point of view. If there one moment and gone the next – before their very eyes – I didn't want to cause undue fright or give reason for anyone to doubt their own sanity. Ah, a small portico would do. I removed the amber from my riding pouch, carefully keeping it in my gloved hand. Apprehension overtook me – more so than it had thus far – like I was sensing something momentous at the other end of this journey. I committed to go, nonetheless. No time like the present. "Ha!" a pun. Off with the glove, and a deep breath to prepare to be whisked away again. And I touched the stone.

"Oh! Paris!" I had returned, just as I hoped. The *Fontaine Molière* was beautiful in the morning light. I replaced my glove and stopped to admire the delectable patisserie, which once again I left behind with some regret. I loosened my scarf and basked in the comparative warmth of the day as I strolled the rue de Richelieu. Almost too soon the same bookshop loomed before me – with a sign reading, Librairie d'Occasion Curiosità as Thomas had said. So I didn't appear at the station I left from. There was apparently something else that chose the space for arrival. It was like a beacon called me here. Could it be some trick of Mr. Niccolò Manush? But I didn't feel the dread of him, just an urgency beyond explanation, like I was late for an engagement I'd never made. Late or not, I stopped to make sure the amber was securely back in my riding bag and the Journey key was ready to hand.

The brass bells, so like my grandmother's, startled me as I opened the door, but a quick scan of the front of the shop revealed no threat. I ducked into a row of shelves to check my father's chronospacometer to verify the time as well as location. It seemed the amber had taken me to a different time than 1941, so my first theory of it moving only through space was apparently not sound. Ah yes, same year as the first time the amber brought me to Paris, not matching the year I just left. 10:01 AM APRIL 23 1910 AD PARIS EUROPE. Oh dear, it was the day after I left Snoqualmie. Worry consumed me and it was urgent to get back to my horse and home.

My search was for one of two stones – or the pair if such was granted – the crystal and the ruby.

I saw the shop much differently now. Each shelf, table, desk and chair was no longer a holder of books, but rather a possible place to hide a stone. Once again the sunbaked woman attended the counter. I took notice of her dark hair, shawl and gold earrings – just as Thomas described the haunting woman who visited his shop in Snoqualmie. Though he didn't mention there was amber with the gold. She indeed appeared to be a gypsy of France.

I remembered I'd unwittingly stolen the strange book from her on my last visit to this place, and was consumed with fear. Would she hold me and turn me over to Mr. Manush?

Perhaps it would help if I made a purchase. I could overpay and balance my trespass. "Bonjour, Madame. Je souhaite acheter ce livre, s'il vous plaît." I emphasized the word for *purchase* and handed her a book I picked up blindly from a nearby table.

I cried out, and the woman tipped her head, regarding me without indication of her thoughts. My unseemly reaction was to reading the headline on an article in the current *La Figaro* next to the counter. It claimed Mark Twain had passed on the evening of April 21st. How could I not have heard news of one of my favorite writers leaving the earth? How remote my new home truly was. But at least the newspaper's date of 23 avril 1910 confirmed the chronospacometer's reading.

She wrapped the book I'd chosen in light paper and tied it with string, without comment. As she handed me the package, her face remained ambivalent. I thought she didn't recognize me, which seemed odd after the intensity of our last encounter. Then her eyes dropped to my locket, and I felt sure she knew what it contained. But she still gave no sign.

"Dix francs," she priced.

When I tried to give her the payment it slipped back into my coin purse. So I pulled off my glove to fish through the francs, and gave her twenty instead of ten. She reached into her money box for change.

"Non. Gardez-le, s'il vous plaît." I put up my hand to insist she keep it, but with a steady gaze into my eyes, she took my hand and turned it. I was about to protest, when she placed something weighty on my palm. There was just enough time to notice the clear crystal stone before I realized I was in a different place.

My quick wit provided a timely jump aside to avoid a merchant carrying a large bundle of rolled carpets. I squeezed up against a mud-brick wall, and noted the shape of the stone resembled the open space in the tray of gems back home. It was the crystal quartz! This time there was no doubt the dark woman intended the gift.

"But why —" The stone jumped from my hand and I caught it with my gloved one as I was bumped by an elbow. The woman carrying fruit — dressed in a rough rust-toned robe — passed me by without apology. I was dodging people without relief. Oppressive heat was dizzying. The noise and rush of the street market overwhelmed me. I didn't know where to turn. The shock of unexpected travel and exotic scents set my head spinning.

"Oh!" My riding boots slipped on the loose sand as I scrambled to the edge of the thoroughfare. My arms thrashed the air to no avail and left me flat on my back on the ground. I lost my breath, but found my equilibrium. As focus resumed, the image above my head resolved into...a palm tree. I'd never seen one other than illustrated in a book.

At least I'd managed to hold on to the crystal, and I promptly stowed it in my riding bag. My hand rummaged furtively for the emerald as I righted myself, then stopped as my jaw dropped in awe. Upon a desert mound was a monument, smaller, but reminiscent of the Great Pyramid of Giza. Instead of the emerald, my hand closed on the chronospacometer. I popped open the fob. 12:01 PM JUNE 30 2112 BC, and the rest of the dials read pure gibberish. What a terrible time for it to stick, as father said it was prone to do. After several rather desperate and violent thwacks on my leg, the mechanism began to whir into place. 12:01 PM JUNE 30 2112 BC UR, MESOPOTAMIA. I dropped the instrument into my bag in alarm. Could I really have traveled so far back in time?

CHAPTER THIRTY-FOUR

∞∞∞∞

In Which Miss Livingstone Seeks the Fastest Escape

My ancient locale shook me to the core. I finally located the emerald, and tucked it into my gloved hand with care. I clung fiercely to my mineral ticket back to Newbury. The emerald led my way, held out before me like a loaded pistol. My wary attention was again pulled into the lively market. Staying out of traffic, I observed the fantastical wares. It was as if I meandered through the Peabody Anthropology Museum's gallery back at Harvard, but with artifacts posing as daily craft wares. Food aromas and perfumes filled the air. There were silks of vivid color, including the yellow-green of the curtain that hung in the bookshop back home. The sweet scent of dates brought an image to mind of Christmas morning back home – so out of place in this scorching melee. Some carved alabaster pieces were inscribed with a language as unfamiliar as the wickedly hot atmosphere. It was hard to feel appropriate awe at seeing these en masse and intact. Flustered, hardly began to describe my condition.

Just as I began to regain composure, my heart leaped into my mouth. The emerald slipped my glove and landed in the sand at my feet. As I bent to pick it up, I peeked at the woman that startled me so. She looked much like Mr. Manush, and like the woman at

Librairie d'Occasion Curiosità but gnarled and fierce, and much older. Her eyes burned with the intensity of Miss Penn's but were so dark they were nearly black. She stared hard at me from her table in the market.

As I picked it up, I made contact with the emerald, forgetting my glove. The fire of the woman's glare and the image of the, now familiar, strange emblem on her gold headpiece followed me through time. I arrived on a proper city street with my mouth open, about to cry out in recognition of the final stone. Or at least I thought that's what I saw amongst the terrible woman's wares. An enormous ruby of a similar shape to the sketch and the space in the tray of stones back home. But instead of excitement I felt only relief to be away from her. I hadn't the nerve to return to that foreign place that was lost in time – despite the ruby I sought.

I recognized the street around me as Newbury, but wasn't certain when. I stepped aside to pull the chronospacometer from my bag and stow the emerald away for safe-keeping. When I clicked open the fob, it spun from MESOPOTAMIA to 03:33 PM DECEMBER 16 1941 AD BOSTON NORTH AMERICA. The street appeared as if I'd never left, except for my internal tremors from the trauma I felt. I shivered violently, and not just from the drastic drop in temperature. My feeling of dread deepened. I ran toward the station to board the train.

My intuition had apparently picked up on Mr. Manush. He was at the station waiting for me, and pinpointed my location immediately when I came into view. I was keenly aware of the crystal stone. It was as if he could see it and was drawn to me. There was no way to shake him from my trail, so I sought the quickest escape.

I wasted no time at the ticket booth, but ran straight to the boarding train and fumbled in my bag for the key. While seeking a slot on the train's side to insert the Journey key, I sensed heads turning to watch his pursuit – not far behind me. There was no time to worry about the attention we were garnering. I just wanted a place for the key. "Aha!" It was a race as I pushed the key into a small gap and turned it, and...I was inside the train!

The whoosh of wind, knocked Mr. Manush backward just as he reached me. I could only imagine the blindness the flash must have caused him as I prolonged my own blink against it.

Once inside, I dropped the Journey key into my bag and kept on moving. If I could only evade him until the train pulled from the station, I could travel again. My hand hovered – partially in my riding pouch, ready to contact the stone and go home.

I presumed he'd entered the car when I heard gasps and chaos erupting behind me. I was causing similar disruption as people were thrown from their balance in the press of my rush onward. *Woooot woooot.* At last! I thought the departure whistle would never sound. We were bound to pull away from the station at any moment.

When I risked a quick glance backward, Manush was much closer than I'd imagined. I regretted my release of the Journey key as loss of a desperate chance to escape if needed. I reached a bit further into my bag, but was afraid I'd contact the wrong stone. I didn't want to go back to that barbaric ancient market. I couldn't face that woman again, and if Mr. Manush followed me there, I'd certainly be lost.

"Janie! Father!" I cried out as if they could find me here and pull me out of trouble. The train seemed to refuse movement. No matter the risk, I thrust my hand fully into the bag. I stumbled as the train lurched forward, and my knee stabbed with pain. I was horrified as I lost my footing. Surely Manush would catch me where I'd fallen!

In helpless peril, I finally pulled the Journey key from my bag. I glanced back to see him nearly upon me. I thrust the remarkable key into a gap between the empty bench seat on which I'd landed and the train's side. With a last breath of hope, I twisted it. My boots slammed hard onto the platform – in Snoqualmie. Pain shot from my knee and my arms swung like windmills. But I managed to maintain my balance. What a relief!

Oddly, it was dark outside. I'd never landed on the platform at night– only in the bookshop. When I'd arrived at the depot before, it was at the usual noontime arrival. I checked over my shoulder and there was no train there at all. The platform was completely deserted. The key must have thrown me out of the passenger car without actually disembarking. Perhaps the train was never really here at all – at this place and time – or not long enough to be detected by anyone but me.

When I recovered my feet and settled my mind, I spotted Summer's Girl tied securely to the hitch by the saloon. What a welcome sight!

I was driven to run again by my excitement to return home, but as I crossed the street, the stones became heavy on my mind. Temptation pulled me toward the door of the bookshop with thought of replacing them under the cover of darkness, but I couldn't shake the feeling of horror and pursuit.

I turned back toward the saloon, untied the very restive mare and hoisted myself up to arrange my seat. I took an instant to pull the chronospacometer from my bag and open the fob with a snap. It settled upon 03:05 AM APRIL 23 1910 AD SNOQUALMIE NORTH AMERICA. Fortunately, I'd escaped notice and was soon off on another ride home under the nearly full moon.

The breeze on my face was brisk, but the cold couldn't penetrate my mood. The night closed in around me, as comforting as a friend. This darkness I had come to know. Everything had changed in such a short time – I was no longer afraid of the shadows that lurked close to home. At least as long as they only contained the evergreens and elk, and not the living characters more sinister than any story of suspense in Mr. Thomas Worthington's Most Excellent Bookshop.

∞∞∞∞

After giving Summer's Girl over to Master Seth, I slowly managed the stairs and then quickly undressed in my chambers. I carefully stowed the tied package and my locket. And just as I eased my throbbing leg onto the bed, and my head touched the pillow, I heard soft footsteps coming down the hall. My bedroom door opened noiselessly. Someone was checking on me. That was terribly close! I rolled as if out of a sleep and kept my voice soft, "Father?"

"Yes, my sweet."

His dear voice soothed my palpitating heart that still flutter from my fear of discovery as I crept in from the night.

"Are you well, Caprice?"

"I'm well, yes, please don't worry yourself on my account. I've had a splendid eve...dream, and no more headaches. Please rest now."

"Very well. It's good to have you home. Goodnight dear."

How curious, I wondered if he knew? No, that was silly. *Yawn*, of course he just meant he's glad I came to Snoqualmie... Of course.

CHAPTER THIRTY-FIVE

∞∞∞∞

In Which Janie's Sweet Giggle Dispels the Horror

"Yes, please assure Father I'm fine," I tried when Camille peeked into my chambers to check on me.

Camille's fist perched stubbornly on her hip. "But you slept so long – and right through your usual book club meeting."

"Oh! Miss Mabel's. I –" had completely forgotten it was Saturday. "That's two weeks in a row." So confusing this jumping through days.

"He wouldn't let me wake you for it. And he's right to be concerned for you. How can I – em, we – know you're well? After all, you were so ill at the Adams' residence Thursday that you couldn't even greet your father upon his arrival."

Would she never let that go?

"One doesn't sleep so much when *fine*," she continued.

She wasn't listening, no matter my persistence. Although to be fair, I'm sure I appeared like I was up for over a day and a half – as I had been – rather than rested and refreshed after a long slumber.

"When I sit down to breakfast – or luncheon, if that's more appropriate...What time is it anyway? – I assure you I'll be as good as new." At least in body, but what about my mind. I would likely lose it if I couldn't see Janie soon. And goodness! How anxious she must've been when I wasn't at Miss Mabel's.

"On second thought, Camille, perhaps you're right. A little more rest would be a good thing." I gave her ample time to gloat. "I'll stay to my chambers and have a tray delivered, please. And after relaying the message to Cook, please return to help me dress and take to my daybed. I'd like a visitor. Please have Jaimeson contact the Adams home and ask that Miss Mary Jane arrive as soon as she's available." I managed to leave off the demand, *immediately*.

∞∞∞∞

"My dear, Lizzie, I've been so afraid for you. When Jaimeson came by to call for me, I feared you were in dire need, especially when you missed book club again." Janie whizzed into my chambers in a whirlwind of worry.

"I regret upsetting you so, dear. As you see, I'm whole and well. Though I've had many adventures and not a few frights since last we spoke. So the new literature raised good discussion?"

My attempt to deflect the point had no effect. "Certainly, but what about you?" Her clear blue eyes settled upon my face expectantly, but I didn't know where to begin.

"Oh! I read that we've lost our dear Samuel Clemens on, em, Wednesday, it was. It's hard to imagine life with no more Mark Twain stories. I read the headline in Paris." I raised the point sadly.

"That's terrible news, to be sure." She paused. "But what happened to you? Please tell me the full tale." Janie encouraged. "No matter how frightful, I shall support you, dear friend."

"Yes, em...I had a good talk with Thomas – the elder Mr. Worthington, that is. Things are well with him, and I got some further information on his partner's history."

216

"Will it help you find the rest of the stones?"

"Indeed. In fact, it already did. I found another one – at the bookshop in Paris. A woman at the Librairie d'Occasion Curiosità gave it to me, and Mr. Thomas told me the shop is owned by Mr. Manush's family."

"Oooo," she squealed.

"But I'm too frightened to use it."

Janie's brow furrowed and her hand flew to the end of her braid, "You...afraid? Did you find out Mr. Manush is truly after you? Will he hurt you if you use the stone?"

"If you give me a moment, I'll tell you."

Janie's sweet giggle dispelled the horror that was growing in me as I approached the memory of the market in Ur. She dropped her hair, and I took a deep breath.

"The woman I met at the bookshop when I was first in Paris was there again. She dropped the crystal quartz stone into my hand instead of change for my purchase, and I traveled. So I have used it once, but... I'm convinced she meant to give me the mysterious book as well as the crystal. But I don't understand her motive." I wished I'd been bold enough to ask questions of Miss Penn.

Janie went quiet – focused on my tale.

"I'm quite certain she's related to Mr. Manush – there's a resemblance – but she seems to be helping me. And I encountered one other on this journey that I suspect is related to them both. But I can't imagine her helping anyone. She's completely other. She may be an enemy – whether to him or to me I couldn't begin to guess. But I saw her unbelievably far back in time. My father's chronospacometer read 12:01 PM JUNE 30 2112 BC UR, MESOPOTAMIA."

"Mesopotamia? Your father's what?"

"Oh, my apologies. His device for measuring not only time and location like a chronometer, but also the date throughout space and time. I... picked it up from his workshop when we spoke the other day. It's just like the large watch-like contraption that Mr. Manush carries. The readings in other places were accurate when cross-referenced with newspapers, so I have no reason to doubt the reading – 2112 BC."

"Oh Lizzie," Janie gasped. Her hands flew to her rosy cheeks, perhaps looking for something comfortably known to hold on to.

My upset didn't allow a stop for her comfort. "The setting itself was daunting – stifling heat and nothing like Europe or America. Uncivilized or...that's not accurate. There was art and written language and remarkable architecture...but not anything like the civilization I'm accustomed to. But they did have one thing that tempts me to return. I believe I saw the final stone. Just as I traveled away, I saw an enormous ruby. And the shape...but it was on *her* table in the marketplace. The darkest woman I've ever encountered. With that suffocating atmosphere and the threat of that gnarled face, I'm not sure I can muster courage to return no matter how tempting."

"Perhaps it's enough that you've found where it is and answered your mystery," Janie offered.

I raised a brow and took a deep breath to help me find patience to answer such nonsense.

Janie jumped in with a knowing laugh. "Yes, I assumed as much."

"Now that I know where it is, I'm even more anxious to see the set together in the cabinet. You've suggested sets of amulets may have more power than each alone. They're not actually together just because I know their whereabouts. We can't know for certain it's the proper stone until it fits the empty groove in the tray."

"And of course you must know for certain. But perhaps you should take some time and find out more before taking the chance."

"Sound advice – as always, my dear. But I feel terribly urgent. I fear I've led Mr. Manush to it, and I must keep him from securing the ruby. I didn't encounter him until I'd left the ancient place, but he was tight on my heels."

"He was after you again? Oh Lizzie, please, do tell."

I was amazed when speaking of it, that it was I who had traveled to these places, and just last night. Telling of my leaving Thomas saddened me again, and I hoped Janie didn't guess too much of my affection. Though it was harmless enough to find an old man dear, perhaps.

"So after I saw Thomas again, I used the amber to return to Paris. I arrived near the bookshop, just the same, and I'm gaining confidence that the stones always take one to the same places – or very nearly. But since I left from 1941 and arrived in 1910, the amber has proved to jump times and not just places, as I first thought."

"It is useful to repeat the same stones, just as you'd hoped. But please, what happened in Paris?"

"I picked up a book at the shop and bought it from the woman who appeared related to Manush. The symbol from her strange gold and amber earrings was also represented on the headpiece the ancient woman wore." And is hanging around my neck, I didn't add. "It's that odd parasol-like symbol on the front of the book that's blank from your perspective, and it's, em, in the carving on the crown of the desk in Mr. Worthington's shop. The one that holds the stones." I kept the property of its secret lever trigger to myself, and continued. "I've got the new book right here." I pointed to the table near my daybed where I thought I'd set it before resting, then remembered I'd tucked it out of sight.

"I'll have to find it for you later, Janie." I was terribly curious to know what I had procured. "The woman priced and wrapped it for me, so she must have seen what it was," I told her. "Do you think it played a part in her choosing to give me the crystal? I can't imagine why she would do so otherwise – unless she remembered me from when I visited before." I remembered feeling that she could see right into my locket where the tiny tile lay.

"Hmm, it's hard to guess without seeing the new book. What a lovely locket," she noted as if she'd read my thoughts.

"Em…it was my mother's."

Janie looked around the room, and got up to move the coverlet. "Is this it?" She brought the wrapped tome up from under the bed where I had tucked it.

"Indeed…" I tore the paper off without thought of decorum. "Oh! I had this edition before and mistakenly left my copy back at Newbury Street. It's a definite favorite of mine."

"The Time Machine," she read. "I heard of this book when I was ten…Of course it had already been published for several years by then. I've always wanted to read it. How exciting!"

"And interesting…But wait," she caught my attention, "you haven't read it? Oh please, my dear, you must take it to read before I do."

"But…"

"I insist." The rest of her objection died at my gentle proclamation, and I released a smug laugh as I recognized the faraway look of a bibliophile in love, swept away in her imaginings as she stroked the sphinx on the fabric cover. I was delighted I'd found a way to reward her kindness.

"Oh!" The intensity of my shout not only got Janie's attention, but brought Camille running with the pot of tea she'd planned to deliver, her face lit with alarm.

"I'm fine…perhaps some lemon tarts?" I challenged Camille to get Cook baking. That would give us some much needed time.

"Lizzie, whatever made you startle her so?" Janie whispered, furious with curiosity. She pulled on her hair with such ferocity I feared she'd remove it.

"The sphinx on the cover brought my thoughts back to the ancient place," I admitted.

"You haven't even told me the rest! How silly of me to get sidetracked."

"By my distress – you dear girl. But I must tell you the details, I suppose." I commenced the full tale of my fearsome journey.

∞∞∞∞

"Ur!" Janie remarked. "That *is* far back in time. What an adventure to see a place so ancient. New digs have shown it as a seat of culture."

"It's exciting when one's reclining safe upon one's daybed and has a pleasant tray of biscuits and piping hot tea to hand. But I assure you there was more fear than excitement in the moment. I was completely out of my element, and it was as if the whole scene was cast in the shadow of black magic."

"I thought you didn't believe in such things."

"I merely reserved judgment to consider the evidence. There was definitely some kind of power evident to my psyche when I saw that dark woman – or perhaps emanating from the ruby stone itself. Even had I not traveled away just then, I'm not sure I could've steadied myself to negotiate with her for that jewel. The power at stake was palpable, and I'm even more afraid of Mr. Manush, now that I know it may be this power he desires."

"But how can you be sure if you don't go back?"

"If only there was some other way to research it…"

"Did you check the book that only you can read? What did it say about the crystal?"

Her trust was reassuring. "It's a stone of power, communication and focus."

"It's good you have such heart to balance and consider its strength. Well, we've theorized that the stones may behave differently as a set." She gave her braid one small tug. "What if you try adding the new crystal stone you've gained to those that are already there and observe if there are changes."

"Brilliant, my dear Janie, you really are a gem." My eyes twinkled at her, and we shared a good giggle.

"Tonight?" she suggested.

"Why wait, I think we should go to the bookshop this afternoon, as soon as I can be made presentable after our tea. We'll arrive close enough to closing that we can linger and return after Mr. Worthington has departed."

"Excellent! Are you sure you're quite recovered? I don't want you to harm yourself."

"The only thing worse than fatigue is curiosity unrequited. Now that you've posed the question I won't properly rest until I know its answer. Besides that, I'm interested to learn more of Mr. Worthington's brother, Mr. Scott. Since he's newly arrived, I'd imagine he'll be with him at the shop today." I kept the older Thomas' reaction to the time of Scott's arrival to myself – not sure of its significance, or if it mattered at all.

"He's certainly handsome," Janie confirmed, understandably mistaking the nature of my interest.

"Indeed." She covered my blush by giggling louder than I. "Why, we're as silly as a couple of goops," I remarked as I gained composure.

"He rather makes me feel like one," she admitted.

I smiled and nodded. His charm was undeniable.

CHAPTER THIRTY-SIX

∞∞∞

In Which Miss Livingstone and Mr. Scott Worthington
Share a Magical Exchange

The small brass bells rang as we stepped inside the door out of the soft spring rain. The shop felt lighter than usual, and my perusal discovered Mr. Thomas Worthington, and only young Thomas Worthington. There were no other patrons, no Mr. Scott, and no Mr. Manush. My shoulders relaxed into an easier posture.

"Good afternoon, Miss Livingstone, Miss Adams." His warm eyes rested on me just a moment longer than on the beautiful Janie.

"Good afternoon, Mr. Worthington, we've come to continue our conversation about my trade. I shall be happier without an audience." He gave me a knowing grin, which I pointedly ignored. Janie was no support, as she had already buried her nose in the stacks near the yellow-green curtain. It gave me shivers as I recognized the color so much like that in the ancient market.

"Where is your partner, Mr. Manush today? He seems to always be about." Lurking about, I was going to say, but it didn't seem polite.

"He has gone to bring my brother from my home. Scott needed further rest but wanted to come by the shop before closing today."

"And since your partner speaks only French, he's not the best to greet patrons if you had gone instead?"

Mr. Worthington gave me the most curious look. Perhaps I wasn't to know that? He didn't tell me that in this time period, but I thought it was common knowledge. Come to think of it, Mr. Manush had always remained silent. Maybe they didn't wish for his origin to be known? How intriguing.

The small bells rang greeting to Mr. Manush and Thomas' dashing brother. I heard a small sigh from the region of the silk curtain. I hoped the gentlemen didn't mark Janie's reaction, though she was close in their proximity. Scott's features were similar to Thomas' but sharper, more defined, and without the encumbrance of moustache and beard. I could see by the heaviness of Thomas' beard that he was attached, but it made me want to ask Thomas to shave – even just once – to see how deep was their resemblance.

"He's even more handsome than I remembered," Janie whispered in my ear as she left her precious books to join me near the center of the shop.

I agreed with a smile.

"Good afternoon, Miss Livingstone, Miss Adams," Mr. Scott Worthington greeted us with gusto.

"Good afternoon," Janie curtsied with a winning smile.

"Afternoon," I blushed while curtsying too. I couldn't even steal a glance at Thomas to see if he noticed the flush of my cheeks. I hoped they weren't as red as they felt.

"We were just about to commence settlement of the trade that Miss Livingstone has proposed," Thomas explained.

"You're a lucky man to negotiate under such pleasing circumstances, Thomas." Scott's green eyes flicked at Janie and lingered on mine, as mine darted to the side.

"The shop is coming together fine, Thomas – just fine," Scott continued as he stepped to his brother's side near the window. "Father would have been proud to see the establishment."

An uneasiness crept over me. I wasn't certain if it came from tension between the brothers or from Mr. Manush's presence. He withdrew to the corner near the curtain, as usual, and became as part of the furniture. I was just as aware of his oddity as that of the desk's. My furtive glance twitched from one to the other, as I fidgeted with my mother's locket. The man shifted and tipped his head, as if noting my discomfort. I felt he could see the stones I carried and had guessed my plan for later in the evening.

After a pause, Mr. Thomas answered, "Yes, and I'm pleased that you can be here to see it and be a part of it, Scott. Welcome again to your new home."

Thomas gave him a strong hug that showed outward affection. It dispelled my deep concern raised by his strange reticence when we first spoke of Scott in the future. If he cares for him so, then I'll not withhold my affection, though I'm still wary of what kept the elder Thomas guarded.

"Are you rested, Scott?" Thomas asked. "I would value your opinion in the fulfillment of this bargain, which has become a challenge of integrity now that Miss Livingstone has placed it in my hands to choose the final terms. I'm sure you recall I've been charged with the recommendation of literature that's of equal value to that offered and also suited to her particular education and enjoyment. We had settled on new books that arrive, but I'd like your help in choosing the best of the package when they are here, so the challenge is renewed."

"Yes, and it's an interesting challenge indeed," His green eyes sparked at me, accenting a discomfiting smirk. "I believe our collective opinions will be of even greater value to her than just your own. Although to give the best advice I need to become further acquainted with Miss Livingstone. It will be my pleasure to assist." His leering eyes flashed at me again.

I shrunk back, perhaps in remembrance of what followed yesterday when the first Mr. Worthington proposed such a thing. I wondered what Mr. Scott Worthington would ask of me?

"Very well. I will give you one question to Miss Livingstone," Thomas allowed.

Scott tipped back his head and squinted at the beams overhead for a time. Then he leveled his gaze at me, "What do you consider the most enjoyable book you ever read and why was it such for you?"

"Oh...oh my. I've never received such a subjectively phrased question on literature. It's generally about the most valuable or prestigious or most educational. 'The most enjoyable?' I shall have to ponder it, for it concerns my own preferences."

"Exactly, Miss. For what better way to gauge value than by what you desire?"

I avoided his eyes, but couldn't seem to hide my smile. He was bolder than his brother with no encouragement whatsoever. At least I was aware of giving Thomas open return of his earlier advancements before he came at me so. Oh dear, but I had to answer Mr. Scott in some way.

"Thirst for good literature is a noble desire, indeed," I offered to foil his attempt at flirtation. Though flattered, I was also appalled he'd speak that way to a woman in whom his brother was interested. Though Thomas likely hadn't admitted it to him, Scott did witness yesterday's display between us.

"Not to be denied." His eyes glittered as he raised an eyebrow suggestively.

Now that it was clearly about literature, I laughed freely. Thomas did not look amused.

"There are many worthy texts for various reasons," I began, "but on the merit of enjoyment, I would choose, *The Arabian Night's Entertainment.*"

This was met with various nods and head bobs – as my audience weighed the choice.

"It brings seemingly endless enchanting tales of adventure and things that can be imagined and pondered." I expanded, "And it encompasses history and legends from exotic parts of the world in an exciting and intriguing retelling." My eyes dropped briefly as I remembered how eerie the exotic felt when it materialized – or when I materialized in its midst.

"Hm, so you are a woman of pure fancy? Your appearance suggests more education and refinement than to delight in mere magical whimsy." Scott looked genuinely perplexed and somewhat disappointed. "Or is it about the treasure?" He nodded, expecting agreement.

"I don't see why the magic in the stories should not be contemplated as things not yet explained. After all, the tales come from traditions that are centuries old," I defended.

"I think the magic in the story is for the entertainment of women and children – which has its value, I'll admit." His eyes flashed toward the men. "But the real thrust of the story is the treasure they gained through taking the risk of adventure." Scott declared.

"The element of adventure met with reward has appeal, but there are also many cautions against greed." I hadn't thought of my own sense of adventure as reaching for reward, but admittedly there was more motivation to travel when there was something to gain beyond mere experience. But I also sought adventure to learn what was around the next bend. To find the truth about things that had only been imagined. "Why should there not be magic? Or rather, why should that which is labeled magic not turn out to be something real. Education and experience often bring to light the trickery behind what was deemed magic to start."

"I can't argue with that, but *Arabian Nights* thrives on magic, it doesn't seek to explain it, but rather implies there are things beyond us that will never be explained."

"Perhaps that in and of itself is an explanation." I had apparently come around to more agreement with Janie's position.

"I will need time to choose. Can we beg further delay with promise to see you again?" Scott offered after a moment.

To my surprise, he'd let the matter drop. I seemed to have won the point.

"Certainly, Miss Adams and I will return. You shall have all the time you require." I gave him a formal nod, relieved to retreat from the discussion for the time being.

"Haste ye back," Mr. Thomas Worthington addressed to me. My breath caught as I recognized the same lovely directive that the older Thomas had left me with. "And you shall have my advice to consider, Brother. I have some suggestions which you and I can discuss that consider my prior acquaintance with Miss Livingstone's preferences." I heard an aggressive edge in Thomas' tone – like a warning. But I'd never seen anger in him, and it wasn't evident on his kind face. "And we may discuss it further on our way home, it seems. It's time to close the shop for the night."

My heart began to thump in anticipation, and Janie's blue eyes flashed at me knowingly. They would be out of our way soon, and we could return the amber and emerald and try the new crystal in its slot. "We bid you adieu, gentlemen." I offered.

"With the promise of your return, we shall manage to endure your absence," Scott laughed.

Thomas joined in at the obvious exaggeration. Janie and I returned their jovial smiles and went out the door with a merry jingle of the bells. Mr. Manush had disappeared behind the curtain so there was no need for an awkward farewell.

CHAPTER THIRTY-SEVEN

∞∞∞∞

In Which Janie's Trust is Undeniable

"I believe if we pace down the block we can make ourselves scarce as they pass on their way home, Janie."

"Can you walk that far? I don't want you to hurt your knee?" she asked with care.

"It's improving, and we can take our time." We walked around the corner to pass the saloon toward the Lucile Hotel. Thankfully the rain had remained a light mist. I broadened my scarf to cover my hat from the moisture.

"Miss Livingstone, so nice to see you here again."

Oh my, it was that pesky gent that was outside the saloon the other night. What a bother. Janie tipped her head, brows furrowed with curiosity.

"Are you tying off a horse again for the currier's son?" His eyes were full of the most inappropriate familiarity and tease.

"No, I shan't be stopping here at all," I stated firmly, and successfully clipped off any further attempt at conversation.

"My goodness, Lizzie, you're exceptionally good at the cold shoulder. Few can resist the charm of Mr. Dionis Reinig. Mr. Dio is famous for his adventuring." Janie whispered as we passed along.

"Reinig – so he's related to Miss Abigale? I should have known."

"Yes, her youngest uncle. But I should hate to be a gentleman vying for your attention if you hadn't already granted it. When I watched you with the Mr. Worthingtons I thought you a woman who readily encourages flirtation, but I see now they've been greatly favored in speaking with you at all." Janie was full of, well, caprice.

"I'm not that difficult," I insisted. The memory of Thomas' comment on my distance drifted in.

She laughed uproariously, leaving me glad to be outside with an outburst of that magnitude.

"Am I?" I amended.

"You're not an easy woman, my dear. But you aren't truly difficult either – just a handful in your way." She smiled and her blue eyes danced merrily.

"If you mean by that I have my own mind, I cannot deny it. But why a man would want anything less from a woman I can't imagine. Unless they'd only like a child-maker and someone to nod at their every whim, and what kind of man would that be? I wouldn't respect him at all."

"Quite." She looped her arm through my elbow, and we strode together with much verve.

As we rounded the next corner to circle the block, she nearly pulled out my shoulder as I froze.

"What's wrong?" Janie asked, frightened.

"Look, there in the shadows. Do you see?"

"No, I'm not certain where you're looking."

"There in the doorway of the hotel. I can't see him now, but I'm sure it was...Mr. Manush."

We livened our steps to the next corner, and after we rounded it, I pulled her back to spy again at the hotel's doorway. The shadow was less deep from that direction, and it was clear there was no one there.

"Are you sure you saw him?" Janie asked.

"I thought so, but now I'm not certain. Perhaps my eyes were deceiving me. If he was there, then where could he have gone?"

"Well, let's hurry back to the bookshop. I'm sure we've allowed enough time. They were gathering themselves to leave as we went out the door. And I'm getting damp through."

"Yes, I'm sorry to discomfort you, my friend," I told her, "the sooner we're inside the better I shall feel. You'll still come with me won't you – inside I mean. I'd like you by my side to see what happens when I add the crystal quartz into the batch."

"Y-yes. Alright, my dear." Her eyes were round with fright.

Janie usually relied on my courage, but I had none to spare.

As long as we were in view of the hotel, I continued to glance backward. Janie gripped my elbow ever more tightly until I had to pat her hand gently and pull it from where it pained me. Still she huddled at my side, and the tension grew almost unbearable.

When we turned the corner and the bookshop's sign came into view, we were leaning on each other like erring children approaching an angry parent. We all but tiptoed to the door.

I pushed back my damp scarf and pulled the Journey key from my pouch. With a glance at Janie's wide eyes, I took her hand and hooked it through my elbow again. I hoped, as with Harriet, that it would bring her with me when the wind blew and the light flashed. I could let her in once I was inside, but I'd rather we were both gone when attention was drawn by the sudden brightness.

I put the key into the slot, met her eyes one more time, and turned it.

Whoosh, flash and we were in.

"Oh!" she cried out, startled.

"Yes, it's rather surprising the first time, isn't it?" I laughed, releasing my tension as well as her arm.

"I'm not sure I could do this as you have done. You're the bravest woman I've ever met."

I hoped she hadn't felt the quaking of my knees. The haunting visage of Mr. Manush on the street quite unnerved me. Though he hadn't seemed to follow us after all.

"Now what?" Janie's voice startled me.

I knew she saw me jump that time. "Now we open the desk." I took charge to cover my upset.

Climbing up on the small table, I had just the slightest twinge of protectiveness before pushing at the crowning symbol revealing the lever to my friend. I stepped back down to her and gathered her hand into mine.

"Oh my," Janie murmured, pulling her hair with her free hand as the gears began to whir.

Her awe caused me to marvel again at the wonder of its intricacy of movement. As the carved emblems traveled smoothly across the face of the cabinet I noticed a pair of spiral-shaped ones that matched more symbols from the headpiece of the woman in the ancient desert.

"Are you alright? Oh, Caprice!" Janie's use of my real name snapped me out of my swoon. Seeing the strange symbols had taken me back to what seemed a nightmare to me now.

"Yes, yes, of course. I just...I'm fine," I assured, dropping her hand from mine.

The doors opened wide, revealing the glowing gems within. When Janie turned her eyes toward the cabinet, her face tipped up and her jaw fell. I stepped back up on the table and set the amber and emerald in their places. Then I pulled the crystal gem from my pouch with my gloved hand – and I almost dropped it!

"Are you sure it will be alright?" I heard Janie's question as if from a great distance.

"Come. Step up here beside me," I encouraged. I pushed away my possessive feelings in favor of greater friendship and fortitude. If she was to be a part of this, it would be good to have her truly alongside, she deserved my devotion and had certainly earned my full confidence.

Janie took my hand and stepped up. I looked toward her, and she met my eyes steadily, her expectant blue orbs full of trust. They gave me the courage I needed.

I studied the two spaces and the stone and placed the crystal in the one that seemed to match. A bright glow emanated from the cabinet when the stone fell into its place. The light throbbed and grew until both Janie and I turned our heads away and partially covered our squinting eyes. But nothing further happened. It dulled back down again and remained just a little brighter than it was before the crystal was added.

"That's it?" Janie remarked, somewhat unsure. She dropped my hand.

Truth be known, I was pleased, it'd been quite a day already.

"It didn't complete the set. Perhaps there'd be something more if we had the final gem," I conjectured.

"Yes, I suppose you're right." Janie's brow furrowed, and she displayed a small pout. I'd never seen her quite so disappointed.

"Perhaps, if you're willing to try, you could come with me? I might bear going to the ancient place if you were at my side."

Her eyes lit with excitement. "Truly? Can we go now?"

That shining blue would be unbearable to quench. "Yes, of course," I agreed with trepidation.

Janie nodded her encouragement. I couldn't deny her.

"Hold on," I said, and she put her arm through my elbow once again.

Slowly, I removed my glove. I held up my bare hand. Janie tugged her hair and nodded her support again. We leaned in toward the collection of stones and I reached for the crystal.

As my hand approached the clear gem, it was as if the world throughout all time held its breath. I had almost contacted it, and was beyond changing my course, when I heard Janie cry out. I touched the stone.

CHAPTER THIRTY-EIGHT

∞∞∞∞

In Which Miss Livingstone and Janie Nearly Bare All

I recognized the marketplace of Ur but was otherwise disoriented. Janie pulled me along at a most insistent run. I stumbled as I looked behind, unable to resist the curiosity of what caused our urgency.

There he was, Mr. Manush, bearing down on us like a stooping bird of prey, until he ran into a girl with a basket of fruit on her head.

"Where did he come from?" I cried out in my fright.

"The curtain. He came from behind the silk curtain in the shop when you touched the stone." Janie squealed.

My wits returned. He would be on us again in moments. I had the advantage of knowing where the woman would be, and decided to lead Manush astray. He must not have known exactly where we were going since he'd spied and then revealed himself by following so closely.

Among the mud-brick structures I spotted a tent of sorts, made with various patterned cloths, rough and reddish like the woman's robe I saw when first here. I steered Janie toward it, hoping it belonged to a traveling merchant and would be unoccupied at midday.

Hope dropped away as we were met by the surprised expressions of a group of men lounging on stacks of cloth and smoking from stone pipes. I assumed our outlandish dress didn't help matters, but also wondered if women were not permitted.

A large man with a very black beard drew his thick brows down atop his terribly long nose. He raised to his knees and scolded us furiously in a flood of words we couldn't understand. His hands flung toward us mercilessly, emphasizing his indecipherable point. A smile could be disastrous, so I set my mouth in a line and opened my hands. I shook my head from side to side. The intensity of his ire pushed us toward the door flap where Manush would soon appear. My determination not to go there gave me an idea.

I gave Janie what I hoped was a meaningful glance and began to pull off clothing. Nothing crucial, certainly, but it achieved the attention I desired. And, more importantly, I'd frozen the press toward the door. I slipped a look at Janie and received a wry wink of her eye. She'd caught my hint. We moved in a subtle arc around behind the group of men while very slowly removing items of clothing. I started with my hat-scarf, my hat, my wrap. I suddenly wished for the multi-layers of old. One of the men set aside his pipe and began playing an eerie tune on an odd wind instrument – no doubt the equivalent of some bawdy tune in a French cabaret.

Mr. Manush came rushing in, but we had a whole tent full of men safely insulating us from him. We'd gained every man's allegiance. They wouldn't let him lay a hand on us as long as we continued our show. But what then? My wit could only take me so far.

I met Janie's eyes in desperate apology. Rather than orbs of fear or confusion, they were steady beams, directing me toward something I hadn't yet noticed. There was a flap in the tent's side nearby – an escape. It was very small, perhaps meant for venting, but with determination we just might fit through – especially after shedding our bulkier garments. We were down to our petticoats, and our small size was an advantage. The larger Mr. Manush would be slowed or even stopped in the crawl.

I gave her the nod, and we shook our gloves flirtatiously toward the men as we backed our posteriors away toward the vent. The cheers and leers of the men were horrifying, but I persevered and tipped my head to her to go first. She was gone, suddenly ducking behind me. I quickly turned and squirmed through the gap close on her tail.

As I jumped to my feet, Janie cheered in a stage whisper, "We're free!"

Hardly, I thought with a glance back at our escape hatch. But there was no one yet on our trail. "Quickly!" I shouted to her and rushed away toward the woman I didn't want to face. There was no time to lose, and I couldn't let Janie down.

Winding our way through the market's traffic, the heat once again caused my head to spin. Or perhaps it was the anticipation, both fearful and ecstatic. The mystery hung in the balance and would be solved shortly, for better or worse. I blinked and tried to focus, wishing I could shake my feeling of dread.

As we neared the place in the street market where the woman's wares had been before, I couldn't fight the dizziness any longer. I fell into a near swoon only vaguely aware of Janie pulling me along. In my mind's eye I saw the face of the woman in Paris as she appraised my worth when I was in her bookshop the first time. Then I felt the weight on my palm as she gave me the crystal stone when I returned. The book! It seemed terribly important, like there was something more I should know. I had fallen asleep last night while pondering the new words that described the stones. It was as if I'd kept reading during my long sleep but had forgotten the words in the morning. And now that the dark woman's face had appeared in my mind, the dream and the words had become clear to me again.

The book contained explanation of the power to travel anywhere through time at will – if only one was able to see it. That power would belong to the one who placed the last stone with the others, to complete the set. When the stones were brought together, the rust stone – the one that seemed to contain a thousand stars – could be removed and carried as a single talisman. I understood so much more now, and the fathoms within Miss Penn's eyes felt like they were burning within my own. The stone of stars would summon the power of each of the other gems, directed by the command of the set's owner. I needed only to bring them all together at the bookshop and then take the ruling gem, and I would be a master of time.

But there was something more. When I tried to read it in my dream, the language had become foreign. I'd struggled and become frustrated. I could see that section of the book before me again now, in my strange trance-like swoon. But still I was unable to decipher the meaning. As I strained to make sense of it, an image of the gnarled woman from the market appeared beside me. I felt no fear of her in this strange nebulous space and didn't resist as she removed the strange headpiece from her fiercely black hair and placed it over my unruly curls. Then I understood. An innocent. Only if the last stone was collected by one who was innocent of greed for power would the power of the set of stones be pure – to be used for good. That was what the lady wished. Perhaps it was the reason she protected the stone from Manush, and many others before him. Would she also protect it from me? She and her family had led me to this place, but I wished so much for the power to travel. Was I innocent of greed?

I shook the grogginess from my consciousness and worked to regain my wit. "Oh!" I cried out in my effort.

Janie still moved us along. "It's alright dear, he hasn't found us. Are we going the right way?"

I was unable to answer her but focused on the goal. I would try to get the ruby stone, and I would do my best to protect it too.

At last I saw the woman before us through the fray. "Janie, she's there," my voice said. I felt my arm point ahead as if it belonged to someone else. I stumbled forward again, and when I couldn't continue Janie caught my fall. We stopped.

The woman stared at me impassively where I leaned at the edge of her table, crumpled upon the arm of my friend. She simply waited.

It was a standoff, like all of time quit moving forward, and everything came down to this moment. We hung in a void of darkness. Neither of us willing to start the clock.

"Oh, what a beautiful gem!" A voice came from beyond the void, and there was light.

Janie's hand reached toward the box of stones amongst the woman's wares. One in particular glowed from within and took over my view. As my dear friend's hand came down to touch it, I looked up at the woman who had terrified me so. The woman's expression was clear and open. Her gnarled features were transformed with peace. She gazed upon Janie like a dear child whom she'd lost to the world and who now crossed the threshold to come home at last.

I reached out to catch Janie's elbow as she picked up the glowing ruby. A burst of light pressed my eyes tightly closed and opened my heart to pure joy. When I could finally see again, I recognized the interior of Mr. Thomas Worthington's Most Excellent Bookshop. I was elated.

We'd been transported home into the center of the shop – near the ornate desk – but with Mr. Manush in tow. He must have caught the hem of my petticoat! The cabinet of gems stood open to us. Its glow called me to urgency. Mr. Manush was recovering from a tumble onto the floor. I saw my cat, Timber, shoot away from the overturned chair that tripped the villain. Whatever was the cat doing here? There was no time to puzzle! Manush's eyes were fixed on the ruby in Janie's hand. The light within it brightened to a glaring red. He struggled up toward it like a beacon that he couldn't resist.

Taking my chance of slipping his attention, I climbed up to the cabinet. Protecting my hand with my petticoat – for lack of other garments – I dropped the crystal stone back into its place. The glow from the set of stones became brighter again, attracting Janie's gaze. Mr. Manush was still intent on his prize. Quickly, I slipped my hands into the folds of my petticoat and prayed I wouldn't lose my grip. I nodded and held out my makeshift net, encouraging Janie's throw.

She responded instantly, and the fiery red orb flew into the air bringing Mr. Manush's fixed attention solely my way. I fumbled the catch briefly but secured the stone in my grasp through the scalloped hem. I turned to the tray of stones haunted by the horrible visage of the furiously desperate Manush lunging toward me, Janie lunging at him, and Timber running in between.

"No!!!" tore the air behind me, ripped from Janie's body in determined defense. I resisted the urge to turn and see which person landed upon the floor with a terrible *flummph*.

I leaned forward and dropped the vibrant stone into the one remaining space.

The warm glow from all the stones raised in intensity until blinding and then knocked me off balance with a burst of energy. Miraculously, I regained my footing. I clutched the rust colored stone – still shimmering with stars – and dropped it securely into my pouch.

Just as it slipped away from view, Mr. Manush appeared at my side. He looked at me with a horrified expression and then looked down at the wide open hole that spilled light into the room from where the shimmering stone had been. He reached his hand toward the space in disbelief and contacted the edge of the hole. *Whoosh* a fierce wind blew up through the hole into the store disturbing the pages of the books. It continued like a gale. The sound was deafening and light shone from the hole, all around Manush, brightening until the detail of his being, dispersed in its glory. The direction of the wind suddenly reversed and the painfully glaring light was sucked into the stone's space and was gone. Manush was no more.

CHAPTER THIRTY-NINE

ထာထာ

In Which Some Things Never Change

My first reaction to Mr. Manush's disappearance was a heavy sigh, but the exhale went beyond relief. I was dizzy again and fell from my perch into darkness.

I revived, facing a fevered flurry of words from Janie, kneeling next to me on the floor of the bookshop. Her hovering face ached with concern. She was apparently asking me if I was alright, but I couldn't reply just yet. Timber curled into the space between my shoulder and elbow and stared at me intently. I was buoyed by his steady gaze.

"Janie, my dearest girl and sweet friend, I assure you I'm well." I tried out my limbs by bending each, just to be sure. "Please calm yourself and don't be strained on my account." My hand checked the locket – still at my throat.

I sat up and Timber moved to my lap. "Good kitty," I assured and stroked his soft long grey coat.

"Oh! Thank goodness," was released from Janie along with her pained expression. Her face bloomed with excitement. "He's gone. Mr. Manush...If it weren't for Timber...I couldn't reach him in time to protect you, but Timber ran through his legs and the brute hit the floor with a grunt. I was terrified when he recovered so quickly. I pulled at him, but he yanked away from me and stepped up beside you. Then the wind howled and I ducked and sheltered my eyes from that incredible light. I've never been so afraid! I felt the wind shift, and when I looked up he was gone! Where is he?"

"I couldn't begin to say, but the whirlwind centered in that hole – where the starry rust stone once lay. And after he blurred into the light, it sucked away the brightness and, apparently, our foe. It's completely still and dull now, like none of it was ever there at all."

"Oh, Lizzie, do you think he's truly gone?"

"Perhaps." But he could be in other times. The thought was unavoidable. I'd been assured I'd be entangled with him for a long time to come.

"Where's the sparkling stone? Did he take it with him?"

I opened my pouch and pointed at the shimmering stone inside. Janie's impassioned use of my nickname – for such it must be called – warmed me to my toes. I felt quite myself again. Or perhaps newly so. "It certainly appears he's vanquished, and I'm inclined to believe my eyes. Though nothing in this world will ever be certain to me again. Not in the way it once was. I need to check over what is and what's not, as though I've never learned a thing."

"Yes, it's been eye-opening indeed. Quite an adventure. It's bound to leave one feeling tossed and looking for anchor." Her blue eyes were comforting.

"And there's much more journey to be had. The answer was in the book – in my dreams. It's the starry stone."

"Easy dear, I think you're still undone." The crimp in Janie's brow returned.

"I know I sound mad, but the woman, she...passed the knowledge to me. She chose us. Chose you actually. For it was you that collected the ruby. I don't know if she'd have found me worthy. You're the real master of the set of magnificent stones. Here, take the rust-colored starry stone from me – the one that carries the energy of them all. With it you can travel anywhere in any time. The adventures are yours to choose." I fumbled with the pouch, trying to pull out the stone without touching it. I held it out to Janie, wrapped in my hem once again.

"Nonsense, of course you are worthy. And it was you that was given the crystal and book that led us there. You've got to help the older Mr. Worthington, and I'm convinced it's your fate to chase the keys to the mysteries of time, my dear. I've had enough travel and am content to stay here at home waiting for the books you discover and the marvelous tales you bring back to me. Please – the stone – it's yours."

As she pushed my hand that held the gem back toward my heart, I gasped.

"What is it?" she cried out in concern.

"There...but it's gone again now. The trim on the desk formed the words of a message. It seems I'm meant to continue my journeys after all."

Janie's eyes scanned the carvings, full of curiosity. She stroked her hair like pulling its tress would magically reveal the answer. "I can't see it."

"Of course not, it's gone now. *'Find the keys to your fate and your past future recreate,'*" I recited. "Whatever can it mean?"

"Don't you see?" She lit with the prospect of new adventure. "You've got the chance to live your life again, differently. Like in Thomas' twist. He wanted things to change in your future."

"But I don't even know how it will be once. And now I'll have the chance to choose? How exciting!" and daunting, I didn't add aloud. I thought of the tile that was my charge until I understood the purpose of Mr. Manush. Then I remembered the second message that had come to me from the desk, that now seemed so long ago. *If you travel where you've been, you'll wish you could do it over again.*

The image of the shimmering stars within the stone sparked in Janie's lovely blue eyes. I watched the silvery glitter of the reflection fade from them as I secured the stone back into my bag, but bright affection shone in them nevertheless.

"I will take the challenge to find these 'keys'," I decided. "I don't know what my further journeys will bring, or what things in life I'd want to alter. But one thing's sure, I've found the best of friends in you, Janie. And I believe I can count on my cat."

Timber seemed to answer me with his loudest purr. He would hardly let me rise, so busy was he rubbing about my legs as Janie helped me to my feet.

"Shall we go home? ...Oh my!" It was my turn to exclaim. "We're in nothing but our petticoats. I hope we're not seen. How ever will we keep our dignity?"

Janie burst into giggles, and I loudly joined in. Some things would never change.

END BOOK I

MORE Miss LiV Adventures···

THE UNWITTING JOURNEYS
OF THE WITTY MISS LIVINGSTONE
BOOK II: MEMORY KEY
Coming Fall 2017

Just when Miss Livingstone seems to hold the key to her journeys, she touches a new kind of key and slips into an alternate timeline with no memory of the one that just occurred.

Life in 1910 Snoqualmie is much the same, but in the new timeline there's no trace of the elder Thomas's purposeful twist. Miss Livingstone and Mr. Scott Worthington have pursued the mystery of the stones together.

When the dreaded Mr. Manush makes flashy appearances on the heels of a future-girl, Miss Livingstone is drawn into another mystery of life and love, which could affect her own past and future.

Miss LiV Adventures is a five book series that follows the Unwitting Journeys of the infinitely curious Miss Livingstone through time. Collecting books for Mr. Thomas Worthington, she becomes tangled in life and love as she learns of her relationships with Mr. Scott Worthington and Mr. Thomas in alternate timelines. Further complexities unfold with family and friends, as she finds keys to her ultimate choice of which life to live. All while being chased by the powerful family of the mysterious Mr. Manush.

freevalleypublishing.com

OTHER BOOKS BY THIS AUTHOR

SECRET ORDER OF THE OVERWORLD by Kennedy J. Quinn

In this inspiring and thought-provoking fantasy, Gabrell and his beloved Majeska are pulled into a power struggle caused by men's corrupt control of the Overlings' government. These men dismiss a way to societal harmony that women find Traveling the Catalyst. In response a Sisterhood forms. They use secret knowledge gathered with Visionary prowess to punish corruption in a hidden realm Underneath. But their justice becomes high-handed like the injustice they set out to destroy.

Books One: UNDERNEATH & Book Two: OVERCAME - the complete saga - included under this cover.

LIKENESS a novel by Sheri J. Kennedy

What if everyone became the same?... In LIKENESS, early millennium Seattle-based workers Charlie and Emmaline are thrust from their comfortable and quirky marketing department to the Worldwide Pharmaceutical Conference stage. They present their ad for a new drug, *Assimilaire*, that minimizes social anxiety by making one feel the same as those around them.

In a strange twist, a free sample causes the audience members to not only feel like, but to become like athletic geek Charlie and adventurous artist Emmaline.

Forced to stay at the conference by a bomb scare, the affected hotel guests are caught in a grand experiment and a madcap romp exposing the nature of similarity and difference.

This snappy contemporary novel provides much to think about and plenty of humor as it considers the value of who we are.

Available on Amazon.com

ABOUT THE AUTHOR

Kennedy J. Quinn, aka Sheri J. Kennedy, is an individual who thrives on creating. She's a visual artist, photographer and writer. THE UNWITTING JOURNEYS OF THE WITTY MISS LIVINGSTONE -Book I: Journey Key, is her fourth novel. She studied philosophy, literature and communications which gave her a B.A. in Humanities. Thoughtful curiosity influences all of her pursuits. She enjoys participation in her community and life with her husband in a small house on the banks of the Snoqualmie River in the mountains near Seattle, Washington. If she had it all to do over again, she wouldn't change a thing.

sherijkennedyriverside.wordpress.com
misslivadventures.com

Made in the USA
San Bernardino, CA
25 October 2016